THE DEVIL'S DUE

Also by Bonnie MacBird

Art in the Blood
Unquiet Spirits

The Devil's Due

A SHERLOCK HOLMES ADVENTURE

BONNIE MacBIRD

COLLINS
CRIME
CLUB

COLLINS CRIME CLUB

An imprint of HarperCollins*Publishers*
1 London Bridge Street
London SE1 9GF
www.harpercollins.co.uk

Published by HarperCollins*Publishers* 2019
1

A catalogue record for this book
is available from the British Library

Hardcover: 978-0-00-819507-6
Paperback: 978-0-00-819508-3
US Hardcover: 978-0-00-834810-6

Set in Sabon by Palimpsest Book Production Ltd, Falkirk, Stirlingshire

Printed and bound in Great Britain by CPI Group (UK) Ltd, Croydon CR0 4YY

MIX
Paper from
responsible sources
FSC www.fsc.org **FSC˚ C007454**

This book is produced from independently certified FSC™ paper
to ensure responsible forest management.

For more information visit: www.harpercollins.co.uk/green

For my cousin, Chris Simpson

Contents

Prologue   ix

PART ONE – LONDON

1   Fog   3
2   221B   9
3   Attack!   17
4   Devil and Hyde   23
5   Brotherly Love   33

PART TWO – GATHERING THE TROOPS

6   The Greater Goodwins   45
7   The Spice of Life   57
8   The Lady   65
9   A Question of Taste   79
10   The Snake and Drum   91

PART THREE – ALLIES AND OTHERS

11   Heffie   101
12   The Dogged Detective   109
13   The Baguette Brigade   117
14   Death at the Opera   127
15   A Voice Stilled   133
16   Italian Air   141

PART FOUR – SETBACK

17 Snap   151
18 Helping Hands   163
19 Pack of Foxes   179
20 Might Makes Right   189

PART FIVE – BACKWATER

21 Cat and Mouse   205
22 One Flask Closer   225
23 Zebras   233
24 Fabric of Doubt   245
25 Deep Waters   259
26 Into the Mud   269

PART SIX – OUT OF THE FRYING PAN

27 Aesthetes and Anarchists   287
28 Conflagration   303
29 Embers   309
30 The Baker Street Bazaar   329
31 The Bizarre   343
32 221B   355

    Acknowledgements   367

Prologue

On a recent late September afternoon in London, as torrential downpours skittered down the bow window of my flat on Chiltern Street, I stood looking at the grey wall of water battering the vista below. Off to the right, across Marylebone Road, umbrellas crowded the Baker Street Station tube entrance, collapsing like evening blossoms as their owners, clad in puffy jackets, windbreakers and trainers, dashed into the building.

Those doors first opened more than a hundred and fifty years ago.

I blinked and imagined it was 1890, that same station, but beneath the jumble of umbrellas was a sea of top hats, bowlers and a few flowered bonnets, well-cut suits and the occasional long dress trailing across the muddy pavement.

Deep below street level, noisy black engines belched

steam and thundered through the darkness at terrifying speeds. Some superstitious Londoners would not venture into the depths. Who knew what devilish vapours might be swirling around down there?

In 1890, London was the reigning centre of culture and commerce. But even as we romanticize those late Victorian times, we must also acknowledge that this magnificent city had her woes. What astonished me about the tale I discovered that day – inscribed in neat penmanship on a faded schoolboy notebook – was how little things had actually changed. Crime, yellow journalism, mob thinking, homelessness, murder, police brutality, fear of immigrants, dark politics – all in full flower then – and now.

But who better to slice cleanly through the shifting morass of murder, chaos and moral ambiguity than the remarkable Sherlock Holmes? It was time for a dose of his clarity, courage, and intellectual rigour.

So, once again, I sat down with the battered tin box which had been given to me by a mysterious woman from the British Library. What might be revealed today? I opened the box and immediately my eyes were drawn to a glint of gold. A bright coin had been glued to a thick envelope sticking out from the others. I pulled it out to have a look.

The coin was old, two hundred years or more. What could it mean? Its date was long before Watson and Holmes walked the London streets. A small voice inside me said that the time was right to open the package to which this coin had adhered.

As I removed the string tied round the musty envelope,

a playing card fell out. On the back was a faded design in blue. I flipped it over. It was no ordinary playing card, but a Tarot card – bearing the image of a monster with a remarkably frightening visage – horns, forked tongue and a lean, muscular body. *The Devil.*

And then a strange thing happened.

As I stared at it, the power suddenly went off in my flat, silencing a Vivaldi violin concerto mid-*arpeggio*, and plunging me into near darkness. Outside, the rainy dusk was a dim glow.

I am not the superstitious type. I got up, lit a few candles, and sat back down. I gently eased the dog-eared notebook from the envelope. On the cover, *The Devil's Due*, was inscribed in Dr Watson's distinctive, neat handwriting.

Consuming this by candlelight seemed entirely appropriate. Here is what I read.

—Bonnie MacBird
London, April 2019

PART ONE

LONDON

'Sir, if you wish to have a just notion of the magnitude of this city, you must not be satisfied with seeing its great streets and squares but must survey the innumerable little lanes and courts. It is not in the showy evolutions of buildings, but in the multiplicity of human habitations which are crowded together that the wonderful immensity of London consists.'

—Samuel Johnson

CHAPTER 1

Fog

ondon could be heaven; London could be hell. I thought I knew the city well following more than eight years of adventures with my friend Sherlock Holmes, but the extremes of my adopted home had never revealed themselves to me so clearly as they did during the adventure I am about to relate.

It was in November of 1890 that Holmes faced one of the worst villains of his career, a monster responsible for a series of high profile, grotesque murders that both terrified and titillated the city. These violent deaths were strung, like so many blood-soaked pearls on a devil's necklace.

Only Sherlock Holmes could have traced the gossamer thread that tied together anarchists and artists, politicians and prostitutes, grocers, grafters, and even royalty. But in the process, he was nearly consumed himself by the fires of hell. Or in this case, St James's.

My name is Dr John Watson. At the time of this tale, I had been happily married to our former client Mary Morstan for close to two years, and had resumed my medical practice, now in Paddington. One icy Tuesday morning in November, Mary and I lingered in our quiet dining-room over coffee and the newspapers.

The Russian 'flu, which had kept me monotonously occupied was at last waning and no one awaited me in my surgery. The grandfather clock ticked, crisp toast cooled in its silver rack, and time stretched on. I poured myself a third cup of coffee. It had been weeks since I had seen my friend Sherlock Holmes.

Meanwhile the newspapers reported that just outside our windows, London seethed under the tumult of a rising tide of immigrants from France, Italy, and Ireland, shuddered with terror as anarchists (mainly French) set off bombs, groaned under the weight of poverty and a rising crime rate, and twisted in circles over government intrigue, royal scandal, industrialism, and 'The Woman Question'. At the same time, the city glittered with new operas and theatrical galas, and art, music and entertainment lit up her evenings.

I flung down my paper and stared at the rain outside our window.

'Listen to this, John,' said Mary. 'There's a newly installed "Chief Commissioner of the Metropolitan Police" – now there's a title – named Titus Billings who "promises to make London safe from the hordes of foreign criminals flooding our city".'

I sighed. 'Hmm. I am sure there are a few home-grown ones as well.'

'There is more. He's planning to do this by "arming the police, putting more boots on the street, and banishing all amateurs from criminal investigations".' She handed me her pages in disgust. 'Looks an awful fellow. You don't suppose he means Mr Sherlock Holmes?'

I stared at the image of Titus Billings on the page. He was an imperious, military type with a thick black moustache and fierce eyes. It was a case of instant dislike. 'He'd be a fool if so,' said I. It would not surprise me if Holmes had already tangled with the man.

'Perhaps a visit to Mr Holmes is in order?'

'I am sure he is quite busy, Mary. He is no doubt behind the scenes on that strange Anson case.'

'The man found drowned in his bed? An impossible death!' She shuddered.

'Yes, an odd one,' said I musing at the image of a wealthy man found dry, clean, and in his nightclothes, upright in his bed, yet drowned, a 'Devil' Tarot card in his hand. The reports had been intriguing. Mary was staring at me. 'Well, yes, it has been quite the season for unusual murders,' I added.

'And Danforth, that paper magnate, stabbed to death with a letter opener,' she urged, regarding me closely. 'That is an odd one!'

I laughed at the irony of the crime. 'Oh, indeed,' I said. Holmes was no doubt enjoying that case.

'You share Mr Holmes's morbid humour, John!' she

chided, but I knew she was as fond of Holmes as I. 'You know, he may have run into trouble there,' she added. 'Take a look.' She laid *The Illustrated Police Gazette* in front of me. There, on that lurid rag was the headline '*False Conjurer Sherlock Holmes Fails Spectacularly!*'

'False conjurer? What on earth?'

I quickly read the article, and as I did so, felt a rising anger against the writer, one Gabriel Zanders. He hinted that Sherlock Holmes had 'an unhealthy affinity for blood and death', had 'attempted to misdirect the police in the manner of a carnival magician', and 'caused the arrest the wrong fellow in the spectacular Danforth murder'. It ended with: 'What dark motives are hidden behind that sallow, sinister face? Who can understand the mind of this inhuman automaton who haunts London?' An unflattering illustration of Holmes appeared next to the article.

Mary began clearing the dishes. She lingered near my chair, looking at the article.

'John, what about a short holiday? Take some time off. Perhaps go see Mr Holmes. You are the wind under his wings, I think.'

'The ballast in his hold, more accurately,' said I, smiling at the image of my friend as a fast moving though slightly unsteady ship. 'But if I am to take a holiday,' said I, 'it must be with you, Mary. I am worried about that cough.'

'The Trowbridges have suggested a fortnight's visit to their Cotswold manor, John,' said Mary.

'Fresh air. Good idea,' I said, my heart sinking.

She laughed. 'Oh, John, you despise the Trowbridges! I

will go there, and you go to Mr Holmes. Do not argue.' She smiled and kissed me on the cheek. 'We shall both return refreshed.'

What man has ever had a more understanding wife!

With the notice of a holiday posted on my surgery door, and a word to a colleague who would take up any urgent cases, I was off within the hour.

CHAPTER 2

221B

t was thus with considerable pleasure and a free conscience that I found myself later that morning in the sitting-room of 221B Baker Street, awaiting the appearance of my dear friend. Whether he would welcome an extended visit, I had no idea.

The room, as usual, was awash in newspapers, dirty ashtrays, and odd items. The chemistry table held a series of jars containing what appeared to be human fingers, and on one table was an elephant's tusk, stained brown at the pointed end.

How I missed our close association!

I noticed that several newspapers including two weeks' worth of *The Illustrated Police Gazette* had been laid out on the dining table, their pages folded back to specific articles. I was reading the third, tirades much like the one

Mary had shown me, with mounting alarm when I was startled by a voice inches behind my left ear.

'Dear Watson, are you finding the *Gazette* edifying?'

I started and turned to see my friend, who must have entered the room on a cushion of air, for I had heard nothing.

'Holmes! You gave me such a fright!'

'Apparently I am having quite an effect on any number of people,' said he with a laugh. He was still in nightclothes, his hair uncombed, and a cigarette already in hand. 'Coffee, please, Mrs Hudson,' he called out over his shoulder. Then to me, 'You will join me, Watson?'

'Thank you, no. I have been up for hours. My God, these articles! This Gabriel Zanders, fellow—'

'Disregard him. He is a muckraking master of *schadenfreude*. He's first to the scene of any crime and loves nothing more than to publish lurid details even before the family is notified. I took him to task for this in front of the man who happened to be his editor. He has been going after me ever since.'

'I am sorry to hear it. He seems bent on doing you harm.'

Holmes shrugged dismissively, then turned his focus to me. He smiled. 'You have been busy of late, but you have decided on a holiday. What brings you here, instead of to some pastoral paradise with Mary?'

'Do not make me ask how you deduced this!'

'Perfectly simple. You have discarded your professional costume. You lack the expensive polished boots with which you attempt to dazzle your new patients, but which cause you pain in your left big toe, and the rather ostentatious gold watch which announces that you are more well established than you actually are. Instead, you are in your old suit and your comfortable brogues, which have served you well on our many wanderings, and with that old timepiece of your late brother's, also gold but rather worn, which provides sentimental value but conveys less prestige.'

'All right, Holmes. I know that you— Wait! The left big toe?'

'Remember I have visited you in your surgery, Watson. I have noted your very different attire, shoes and watch, which I have never seen you wear elsewhere, and have drawn an obvious conclusion. In those terribly shiny boots which complete your impressive costume, I discerned a small protrusion in the area of your left big toe, and having seen your feet free of encumbrances on a number of occasions while you lived here on Baker Street, I am aware of a slight deformity which makes shoe-fit difficult. Those you are wearing now you had stretched by the cobbler on Paddington Street in March four years ago, and you have since worn them for some time, and on some very long rambles.'

I sighed. It was simple observation, coupled with that prodigious memory. 'Really, Holmes, you risk overcrowding that brain attic of which you are so proud.'

Holmes laughed. 'You need not worry, Watson.'

'Though it has served you well. I read you were being considered for Queen's honours!'

'And today dismissed as a fraud!' exclaimed Holmes. 'Or

rather a false conjurer. Ah, the press. It is as worth riling oneself over them as it is the weather.'

'Today was a particularly vitriolic attack, Holmes. Were you wrong about the Danforth case?'

Holmes yawned. 'Of course not. Do not believe all that you read, Watson,' said he. 'The press seeks to create heroes and villains, angels and devils, where mere mortals exist.' He took a deep draw on his cigarette and sank into the basket chair.

Mrs Hudson entered wordlessly and set down a coffee service on the table, not bothering to remove the newspapers laid there. With a friendly nod to me and a look of remonstrance at Holmes, she exited in silence.

I had meanwhile glanced at two other Zanders articles. I shook my head in anger.

'Good old Watson. Like most people I see that you are drawn like a moth to a flame to a trifling bit of opprobrious news.' He looked at me closely. 'And you are transparently outraged!' This appeared to amuse him.

'Here's another headline: "*Baker Street Braggart Sherlock Holmes fails spectacularly.*"

'I know. Let me apply some coffee to my fogged cerebrum.' He poured himself a cup and once again sank into the chair.

I drew the offending paper from the table and sat opposite him in my old chair. 'Shall I read it aloud?' I asked.

'No, thank you. I have tasted those bitter spirits an hour ago.'

I turned my eyes to the article and finished it with

increasing revulsion. I looked up. Holmes was lighting a second cigarette to accompany his coffee.

'What a ghastly business, this Sebastian Danforth murder!' said I. 'A well-respected MP and esteemed philanthropist who made his fortune in paper, stabbed sixteen times with a dull letter opener by his own son!'

'Seventeen times. And yes, a son did it.'

'This article says you named the wrong person.' I pointed to the fourth paragraph and read aloud '"The erroneous evidence provided by that deranged poseur Sherlock Holmes" – "*deranged poseur*", great heavens!'

'Your indignation should be directed at the word "erroneous", Watson, not "deranged poseur". My evidence was flawless and damning. The eldest son Charles Danforth was clearly the culprit. There were a number of indications, but a tiny splatter of blood on the murderer's watch chain was conclusive.'

'Well, this Titus Billings fellow disagrees vehemently. Why? And who is he?'

'Billings is an unknown quantity, late of the foreign office and has been given some kind of sovereignty over at the Yard that I cannot fathom,' he remarked casually – then vigorously exhaled a plume of smoke. I noted his foot tapping silently.

'Tell me of the case, Holmes.'

Holmes leaned back in his chair. 'This murderous son, Charles Danforth, who was initially gaoled on my evidence, believed his father had suddenly written him out of his will. Charles was already known to be unstable, and upon hearing this news – false, as it turns out – a shouting match ensued, with the son cursing like a fiend at his father. Shortly after, the old man was discovered, expiring from multiple stab wounds. Upon my evidence, Charles was arrested, but "new evidence", to which I was not privy, was submitted, supposedly implicating Sebastian Danforth's *younger* son. As of last night, Charles was running free. His younger brother – quite innocent – was charged with the crime and waits in gaol. But it will all be set right soon.'

'I should hope so,' said I, 'if nothing more than to clear your name.'

'My reputation is nothing in the grand scheme of things,' said Holmes. 'But this gross error allowed a monster to roam free throughout London last night.'

I was astonished at this last. 'It is unlike you, Holmes, to be sleeping late when there are such doings afoot.'

Mrs Hudson entered with a tray of sandwiches. 'Mr Holmes has been in his bed for less than two hours, Doctor.' Turning to her lodger, she remonstrated, 'You endanger your health, Mr Holmes, with all this gallivanting about at night.'

She poured me a coffee without asking. Handing it to me, she added, 'Just see how tired he is!'

Holmes sighed. 'I located the villain and communicated his whereabouts to Inspector Lestrade some four hours ago. This worthy endeavour involved a rather dangerous chase at the docks, and a visit to a brothel in the guise of a doctor.'

'Remarkable! I take back my remonstrance. Apologies, Holmes.'

He smiled, but the smile dropped as he added, 'I have had to proceed unofficially, as I was blocked from the case by this new man, Billings. But Lestrade has the facts in hand now, and no doubt the murderer as well. I am confident he will see things through to conviction.'

Once more my friend had brought justice to bear, while giving all credit to the local police. His selflessness was one of the things about him I most admired.

'Holmes, what a remarkable night's work. You are to be congratulated! Perhaps you may want to rest. If so, I am happy to stay and read until you arise. We might enjoy a meal out later?'

'If you wish, Watson. But I shall first pay a visit to the murderer's rather delicate wife. Constance Danforth will surely be relieved at her husband's capture. I interviewed them both, separately of course, and perceived that she was terrified of him. Although she would not admit it, I saw evidence of burns along her arms, as if from a cigarette.'

'Good God!'

Holmes got up and began to stir the embers of the fire, which had nearly gone out.

'While one cannot resurrect her late father-in-law, I am convinced that this investigation will at least serve to save the life of that innocent young woman. How much time have you free?'

'A fortnight. Mary has gone—'

'Splendid! Your room is vacant, should you care to stay.'

He began to add coals to the dwindling fire. I found

myself uncommonly pleased and surprised at the extremity of my emotion.

'I shall retrieve my luggage, then—' I began, when a sudden bang drew my eyes to the door, and a heavyset, muscular man of about thirty-five exploded into the room.

CHAPTER 3

Attack!

y first impression was of a whirling black coat and silk hat, and a silver-tipped walking stick. But it was the man's reddened face – wild-eyed with fury and venom, his eyes nearly popping – that froze me in alarm. Spotting my friend kneeling by the fire, the intruder crossed the room in three bounding steps, stick raised to strike.

I had only time to cry out, 'Holmes!'

Just as the fiend was about to smite my friend with what threatened to be a fatal blow, Holmes leapt up, and with the grace of the fencing master he was, whirled and blocked the descending stick with the fireplace poker in his left hand. It clanged like a church bell. In one continuous move, Holmes dealt a hard right to the man's jaw. There was a sharp crack as his fist connected, and the strapping fellow dropped like a stone onto the bear rug in front of the fire.

There he lay still, face down and pressed against the great beast's grinning countenance.

It was as if Holmes had eyes in the back of his own head, so smooth had been his remarkable defence. He now stood, gazing calmly at his attacker. With one slippered foot, he nudged the shoulder of the unconscious man, rolling him onto his back.

'Charles Danforth,' he remarked, as though commenting on some fruit selection at an outdoor market. 'Truly one of the most vicious murderers London has seen in some time.' Holmes looked up at me. 'It took tremendous strength and rage to kill his father with a dull letter opener, Watson. A ghastly way to bring about an end.' He rubbed his forehead tiredly. 'Though I did think Lestrade would have had him in custody by now.'

Just then the wiry little police detective and two constables burst through the door, Mrs Hudson behind them.

'Mr Holmes! Are you all right?' cried Lestrade. Spotting the man on the floor, the policeman exhaled in relief. 'Well, of course you are, sir. He slipped us once, but we got onto his intentions, and it was a race to your house. If only I had come in time!'

'Yes, well, you are here now,' said Holmes. 'This man's intemperate attack, Lestrade, can only bolster your case.'

'Oh yes, Mr Holmes. No question. Take him away, boys.'

Lestrade's constables hoisted the unconscious form of Charles Danforth and conveyed him out the door.

Lestrade turned to Holmes. 'Excellent work, Mr Holmes, and once again the Yard is grateful to you. And between us, sir, I am pleased that you, rather than Mr Billings, have brought the villain to heel. I will make sure that everyone knows.'

'Please do not do so, Lestrade. I wish you to take the credit.'

'But Mr Holmes, I—'

'I must insist.'

Lestrade looked relieved. 'As you see fit, Mr Holmes. You were right about it all, including his poor wife, may she rest in peace. True about the burns on her arms. Cigarette, I would say. Oh . . . Charles Danforth is a beast!'

Holmes had frozen in horror. 'His wife? Dead?'

Lestrade nodded wearily.

My friend was galvanized. 'How did she die? I advised you to post a guard to Constance Danforth's house the moment I heard of this man's release! Did you fail to do so?'

Lestrade shook his head. 'We followed your instructions, Mr Holmes, and posted a guard directly. She was alive when we did so. 'Tweren't her husband, though. She killed herself, the poor little dear, thinking her husband had gotten away with murder and would be back.'

'When? How?'

'Naught we could have done. Found by her maid last night. I was informed just after I saw you a few hours ago. That would make it perhaps around midnight?'

'How, I ask?'

'Poison. There was a note.'

'I must see it.'

'I'll have it brought to you straight away.'

In a moment, the police had departed with the unconscious criminal. I closed the door behind them and turned my attention to my friend. Holmes had sunk motionless in the basket chair, head in his hands.

This reaction was far more than the sudden collapse of energy I had witnessed often at the end of a challenging case. The woman's suicide had hit him hard; clearly he had been unprepared for it.

I sat opposite him and waited.

'Holmes?' I whispered after some minutes had passed. 'You asked for her to be guarded. What more could you have done? Surely she felt safe with police protection.'

'I should have gone there myself.'

'You could not have predicted.'

'She was delicate. Frightened. Despairing. She had loved her father-in-law deeply, and he had been, I inferred, her protector.'

'You are a detective, not an alienist. Or a fortune-teller. How could you have foreseen a suicide?'

Holmes did not answer.

'Instead, you went after the brute and succeeded in locating him.'

Holmes nodded but said nothing, sinking further into black rumination.

After a few minutes, I informed him that I'd return in an hour with my things for an extended stay, and that I expected to entice him to a walk or a meal if he was not sleeping off the effects of the night. 'Doctor's orders, Holmes.

Whatever lies ahead, it is time for recovery, not remonstrance.'

He said nothing, and I left, determined to return as quickly as possible.

CHAPTER 4

Devil and Hyde

n hour later, I returned. The rain had abated for the first time in days, and I convinced my friend that a ramble in Hyde Park would offer refreshment. We usually frequented Regent's Park but today I suggested a change of scenery.

We set off at a brisk pace and were soon strolling in the southern end of the park along the Serpentine. I hoped this serene, tree-lined vista would soothe my companion's jangled nerves. Who knew how long we might enjoy the bright sunlight, with rainclouds scudding across the sky. The chill was bracing.

I glanced at his thin figure, bundled in a long black overcoat and blue scarf, his collar turned up for warmth, as he walked beside me in silence, head down. I had forgotten the intensity of those black clouds which periodically rolled in to darken his outlook. He seemed oblivious to the gleaming waterway and the brilliant golds and oranges of the foliage.

'Holmes,' I ventured. 'What of a dinner tonight at Simpson's? Some roast beef, your favourite, followed by perhaps an opera? *Faust*, by some French composer, is on just now.'

'The composer is Charles Gounod – and I have seen it already. Watson, you despise opera. I am not in the humour for conversation. Is it not enough that I agreed to accompany you on this pointless meandering?'

'It is hardly pointless,' said I.

'Then what *is* the point?' he asked crossly.

'The point is to breathe, to take in nature, and to reset the mind. Look at those trees!'

Above us the canopy of golds, greens and hints of orange glowed like stained glass, sparkling intermittently as the bright sun peeked through.

He glanced up at the sky. 'It will rain again soon. Let us return to Baker Street. I neglected to bring my umbrella.'

He turned left and headed sharply north, in the direction of Speakers' Corner. We had been out for less than an hour.

'Holmes, shall we not concentrate on the good news? Those Queen's honours under discussion? Not a knighthood, do you think?'

It was as though I'd thrown vitriol on his favourite coat. 'Watson! You know me better than that!' His vehemence surprised me.

'It is one thing to refrain from *seeking* accolades, but

can you not at least appreciate them when they are offered sincerely?' I said. 'Surely this would bring in more clientele.'

'Anonymity better serves my work. That journalist simply needed a story,' he said bitterly. 'Today I am reviled. Neither notice means anything.'

'Well, what of this Gabriel Zanders fellow? I am genuinely concerned, Holmes.'

'He is creative, to be sure. He has made it his business to vilify me, alternately deriding my abilities, and ascribing to them some dark origins.'

'Dark origins? But this is laughable, Holmes!'

'To the rational, it is laughable.'

'What does he mean, dark origins?'

'To the gullible among his readers, and those are the majority, he implies my powers are otherworldly, devilish. For his more educated readers, he implies that I have deep ties to the criminal community. Either explanation is apparently easier to swallow than my use of scientific method, keen observation and hard work.'

'Indeed. And the occasional flash of intuition, Holmes.'

'One cannot count on that. In any case, Zanders is to be ignored. Even if he is having me followed. As indeed he is, at this very moment.' He nodded behind us.

I looked about but saw no one.

Holmes stalked on. I had difficulty keeping up. While notorious for not caring about public opinion, Holmes knew better than to inflame a reporter. Dark clouds had moved in rapidly to blacken the sky, and no less the mood of my friend. He scowled and picked up his already furious pace.

'Are you trying to shake him?' I asked, referring to his supposed tail.

'That will be difficult in the park. Just to exhaust him, perhaps.'

'Well, you are exhausting me!'

We continued a moment in silence. I was growing a bit winded.

'You are out of training, Watson.' He picked up his pace as if to challenge me further. 'Rather more tiresome than Zanders is this fool Titus Billings at Scotland Yard!'

'He does have some peculiar notions,' I offered. 'Slow down, please. In any case, you enjoy a challenge, Holmes.'

He said nothing, and we continued in silence. He looked no less grim. The walk was not having the effect I had hoped.

'Holmes, perhaps I join you at an inconvenient time.'

'All I need is an interesting case, and the freedom to pursue it unimpeded!' he exclaimed. 'Nothing more!' He glanced my way again and, with a look of contrition, added, 'I am sorry, dear fellow. No, you are not inconvenient. Rather, in fact, most welcome. I might find bad humour overtaking me if you were not here.'

'Bad humour? You?' I laughed. Holmes favoured me with one of his quick smiles. We proceeded in silence. Our relative peace did not last long. As we drew nearer to the northern end of Hyde Park, I began to discern the sound of a crowd, chanting something unintelligible in unison. We approached the fabled Speakers' Corner, and a loud and melodious voice pierced the chill November air, followed by another unison crowd response.

We came upon a makeshift dais of several wooden boxes on which stood a tall, muscular figure garbed in the long black coat, wide-brimmed hat, and white collar of a pastor. His was a handsome face, rather more sun-darkened than one associates with a London man of the cloth (but perhaps he had served his church in southern climes, I thought). Despite his sober clothing, there was something of the salesman to the fellow.

His words enthralled a highly animated crowd of nearly one hundred people. 'We must give up our vanity, give up our greed, give up our lust,' he exhorted. 'Because the Devil is always near. We must be on the lookout. For the Devil walks among us. Who walks among us?'

'The Devil walks among us,' responded the crowd.

'Who walks among us?' he shouted.

'The Devil walks among us!' the group responded, louder this time. I paused to listen, fascinated with the hypnotic effect this man was having upon the crowd. 'We must be on our guard,' insisted the object of their attention. 'We must seek him out and destroy him. Frighten him with your voices. Louder now! Where does the Devil walk?'

'The Devil walks among us!' shouted the crowd.

This must be the kind of 'tent preacher' I had read of, roaming the American South. A rabble-rouser, to my mind.

Holmes stiffened and I followed his gaze to a garishly dressed young man, clean-shaven, with slicked-back hair and an eager, hungry face. He had arrived on the periphery of the crowd opposite us, scanning the scene. As I watched, he took out a small notebook and pen. He glanced our way.

'Holmes, is that—?'

'Zanders? Yes.' Holmes turned to regard the speaker with a strange expression, perhaps irony. He shrugged. 'Come along, Watson, we burn daylight.'

'Look for him always. And what must we be?' cried the speaker.

'On our guard!' shouted the crowd.

I could not tear myself away. Something about this scene and this speaker utterly fascinated me. I grasped Holmes's arm. 'Look at those white lines around his fingers! Many rings, I should think. What preacher would adorn himself so?' I felt sure Holmes would compliment me on my keen observation.

'None, Watson. His name is James Fardwinkle and he runs a pickpocketing ring out of Holborn. I have had him arrested twice, but he is something of a greased hog. The police cannot take hold. Let us move along.'

I laughed. 'Indeed! Look—!' A young boy wove through the crowds, pausing to artfully extract a billfold from a pocket. He began to approach us but then, noting my challenging stare, he changed course. In a moment, he dipped into a woman's reticule, removing several pound notes.

'Stop, thief!' I shouted.

'Watson!' Holmes whispered.

The speaker swivelled to glare at me directly, his face melting into a theatrical portrayal of hurt innocence. But as he recognized Holmes standing next to me, a transformation came over it, which sent a chill down my spine.

'That was not wise,' murmured Holmes, looking down and adjusting his Homburg to cover his face.

'There's a policeman right over there.' I gestured to a constable standing off to one side, presumably monitoring the situation. 'Fardwinkle can hardly weasel out now. Police!' I cried.

'We must be off now,' said Holmes, seizing my arm with an iron pinch.

'Will you know the Devil when you see him?' shouted Fardwinkle. The preacher was staring at me, or rather us. He raised an arm and pointed it at Holmes. 'I can. I do. The Devil is standing here among us.'

The crowd turned to look at us. Their gaze focused on Holmes. Admittedly, his gaunt pallor, intensity and swirling black coat were not at that moment helping to portray the angel of justice I knew him to be.

I would not let this situation intimidate us. 'You are an utter charlatan!' I found myself shouting at Fardwinkle. 'Watch your pockets, ladies and gentlemen!' Turning to Holmes, I said, 'How can this crowd be so gullible?'

Holmes shook his head but did not release my arm.

'There he is. The Devil. The Devil in the flesh! You know what to do!' The speaker continued to point at Holmes.

This was an outrage. We were in the centre of modern London. The Devil, indeed!

'This is Sherlock Holmes, you fool!' I shouted. 'The detective.'

'Oh, dear God,' murmured Holmes. He yanked my arm, none too gently. 'Stop talking.'

'Sherlock Holmes, who sends innocent men to the gallows!' shouted Fardwinkle in full preacher voice. 'Charles Danforth! Just this week, an innocent man, freed only yesterday by the will of God. Sherlock Holmes, who has been taken by the Devil. The Devil is Sherlock Holmes!'

A woman moved up to him and batted at him with her handbag. 'The Devil!' she announced, nodding.

'Not me, madam,' he said gently, as he sidestepped her, only to find two men blocking his way. 'Watson, run.'

I caught a glimpse of Gabriel Zanders across the crowd, regarding the unfolding drama with eager excitement. The crowd closed in and Holmes and I were separated. A leering man leaned in to me and shouted, 'Who are you who walks with the Devil?' Two more moved in beside him, giving me their hardest looks.

'My name is John Watson. I am a doctor, you idiot. Now, let me pass.'

Ahead of me, Holmes was engulfed by murmuring congregants. Only then did I realize the true danger of the situation.

They began to push. The man near me knocked the hat from my head. I bent down to scoop it up but upon rising could no longer see Holmes.

From the dais, the speaker continued to excite the crowd. 'The Devil and his disciple walk among us. You know what to do. The Devil! The Devil!'

Suddenly I felt the press of the furious crowd. The situation had ratcheted from zero to lethal in seconds.

'Destroy the Devil! Destroy the Devil!'

A woman slapped at my face and a man tried to wrench my arm behind my back.

I yanked free, then caught a brief glimpse of Holmes, who was attempting to fend off grasping hands without hurting anyone. Above it all, Fardwinkle continued to shout, waving his preacher's hat towards my friend, a malicious smile splitting his sunburnt face.

Two men seized my arms but, with a sudden heave, I freed myself and pushed through the crowd towards Holmes, inadvertently bumping into a young woman. 'Pardon me, madam!' I said, noting the beautiful young face fixed on mine. Her hand snaked into my pocket and she smiled in triumph. I pulled away in alarm, before remembering I carried nothing in that pocket. More people intervened, and I pushed through to my friend.

Holmes and I exchanged a look, locked arms, and rammed our way free. Before us was the path, and beyond that, Marble Arch, and the safety of others.

We ran.

A couple of the men followed hard on our heels, but the policeman's whistle sounded, echoed by another, and our pursuers gave up the chase. We did not slow down until we were safe among the milling crowds near Marble Arch.

It was only when the drizzle became a sudden downpour that I realized I had lost my umbrella in the mob at Speakers' Corner. 'Devil take it,' I said in exasperation. 'My umbrella!'

'Devil did take it indeed, Watson.'

We took shelter under the arch, but the rain slanted in to pelt us, nevertheless. Water poured off our hats and shoulders as crowds of businessmen hurried past under their umbrellas without a thought. We were back in modern London. Holmes and I eyed each other for one tense moment, then . . . burst out laughing.

'You do look a touch satanic,' I said, eyeing the rain dripping from Holmes's black Homburg.

'Apparently so, Watson.'

'What's this?' I had put my hands in my pockets against the cold when I discovered a small card in the left one. I pulled it out. It had a strange, ornate blue and white pattern on one side. I turned it over.

'Look at this!' I exclaimed. 'A young woman in the crowd – she must have placed it there.'

For there, in my hand, was a Tarot card, with a leering, horned figure, ornately drawn in black and white and blood red. The Devil!

CHAPTER 5

Brotherly Love

wenty minutes later, the fire roaring and our wet clothes set before it, Holmes and I sat smoking in our dressing gowns in the sitting-room of 221B. Holmes perused the Tarot card I had been given and retrieved his magnifying glass to have closer look.

'Anything, Holmes?' I asked. 'One of those fortune-telling cards, isn't it?'

'Tarot, yes. Fairly common type; I've seen this deck before. Delarue Franc, it says here, exported from France. The Devil. How apropos.'

I stared at the gruesome horned figure dancing on the card. 'Hmm. I see no resemblance to you. Well, maybe around the eyes—'

'Watson!'

'All, right, not the eyes. But you could both use a bit more meat on the bones.'

We sat in silence as he continued to examine the card.

'What do you say to my idea of Simpson's, Holmes? A bit of sustenance?'

'I do not like this, Watson. A card like this was found at that Anson murder. Who gave you this card? Was it one of the two dippers?'

'The pickpockets? Not one of the two boys, no. It was a young lady, barely more than a girl,' said I. 'I am not sure she was working with them.'

'Why?'

'I . . . I don't know. Better dressed, perhaps?'

'Did you get good look?'

'Yes. Long dark hair, blue eyes, quite beautiful, unafraid. Bold even. Hard to tell her age, perhaps eighteen or so.'

'Have you seen her before?'

'No, and I think I should have remembered,' I said with a smile.

'That lovely?'

I nodded. 'She had a mole here.' I pointed to my right cheek. 'And truly unafraid. Triumphant, almost.'

'Well, she did manage to plant this card on you. Did she get anything in return?'

'No. I keep nothing in my overcoat pockets.'

'Wise. How did you lose your umbrella?'

'I – I must have dropped it in the melee. Nothing else is missing, I checked, Holmes,' said I, growing annoyed.

'If you are sure then,' said he, turning back to examining the card.

'What of that reporter, Holmes? Do you think it coincidence that Zanders was there?'

'I do not believe in coincidence. I told you that he is having me followed. I shall be more careful. This incident will appear shortly in some rag, no doubt.'

'He is going to a great deal of trouble about you, Holmes. You must have truly infuriated him.'

'Leave it, Watson. He is simply fishing. He will tire of it when a better story comes round.'

A knock sounded on the front door and in a moment Billy, our page, stood dripping in the doorway, cap in hand.

'Mr Holmes. Dr Watson. I have a message from Mr Mycroft Holmes, sirs. He would like to see you both, er . . .' he squinted at a small white paper . . . 'Towdee-sweetie?'

Holmes laughed. '*Tout de suite?* Ah, urgent, is it? Well, Watson, our comfort is short lived. The Diogenes awaits.'

An hour later, dressed once again in our city finest, Holmes and I sat near the fire in the Stranger's Room at the Diogenes, the only room where conversation was allowed in his brother's most unusual gentlemen's club. It was a masculine, elegant room, designed to impress with a row of antique globes, thick carpeting, and gilt-edged books. A window looked out on Pall Mall, where rain continued to flood the streets.

It was one of a handful of such meetings I had attended. In each case, I found myself acutely uncomfortable. There was an unsettling discord, a tension between the two brothers that I did not understand. Mycroft wielded great power and influence at the highest levels of government.

He and Holmes worked together frequently, but not always amiably. In this very room, I had witnessed Mycroft Holmes once threaten my friend with a gaol term, and worse.

Today's meeting had started badly, and it was not sitting well with Sherlock Holmes.

'Mycroft, you are full of advice and admonitions today!' said my friend, striding around the room. 'Do not confront this Titus Billings, you say. Steer clear of journalist Gabriel Zanders. Drop my work following the French anarchists. What is it that you *do* want?'

'I am looking out for your best interests, Sherlock,' drawled Mycroft Holmes as he fingered a small gold pocket lens dangling from one of two heavy watch chains stretched across his ample girth. He was, as always, impeccably tailored, from his mirror-polished shoes to his professionally barbered countenance, implacable, and mountainously heavy, so unlike his brother. I felt a small pleasure that the Double Albert watch chain was perhaps somewhat tighter across Mycroft's growing girth than the last time we had seen him.

'First, you must hear a few things, Sherlock. Titus Billings is connected at the highest levels, I believe to a close relative of the Royal Family. One of the Queen's cousins. Steer clear. He is out of my reach for the moment.'

'Extend your reach quickly then, Mycroft. The Danforth case was horribly bungled,' said Holmes bitterly. 'An innocent young woman died as the result.'

Mycroft sighed. 'Sit down, Sherlock.'

'And Billings's aim to arm the police?' continued Holmes.

'The man is a philistine. Most of them should not be trusted with their truncheons, much less a gun.'

'In time, I will discover the wedge, but you must be patient.'

The long thin wedge. I had heard Mycroft speak of it before. It was a metaphor, I suppose, for whatever he did at Whitehall. In the past, Holmes had hinted at his brother's Machiavellian manoeuvring, but always in service of the greater good. However, it has been my experience that the more power a man has, the more challenging it is to retain the moral high ground. Whatever Mycroft did or didn't do in service of the 'greater good', I only hoped that he shared the admirable code of honour of Sherlock Holmes.

I was never sure.

Mycroft Holmes lit a cigarette and offered the box to each of us. We declined and I moved the ashtray closer to him. At last Holmes sat down.

Despite their differences of physique and temperament, the Holmes brothers did share uncanny skills of observation and deduction, and an astonishing ability to store an encyclopaedic range of facts. And both had developed mysterious, though I wager very different, ways of monitoring the events of their relative spheres of operation. I had no idea how Mycroft knew nearly every move made by his brother. It was not a comfortable idea to contemplate.

'I have asked you here today, Sherlock, primarily to discuss this recent spate of unusual murders.'

'At last. Which exactly?'

'First, give me your further thoughts on that Danforth case.'

'Curious. An act of remarkable violence on the part of the son.'

'Out of nowhere, then?' asked Mycroft.

'I think not. There were strong signs of Charles Danforth's instability, the family were aware of it, but the incident must have been set off by something. I do not know yet what that was.'

'Someone gave a push, perhaps?'

'Possibly. I do know that the killer was under the impression that his father's will had been recently revised to favour the younger brother.'

'Had it?'

'No.'

'That is all you have?'

'I have been busy.'

'And working alone. Perhaps now that Dr Watson has rejoined you, you will be more successful.'

I could sense Holmes's suppressed anger. He sprang up again and moved to the bookshelves where he appeared to become unusually interested in the antique globes.

Mycroft continued to goad. 'Up and down. Since you were a child. What about that Horatio Anson case? Unsolved?'

'I was away when that came up. Curious, though, that a former shipbuilder was found dead in bed, fully clothed and dry, yet drowned. I intend to look into it further.'

'And Clammory?' said Mycroft.

'Fellow who made a fortune with a series of barber shops, found with his throat slit with a razor?' I exclaimed. 'That was a strange one!'

'Mmm,' mused Mycroft. 'Sherlock? You did not investigate that either?'

'Away during that one as well. Upon my return, I found that Titus Billing had blocked my access to police files. I have asked Lestrade for a few in particular and expect to receive them shortly. Mycroft, this Billings is most inconvenient.'

He returned and sat down again next to me on the sofa. The two brothers faced each other for a long moment. Something passed between them. I became aware of an enormous clock ticking on the far wall. The clop of horses and sounds of carriage wheels hissing through the wet and icy streets made their way faintly through the curtained windows.

'Anson, Clammory, Danforth,' murmured Mycroft Holmes.

I took a sip of coffee. Something was being considered by the two brothers, I had no idea what. Holmes nodded, then remarked, casually. 'All right. Yes, I see it. Of course.'

Mycroft smiled. 'The philanthropy.'

'Yes.'

'*Significant* philanthropy. All of the victims.'

'Horatio Anson as well?' asked Holmes.

'Medical research, I believe. A rather large donation.'

'And, of course, Clammory and the Veterans of the Boer War Fund,' said Holmes. 'That got quite a bit of publicity.'

'And Danforth?' asked Mycroft. 'Any philanthropy?'

'Literacy programmes for the poor. Very different *modus operandi* in each killing, though.' said Holmes.

Mycroft nodded again.

What was this about? I wondered. All of the murder victims were philanthropists? That seemed a spurious connection.

'And other deaths in the family, immediately attendant,' said Mycroft. 'All apparently suicide.'

'That is most interesting. Let's see . . . with Danforth, yes. Clammory, unsure. No other deaths related to Anson?'

Mycroft smiled. 'A sister in Dover jumped off a cliff, I read.'

They lapsed into silence, allies once more. Most puzzling. A minute passed. The Holmes brothers would explain themselves in due time, I supposed. I needed more coffee and looked around for the attendant.

'But then we are missing a B,' said Holmes.

'Yes,' said his brother. 'Perhaps there has been a B'.

'One that may not have appeared to be a murder.'

'But was taken for an accident or a suicide.'

'Precisely. I shall have a look,' said Holmes.

'What kind of bee are you talking about?' I interjected at last. 'I am not following.'

'Watson, we are considering that these murders are linked, and by the same perpetrator,' said Holmes.

'Yes, but a bee?'

'Perhaps done in alphabetical order. We have an A, a C, and a D. But no B.'

I laughed. 'Well, that is far-fetched.'

'People who murder in series often leave some kind of sign so they will be credited for the kill. They want to be caught, ultimately,' said Holmes. 'Alphabet killings are not unknown. The *"Alfabeto Mortale"* in Rome in the last century comes to mind.'

'And don't forget the *"Alfabetmord"* in Norway,' said Mycroft. He laughed, a mirthless huffing sound.

'Ah yes, the "Norwegian Capper". Left clown hats on all his victims. All quite famous cases, Watson. I cracked the Norwegian one myself three years ago.'

'Clown hats?'

'A double signature, Watson. The alphabet. And the hats,' said Holmes.

'What of that Tarot card, The Devil? Found under Anson's pillow,' said Mycroft. 'It was in the papers. A signature of sorts?'

'I read that, yes. But found at none of the other murders,' said Holmes.

'Unless it went unreported. Or Titus Billings missed it,' said Mycroft.

'Which is credible. He is careless,' said Holmes.

'But not stupid, Sherlock. Take care.'

'A Tarot card?' I interjected. 'Like the one planted on me?'

'Ah, interesting,' said Mycroft. 'Planted? At the park? Do you have it?'

At the park? How had he known this?

Holmes produced it from his pocket and held it up, facing his brother.

Mycroft smiled, not deigning to take it. 'Yes, interesting.' He turned to me. 'Who planted it? Did you notice?'

'A young woman.' I said. 'I didn't recognize her.'

'It was placed in Watson's pocket as we were set upon by a crowd at Speakers' Corner, clamouring to find the Devil in me.'

'Ah yes, I heard about that. I understand Zanders was there. He is employing fellows to follow you, you know.'

'Yes. It is a veritable crowd, with your man following as well.'

I was surprised at this, as I had not noticed any followers.

'Careless of you to become embroiled with that Fagin-esque creature at Speakers' Corner, Sherlock. Let me see the card.'

I felt a tinge of guilt. Had we left when Holmes wanted to, all that might have been avoided.

Mycroft took the card from his brother and examined it with the small glass hanging from one of his watch chains. He handed it back. 'Ordinary. Not likely to be traceable.'

'My thoughts as well.'

'I wonder if it is exactly like the one at Anson's body. Worth pursuing, Sherlock, if you feel you are up to the game.'

'You did not summon me here merely to chastise me!' said Holmes

'No, for several reasons. But primarily to discuss this series of murders.'

'You are holding back something, Mycroft. What is it?'

Outside in the hall there was the sound of high-pitched male laughter and the door swung open.

'Ah, they are here. You have more to learn in a moment.'

PART TWO

GATHERING THE TROOPS

'Do not tell your friend what your enemy should
not know.'

—Arthur Schopenhauer

CHAPTER 6

The Greater Goodwins

ycroft heaved himself to his feet. 'Welcome, gentlemen! Sherlock and Doctor Watson, I have invited this illustrious duo who have something to impart.' Two foppish and very handsome young men spilled into the room on a cloud of cigar smoke, laughter, and the scent of expensive cologne and hair oil.

We rose as Mycroft continued. 'May I introduce to you brothers Andrew and James Goodwin, viscounts both, and members of the House of Lords.'

'I say, Mycroft, is this some kind of Game Day at your club?' cried the taller of the two, garbed in an exquisitely tailored but slightly anachronistic deep blue velvet suit. 'Everyone here seems to want everyone else to shush!' He was a dark-haired gentleman, his long, curly locks coiffed in a Byronic style, giving a bohemian, artistic impression, contrasting with a coiled energy.

'Yes! We were shushed five times – no six – between the entrance and this room,' drawled the shorter of the two, whose deep green velvet attire resembled his brother's. His appearance was differentiated by stylishly cropped hair, groomed straight back from his face and oiled to shine like patent leather.

As strange as their styles were, their suits were expertly tailored, complimenting each man's physique. Sportsmen, too, I decided. Two odd, if very rich, ducks.

'Silence is a policy of the club, gentlemen, except for this room,' said Mycroft. 'Do come in and meet my brother, Sherlock Holmes, and his friend and colleague, Dr John Watson.'

'Sherlock Holmes! The Demon Detective!' cried James, the man in green. 'And his little friend, the writer!'

As if in response to my social discomfort, the taller man drawled, 'He is an army doctor, James, not a "little friend". Relax, gentlemen, we do not bite.'

'Dr Watson! I say, are you a *medical* doctor, then? So sorry!' cried the shorter. 'Because I have a toe—'

'James, not now!' implored his brother, and they both laughed.

At Mycroft's gesture, the brothers claimed the seats on the sofa we had just vacated, the two of them taking up its entire long length, reclining as though they were at home in their sitting-room.

Holmes and I found other seats, then waited patiently as the two young men called for coffee and cigarettes, lumps of sugar, napkins and biscuits, clean ashtrays, Scotch and

Claret, causing the attendant to scurry about, bringing in item after item, only to be sent out again.

Mycroft smoked his cigarette patiently and seemed to take no notice of this odd show. Holmes, however, got up and moved once again to the window, irritated.

I studied them in more detail. Andrew, in blue, appeared to be older, and leaned back, languidly regarding Mycroft through a haze of cigarette smoke, a sardonic smile upon his smooth features. He was clearly a man used to privilege, and rarely challenged. A keen intelligence shined through his relaxed demeanour and I would warrant the man missed very little.

By contrast, his brother James, in green, was highly strung, as though an electric current animated him always, his dark brown eyes glittering in amusement and interest. He gestured with quick movements, smoothing his patent leather hair, flicking ash from his cigarette, sipping from his Claret, taking in the room and us in darting glances. He, too, seemed intelligent, with that air of entitlement possessed by the very rich.

They were a curious combination. I had heard of them, of course. Two of the youngest members of the House of Lords, they were influential and wealthy almost beyond compare. They shared an enormous house near Grosvenor Square, famous for its parties.

These frivolous and foppish first impressions were carefully cultivated, I presumed, as I had also read they had recently championed a major bill in Parliament with new protections for factory workers, against considerable opposition from their own party.

'Shall we begin?' said Mycroft. 'Sherlock, do come and join us. They have news which will be of interest. Mr Goodwin, may I call you Andrew, if only to differentiate you from your brother James?'

'Oh, indeed, do use our Christian names. Everyone does, for that very reason,' said Andrew Goodwin.

'Andrew, then, please advise my brother Sherlock and Dr Watson what you told me this morning.'

'Oh, yes,' said Andrew taking a healthy sip of his whisky. 'Ah, very good, this. We must get some for the house. What is it?'

'A self whisky. Glenmorangie from Tain. And now your news, please,' said Mycroft.

'Tell them, Andrew,' said James.

'Yes. Those recent murders. Anson. Clammory. And then that poor man stabbed by his own son!'

'Danforth. What about them?' asked Holmes.

'They are all Luminarians,' added James.

'Were, James, were!' said Andrew.

'Interesting,' said Holmes returning to sit with the group.

'What is a Luminarian?' I asked.

All eyes swivelled to me. The Goodwin brothers shared a smile.

'It is a very secret organization, Watson,' said Holmes. 'Not unlike the Freemasons, who also exist to promote good works. However, the Luminarians do not spring from the building industry. They are, to a man, a breed of wealthy do-gooders, all self-made, who use their money and influence to "bring light to the world". Hence "Luminarians".

An organization started by the two of you, I understand. That is really all I know.'

Andrew and James stared at Holmes in surprise.

'But you know quite a bit. How is that?' James blurted.

'It is my business to know London intimately,' said Holmes.

James laughed and looked at his brother. 'Well, if Mr Holmes begins to reveal what I did *intimately* in our mutual study at two o'clock early this morning, I'll have him down for a witch.'

'What is a male witch called, by the way?' said Andrew.

'A warlock,' said Holmes, matching their good humour with an uncharacteristic smile of his own. 'I have been called the Devil, but never a warlock. And no, I have no eyes in your study. How does one become a Luminarian? Does one apply and need a second? Do you induct new members?'

'It is not a membership *per se*. There is no applying or formal induction. It's more of a . . . bestowing. Kind of like the Queen's honours,' said James Goodwin. 'Not quite a knighthood, but . . .'

'Oh, James! Being dubbed a Luminarian is *our* honour, given by us, to a very lucky few,' said Andrew.

'And the benefits of this honour?' asked Holmes.

'None really. Just the satisfaction of the honour. A certificate, I suppose suitable for framing.'

Both men laughed at the thought. 'Oh yes, and a rather nice pin,' said James.

'Names, please,' said Holmes, removing a small notebook and a silver pencil from his pocket.

'Oh, we couldn't,' said James.

Holmes sighed. 'If three Luminarians have recently met untimely ends, it would be prudent if you would provide us a list of members. In case this is a . . . trend.'

The brothers exchanged a glance.

'Honorees, not members. What my brother means is that we *really* couldn't,' said Andrew. 'There is no formal list. Besides, no one knows of this group but us.'

'My brother knew,' said Mycroft.

'The recipients of this "honour" know. And those who see the pins,' said Holmes.

'I was joking about the pins. And the certificates.'

'What about meetings?'

'None. It is not a society in that sense,' said Andrew.

'No lunches? No annual Christmas dinner?' persisted my friend.

'You are being facetious. No, just the honour. Mycroft is a Luminarian, by the way.'

'You are forgetting that I declined,' murmured Mycroft, pouring himself a Scotch.

'How is this honour bestowed?' asked Holmes.

'At a private ceremony at our house,' said James. 'Plenty of champagne.'

'Of course, we invite the Luminarians thereafter to our parties,' said Andrew. 'Usually.' Neither Holmes brother reacted. 'It is a rather coveted invitation,' he added.

'Indeed!' I blurted out.

The group turned to look at me.

'I, well, my wife Mary enjoys reading about your parties.

In the papers. They have quite a reputation. The food. Music . . .'

The four men stared at me. I felt myself colouring.

'Well then, surely you should come sometime. Dr, er . . . sorry, I have forgotten.' said James.

'Dr Watson. Make a note of that, James,' said Andrew.

'Please recreate the list for me, the best you can, then,' said Holmes, beginning to lose patience.

'Oh, I can't think,' said Andrew with a wave of his very white hand.

'Neither can I,' added James. 'We have been up all night working on a bill we will bring to Parliament next month. Lunatic law. Inhuman as it stands. Oh, and deciding on the menu for tomorrow.'

'And who to invite shooting in the country next week,' added Andrew.

'It is quite important. Please write down those you can recall.' Holmes extended his notebook and pencil to Andrew, who hesitated, then dashed off a few names, showed the list to James, who added one more. James handed the notebook back to Holmes.

'These are all we can think of at the moment,' said James.

Holmes looked over the list. 'Please try to remember more and send the rest of the list to me later today.'

'We shall,' said Andrew. With a few more goodbyes, the two brothers departed as chaotically as they entered.

As the door closed behind them, Holmes eyed his brother Mycroft with some amusement. 'You turned them down, did you?' he murmured.

'I have turned down any number of honours, Sherlock,' said his brother. 'Now get to work on that list.'

'Why are they holding back on naming its members?' asked Holmes. 'Do *you* have a list?

'No. And I do not think they are holding back. This is merely a hobby, not something they take seriously. Now, do apply yourself.'

'Doing what, Mycroft? I am not equipped to provide protection for seven or eight random men in London, nor can I detect in advance of a crime.' He glanced again at the list. 'An M, an R, an S and a V. There is no B here. Perhaps this Luminarian connection is a coincidence. Ah, but here is an earlier letter. F. How odd. Oliver Flynn!'

'The playwright!' I exclaimed. 'Mary and I loved *Lord Baltimore's Snuffbox*. Brilliantly funny!'

'Watson, please,' Holmes said. 'Mycroft, I have discovered that Flynn is connected to a French anarchist group here in London. I have infiltrated them and, in the guise of an artist, I have been invited to a party in three days' time. I expect—'

'Oliver Flynn is well-meaning, and has sympathy with the downtrodden,' said Mycroft, 'but he is rather misinformed about the methods he is helping to fund. Socialism is one thing, anarchy another.'

'Oliver Flynn with the anarchists?' I exclaimed. 'This seems improbable! Why would a famous playwright and *bon vivant* fund bombers?

'Odd bedfellows. But yes, Watson. I shall explain later,' said Holmes. He turned to his brother. 'What of his connection to the Goodwins?'

'Social, I presume. He gets about. If our alphabet theory is correct, Flynn, as an F, could be a target quite soon,' said Holmes's elder brother. 'I shall use my influence to *convince* him to take a sudden vacation. That should keep him safe while you pursue the Alphabet Killings, Sherlock.'

'Mycroft! The anarchists are my current focus. Flynn's party is vital to my investigation.'

'I know about the trail you follow, including that grocer in Fitzrovia. Those anarchists are terribly dangerous, Sherlock. They are inexperienced young men fooling with explosives beyond their capabilities, driven by youthful fervour and misplaced idealism. One will blow himself up accidentally, mark my words. Stay away.'

I thought that odd. In the past Mycroft Holmes had shown he was more likely to send his brother into danger than to warn him off it.

'Your concern is touching, Mycroft. But, no.'

'Drop it, I say.'

'Why?'

'The French have someone on it.'

'Ah, here we are,' said Holmes. 'Tell me it is not who I think.'

'I am afraid so,' said Mycroft, 'The French government adore him.'

'Not Jean Vidocq?' I blurted.

Mycroft's silence was confirmation.

Vidocq was a handsome, arrogant French operative who considered himself a rival to Holmes. He had occasionally joined forced with us but had proven to be a dangerous and unreliable man. Even his name was a sham. Vidocq was no more related to Eugène Vidocq, the famous founder of the French Sûreté, than I was. He had merely adopted the name for its cachet.

'Jean Vidocq is a scoundrel,' I said. 'Not even terribly competent.' The man was responsible on a previous case for pushing me down a flight of stairs!

'He is useful, gentlemen. And you forget, he is well respected in France,' said Mycroft.

I was unconvinced.

'I will not drop the anarchist investigation, Mycroft,' said Holmes. 'I am close to cracking the group via a grocery in Fitzrovia, and I intend to connect them to Flynn.'

As we stood to leave, Mycroft pinned his brother with a look that would strike fear into most. 'Drop it, I say, Sherlock, and attend to the Alphabet Killings. One by one, men who are creating great works of charity are being eliminated. Think of the loss to those in need. Think of the greater good.'

At that precise moment, a page came in, approached Mycroft and whispered in his ear.

'What is it?' asked Holmes.

'Another bomb went off. The French. Somewhere near Leicester Square.'

'Anyone killed?'

'Five dead. Six wounded.'

Silence as we took this in. Finally, Holmes said, quietly, 'The greater good, Mycroft? Really? I will choose my own cases, and investigate however I please, you and Titus Billings notwithstanding.'

We turned to depart, but Mycroft was not finished. 'Sherlock, that Zanders fellow – remedy that. You know better than to inflame a journalist. You are losing your touch.'

'Perhaps you lack a challenge yourself, Mycroft, and are bored? Here is one for you. Take care. If it is an alphabetical series, H follows E, F and G. The scythe draws nearer, perhaps to you, brother.'

Holmes did not pause for the answer but stormed out of the door, myself following. I was always happy to depart the Diogenes Club.

CHAPTER 7

The Spice of Life

eaving St James's, Holmes directed our cab slightly out of the way to an address in Fitzrovia on Charlotte Street. 'And *where* are we going?' I asked, as our cab wove through the drizzle past rain-soaked pedestrians. He had uncharacteristically hailed a four-wheeler – slower and more expensive than our usual hansom, but I was soon to see why.

'I am in need of some cornichons and a bit of news.' At my puzzled look, he added, 'A French grocery,' and began one of the transformations which I so admired. He donned a pair of wire-rimmed glasses, tousled his normally neat hair into a messy fringe, inserted a set of teeth which gave him an overbite, and altered his expression so that he looked both younger and rather feckless. My friend's theatrical skills never failed to impress me.

'And you are appearing as . . . ?'

'Stephen Hollister. A writer. Stephen does not speak French, and neither do you. At peril of your life.'

'Well, there is nothing to worry about there. I have only schoolboy French.' We rolled on. 'Perhaps a bit more information, Holmes?'

But we were already pulling up to our destination. 'Later, Watson,' said he. We descended and approached a three-storey building with a small shop on the bottom floor. '*Le Bel Épicier*' was elegantly inscribed above the door, and the window was filled with gourmet delicacies from France – mustards, jams, wine and baskets of French bread. There were also demitasse sets, and some strangely constructed coffee grinders – all loops and gears over small metal boxes. Holmes vacillated between ignoring food completely to demonstrating a quite refined taste. The tins of French *pâté* looked quite promising.

Inside, *Le Bel Épicier* was saturated with the strong and wonderful aroma of coffee. Holmes introduced me to the proprietor, a man he had mentioned at the Diogenes. Victor Richard was a jolly and rotund Frenchman, and he welcomed us heartily, pressing a cup of the hot, steaming black liquid into our hands. It was truly the best coffee I have ever tasted, dark and rich, almost like chocolate.

He and Holmes proceeded to chat amiably in English about French lavender honey, wines, and then coffee. From behind the counter, Victor Richard pulled out one of the unusual French coffee grinders I'd spotted in the window.

Holmes explained this was a new and better way to grind the beans for our favourite morning beverage.

Although I knew him to be fluent, Holmes in character as Stephen Hollister spoke no French. In an adjacent room behind the cash register, I could hear voices, and the door to this chamber opened frequently as people passed in and out. When it was open, their voices were quite clear. Several male and one female voice spoke in rapid French, using, I presumed, slang, for I could catch nothing of what they said.

At one point a handsome, intense woman of around sixty, in dark clothing and with a determined air, emerged from the room and walked through the shop.

'*À bientôt*, Louise,' called Richard.

She raised a hand and gave a faint smile.

'Some of that goose pâté if you would, and some of those olives,' said Holmes, and then considered the new coffee grinder, which I noted had the word 'Peugeot' inscribed on it. 'Interesting contraption! If we can only get our landlady to accommodate it. I shall buy one and see.'

I knew full well that Mrs Hudson, who kindly furnished us with food, was a woman very used to routine and would not touch it.

'Let us convince her with a gift of these,' said Holmes with a smile, pointing to a triumvirate of small jars he had selected from the shelves – mustard, honey, and small pickles. 'Oh, and – *a baggetty, sill vooz plate*,' he said, purposely mangling the words. He pointed to a basket of the long, crusty loaves of French bread near the cash register.

'Ah, *non, non*,' the grocer replied. 'For you, one of my best!' He went behind the counter and selected another baguette, this one golden and crusty. 'Still warm from the oven!'

Thus, laden with our treasures, we stood in the street, attempting to hail another cab. The heavy drizzle had turned once again to rain, and Holmes protected the baguette with a carefully angled umbrella.

'Holmes,' I said, 'where to next – more errands?' He glanced at me, reading my puzzlement, and laughed. Once again he flagged a four-wheeler and we climbed aboard. He began to restore his normal appearance as we proceeded north on Charlotte Street towards Euston Road.

'That was obviously not about the food, Watson, although I'll admit it is an added bonus. That little unassuming grocery store is the nexus for the French anarchist activity in London. That, and the Autonomie Club. I have slowly been gaining Richard's confidence. You know my methods. The lady who passed through was none other than Louise Michel.'

'Who?'

'A famous French anarchist, Watson. She is said to have been one of the organizing powers behind the uprising in Paris in '71.'

'What is she doing here?' I exclaimed, suddenly imagining barricades of furniture and bonfires in Trafalgar Square.

'We have welcomed foreigners of all stripes and political persuasions, Watson. It is part and parcel of being a democracy.'

Our hansom turned left onto Euston which became Marylebone Road. The rain had paused, but dark clouds scudded across the sky and a chill wind blew about us. More stormy weather was on the way.

'I do not understand why we should welcome violent extremists,' I remarked.

'I tracked her briefly earlier this year. Louise Michel is writing articles and giving speeches, Watson. There is no law against that.'

'But someone in that crowd has graduated to explosives. Can that not be laid at her door?'

'It is not that simple, I am afraid. We must uphold the freedoms on which our country is based, Watson. A democracy always faces the challenge of discerning what is free speech and what is sedition, what is ardent dissent and what is incitement to criminal acts.'

'But still—'

'Watson, you remarked earlier on the prejudice you heard from Billings. I'm afraid that attitude is growing due to the anarchists, a tiny but very notable minority among the many Italian and French who have come to this country peacably. Most of these immigrants have nothing to do with politics or crime. They are skilled artisans, chefs, woodworkers, and professional people. But along with these come many poor, unskilled labourers, desperate to start anew. For a small subset of these, their poverty and misery make them ripe for conversion to violence.'

'It is a sad situation. Something must be done, Holmes.'

'Yes, but to help them, do you not think? The anarchists

are a small, renegade part of a larger movement who believe strongly in schools for the poor, did you know that? They want to provide a means for the impoverished to raise themselves. Louise Michel has founded such a school.'

'All well and good, but bombs!' I objected.

'They feel their voices are not heard. It is a dilemma, Watson, but I agree there is no excuse for bombing. I shall combat terrorism in any form.'

'There is a lot in the press about the immigrant problem, Holmes.'

'Sadly yes, there is a growing movement – the "restrictionists". They want limitations on immigration, tougher police, all based on fears of economic and racial decline. Titus Billings and his secret benefactor are clearly in the vanguard.'

I looked about me on Marylebone Road. We were passing the elegant Park Crescent dwellings, but even in this refined and lovely part of London there were vagrant individuals begging on the streets.

'Titus Billings thinks the way out of our problems is by militarizing the police. By providing them with ever more brutal crowd control equipment. More deadly batons, handcuffs which break wrists, even guns. Turning them into soldiers, essentially, as if the streets were at war. How do you feel about that, Watson?'

'Well, I . . . it is hard to say. Sounds a poor solution. But . . . bombers are criminals.'

'Yes, they are, Watson. But should we allow fear to turn our country into a kind of police state? It is a delicate balance.'

'This is beyond my ken, Holmes.'

Holmes regarded me thoughtfully. 'Frankly, Watson, it is beyond my own as well. It is more in my brother's realm. But I will help where I can. As result of this stop at *Le Bel Épicier*, I know the exact location of a bombing they are planning two days hence.'

'How?'

'The men in the back-room.'

'You overhead them? How could they be so careless?'

'They were speaking in code, with a great use of *argot* – French slang, Watson. They assume no Englishmen speak their language to such a degree. However, I do. As Mycroft noted, they are amateurs. But still dangerous.'

My friend was wise to ignore his brother's admonition. This new information could well save lives.

He sighed. 'What I do *not* know is *when* this bomb is to detonate.'

Our carriage turned south towards Baker Street and we just managed to make it inside as the drizzle turned into a downpour. Holmes scribbled two telegrams regarding the bombings and sent Billy off to the post office with them. As I hung up my wet things and noted the cheerful fire and tea things laid out, I felt a moment of thankfulness that I was not one of the homeless unfortunates huddling under an awning on Charlotte Street, or Tottenham Court Road, or even in the mews near to this very building. Instead I was comfortable and warm, and quite safe.

Of course, that would not remain the case for long.

CHAPTER 8

The Lady

 settled in again by the fire and cracked open a nautical adventure book I had left behind. Holmes, pacing, checked his watch. 'Do not get too comfortable, Watson. We must go out again shortly. Crime does not halt for inclement weather. The Goodwin brothers have not been forthcoming with the list they promised. Perhaps it is time to pay them a visit.'

'It has been less than two hours, Holmes,' I said. 'Give them a chance.'

'It is ridiculous that they did not have the names in their heads.'

'They are very social. Perhaps between parties and Parliament there are many names to remember.'

'Yes, yes, Watson,' said Holmes impatiently.

I nodded and added a shot of brandy to my tea. Holmes waved away the offer of the same and took out his notebook in which the Goodwins had scribbled the names of the few Luminarians they could remember.

'Oliver Flynn is the odd name on this list. He is the only artistic member. All the rest are industrialists or businessmen. He does not seem to fit. I wonder if something is hidden in the man's past.'

'What a talent he is!' I smiled at the thought of Flynn's play Mary and I had attended at the Haymarket only last week. It was a trifle, to be sure, but a delicious evening of entertainment. His latest was what critics referred to as a "comedy of manners", and we had thoroughly enjoyed his skewering of the aristocratic class, although done with a modicum of sympathy. 'Of course, he is certainly a character,' I said, 'Was there not some scandal brewing? Something about his unusual . . . romantic life.'

Holmes looked up from perusing the articles on the table. 'Raise your view, Watson,' he snapped.

I turned back to my book, irritated.

'Sorry, dear fellow. I should not let slander-by-Zander get under my skin. Flynn engenders more gossip than I do! He hails from Dublin originally, was an orphan who pulled himself up by his own bootstraps. This fact is little known – indeed, he hides it – but he has almost single-handedly funded the orphanage in which he spent his early years.'

'Fascinating, Holmes. His public persona is so different from that.'

'Few of us reveal our true selves in public,' said Holmes, cryptically.

Mrs Hudson appeared with what at less pressured times

was the kind of announcement dearest to our hearts. 'Mr Holmes, a client is here to consult you. A Lady Eleanor Gainsborough.' Her expression conveyed that the visitor had impressed her, and that Holmes had better respond, and quickly.

'I am quite busy,' said he.

'She was most insistent,' said Mrs Hudson.

'Holmes, have you time for this?' I wondered. 'You seem to have a rather full plate.'

'I shall determine that, Watson,' said he, peeved. 'Send her up, Mrs Hudson. When it rains, it pours.'

And although indeed it was pouring outside at that moment, in walked a lady as if blown into the room by a summer breeze, so untouched was she by the weather.

She stood just inside the doorway, a graceful woman of about forty-five. Her wealth and breeding were evident by her poised manner and costly raiment. But she also gave the impression, so common among the very rich, that she was wearing some kind of cloak of ethereal matter, protecting her from rain, dirt, and all the minor inconveniences.

She smiled graciously at the two of us. 'Mr Sherlock Holmes? And the friend – Doctor, er . . . ? '

'Watson, madam, at your service.'

She smiled faintly and turned to Holmes. 'I am so pleased to find you here, and willing to receive me, Mr Holmes.'

She held out her hand, palm down, and Holmes crossed to her, kissing it in the manner of a true gallant. 'Lady Gainsborough! Welcome.'

'Lady Eleanor, please, Mr Holmes.'

'As you wish,' he said.

I nodded deferentially as Holmes guided her to the basket chair which was angled closest to the fire. She placed her reticule on the table, took in the room with its slightly sinister and decidedly chaotic clutter, and then sat, arranging her burgundy velvet skirts around her.

As she did so, I took in the full measure of a born aristocrat, or so I gathered from her gracefully erect posture, her porcelain skin with only the slightest natural blush, her bounteous yet impeccably arranged coiffure of dark brown curls, and the subtle touches of discreet antique jewellery.

Her dress was of the finest quality, with a deep chevron of black lace panels down the front which narrowed into a waist whose tiny size belied her years. She smiled, and it melted any trace of the late autumn chill that lingered in the air and subtracted ten years from my estimation of her age.

'Mr Holmes, I am sure you can help me. I have read so much of you and your remarkable achievements, both by Doctor Watson here, as well as in the newspapers.'

Holmes shot me a sudden glance, indicating the table where the damning tabloid articles were still arrayed. I had forgotten about them. I got up to stack them discreetly before our visitor could catch a glimpse, although I could not imagine a lady of her class taking interest in *The Illustrated Police Gazette*.

'This is, of course, despite recent slander,' she continued, dashing this thought to pieces and eyeing me with amusement. 'My maid brings the *Gazette* into the house from time to time, Doctor. They are hard to resist.' I finished stacking and sat back down.

She leaned forward as if to impart a secret. 'Likening you to the Devil, indeed! For shame! In my view, you are an angel of justice. Your capturing the Covent Garden Garrotter last summer – what a triumph, Mr Holmes! I have followed your adventures for some time. My late husband was an admirer as well.'

Holmes, more susceptible to flattery than he would care to admit, softened slightly, but turned the conversation to business. 'Madam, I can see that you are troubled. How may we be of service to you? It must be a matter of great importance for you to have travelled though this weather, rather than for you to summon us to your school. I read that you have visited this worthy institution before coming here.'

She started at this. 'You read me . . . like a book?'

'It is a figure of speech, madam. Watson, Lady Eleanor is the co-founder and funder of the remarkable Gainsborough School for Young Ladies, a private, charitable enterprise which rescues destitute young women from a life on the streets.'

'Well, my goodness, yes. You are remarkably well-informed. Of course, my girls are not only poor, but have been plucked from very *specific* life on the streets,' said the lady. 'One in which the sad young things have found nothing to sell but themselves.'

'I see,' I said.

'I am surprised you know of us,' said the lady to Holmes.

'Your school is quite renowned, Lady Eleanor.' He turned to me. 'This laudable institution provides education and training which transforms these waifs into employable young ladies – suitable for work in service, is that not correct?' He turned back to Lady Eleanor.

'Indeed, it is, Mr Holmes,' said the lady, pleased at the recognition. 'But we are hidden away in an unfashionable part of town and have had little notice by the larger community. How do you know this?'

'I make it my business to follow everything of importance in London, Lady Eleanor.'

'You must not sleep, then. But returning to my question, how could you have read that I had just now been to visit the school?' she asked. 'The papers do sometimes follow me – as they do you – but not by the minute.'

'It was written on your gloves.'

'My gloves?' She held an exquisite pair of pale lavender leather gloves in her left hand.

'The ink stain on your glove, there,' said Holmes.

Barely discernible was a small stain on one of the index fingers.

'You are far too meticulous in your *habillement* to have left the house with a stained glove, therefore you did some writing elsewhere,' said Holmes. 'Normally, one removes gloves to write, but you left yours on, presumably because you were in an environment where you did not wish to sully your hands. I cannot imagine you engaging the type of barrister or accountant where you would feel the need, but paperwork at the school might have required your

70

attention, and in that undoubtedly less pristine atmosphere you chose to leave them on.'

'I could have done so while shopping. Written a cheque, perchance,' said the lady, who seemed amused rather than offended by Holmes's showy display.

'I warrant you do not do your own shopping, save for very particular establishments, a dressmaker perhaps. And there not only would you have an account, but you would have removed your gloves.'

She laughed. It was a beautiful, silvery sound. 'Well, you are entirely correct, Mr Holmes, and I am even more convinced that it is the right thing to consult you!'

Holmes smiled at the lady.

'It is fascinating,' she continued, 'that Mr Zanders of the *Gazette* seems to attribute your powers, which he declares are waning, to nefarious means. I personally think your past results tell quite a different story. Is it jealousy, perhaps, or does the man hold something against you?'

Holmes's smile faded.

'That is an astute observation indeed, madam. I once took this journalist to task for a gross indiscretion. But please, let us turn to the reason for your visit. How can we help you?'

'An incident occurred at my school and I require your advice, as well as your assistance.'

'Please lay your problem before us.'

'There has been an attack on one of my star pupils, a young woman named Judith. She was rescued from the streets three years ago and in that short time has proven herself highly intelligent, having quickly acquired remarkable fluency in reading, figures, and household organization. I did not know it at the time, but she speaks French, as her mother was French. Although it is French of the streets, she has sought to remedy that, and her colloquial English, with success.'

'Good. This attack, Lady Eleanor? What happened?'

'Judith was attacked in her bed last night as she slept.'

'Attacked!' I cried.

Holmes frowned. 'Details, if you please?'

'Judith, as one of our senior and most accomplished students, has earned a room to herself. It was about two in the morning . . . early this morning . . . when an intruder entered this room, pulled back the covers, grasped her hand, and attempted to sever one of her fingers with a knife.'

'My God!' I exclaimed.

'Which finger?' asked Holmes.

'Er . . . I am not sure. The middle? The ring?'

'It matters. And madam, you are sure? Which hand and which finger?'

'The left, I think. Ring finger. But those are not the salient points.'

'I will determine that. What else?'

'The assailant was masked, hooded. She did not see the man.'

'Is she sure it was a man?'

'Yes. She struck him and he cried out.'

'I see. You said "attempted". I trust he was not successful?' asked Holmes, leaning forward in his chair with that keen expression of a hound on a scent.

'She screamed. Her attacker fled, dropping the knife as he ran.'

'The wound. Deep? Superficial?'

'Just a shallow cut. Almost a scratch. But very upsetting.'

'May I see the knife?' Holmes held out his hand.

She started again. 'How did you know I brought it to you?'

'Lady Eleanor, please. No games. I can see the outline of it in your silk reticule. You are clearly not used to subterfuge, nor violence. Is it bloody, have you wrapped it? If so, you will have removed evidence.'

She paused, and her eyes filled with tears. 'Oh, Mr Holmes,' said she. 'This is a most trying experience.' She then withdrew the knife, holding it with distaste with only one finger and her thumb. It was wrapped in a cloth napkin.

'Ah,' said Holmes, examining it. 'It has been wiped clean. That is unfortunate.'

It was an ordinary kitchen knife. Not distinguishable in any way except for small bloodstains on the blade. Holmes held it to a light on the table next to him, picked up a lens and examined the plain, flat handle and then the blade. He ran his finger along the edge.

'Dull. No fingerprints are left. This tells us nothing,' said Holmes. 'Might it have come from the kitchen at the school?'

'I do not know,' said the lady. 'I am not familiar with their utensils.'

Holmes continued to examine the knife, then he tossed it on a side table.

'I presume you want me to trace this assailant?'

'What I would like, Mr Holmes, is protection for dear

Judith. She is my prize pupil. This has upset her greatly, and this catastrophe will delay my placing her until her wound heals. Most of my girls can only aspire to be parlourmaids or maids of all work. But Judith will be my first to graduate to a position of governess.'

'Impressive,' I said, imagining this tale of rags to respectability.

'I thought it was merely a scratch,' said Holmes. 'Her wound?'

'Perhaps I have not described it correctly. It is a small cut. But it is bandaged against infection.'

'Good,' said I, thinking that few people took such things seriously enough. Holmes shifted in impatience.

The lady continued. 'I would very much like you to come to the school and to lie in wait for this assailant, Mr Holmes. I feel certain he will try again.'

'Dr Watson perhaps could assist. Is there an empty room nearby where he could wait?'

I was surprised at this but said nothing.

'No, it must be in her room. And you, sir. Alone. There is not enough space for you both in the room with Judith.'

'Why do you not remove the girl to a place of safety?' Holmes asked. 'Perhaps lodge her in your own home until this villain is apprehended?'

'Oh, no! I – I could not do that. My staff would be – oh no! But the assailant would not likely return, then, would he? I ask you again, sir. Please come and wait in her room with her.'

I had a sudden thought of our escapade back in '83,

protecting the gentle Helen Stoner, a young woman who nearly met the same gruesome end as her sister Julia – death in her own bed by the improbable means of a trained snake, engineered by her evil stepfather. We had awaited this terrifying event by secreting ourselves, with difficulty, in the lady's bedroom. However, the young person herself had not been present. What Lady Eleanor was proposing was quite unacceptable.

'I am sorry, Lady Eleanor. I am otherwise occupied,' said Holmes. 'But I have in mind the perfect solution.'

'But, sir—'

'No,' said Holmes, firmly.

Lady Eleanor was taken aback. As pleasant and reasonable as she seemed, she was also clearly not used to hearing the word 'no'.

'Here is my solution, madam. I will send over one of my deputies. A young woman who will fit right into your school, a minnow in a school of minnows.'

'A deputy?'

'I have employed her before, and more than once. Her name is Hephzibah O'Malley.'

'That is an . . . unusual name,' said the lady.

Holmes noted this and glanced at me. 'Heffie, as she is known, is an East End orphan, half Jewish and half Irish, and you can well imagine she has felt the brunt of prejudice. She has learned to defend herself masterfully. She is an accomplished street-fighter. But that is the smallest of her skills. Heffie is intelligent, subtle, and observant – an easily underestimated young person.'

Lady Eleanor looked doubtful, but Holmes pressed on.

'The assailant, judging from his lack of success and his willingness to be frightened off so readily, is not a professional. Heffie will be able to handle him, should he return.'

I wondered that I had not heard of her before.

'How old is this Heffie?' asked the lady.

'Sixteen.'

'You would send a child to defend my Judith?'

Holmes sighed. 'Heffie is no ordinary young lady. Her late father was a boxer and wrestler and I have seen her hold her own against several men. Heffie will also fit in perfectly as one of your rescues. There could be no one better suited to watch over Judith. Your assailant, if he is connected with the school, will not even realize that Judith has acquired a bodyguard. Even Scotland Yard has made use of her services. Do you see? Heffie is precisely what you need.'

'I need *you*, Mr Holmes.'

'Madam, I am not free at present. And consider this. I would stand out in that environment like a giraffe in a pen of kittens.'

'I beg you to refrain from referring to my girls as minnows or kittens,' said the lady with dignity. I will admit that I, too, was taken slightly aback by Holmes's colourful analogies. 'But if it is not to be, it is not to be.' She rose, her disappointment obvious.

She glanced once more around the room, revisiting the considerable clutter, including the grotesqueries on the chemistry table. She drew herself up, then ran a hand along the fireplace mantel. A finger came away dirty. She tapped some books, lying askew on a nearby bookcase.

'Mr Holmes. You could benefit from more meticulous housekeeping. Order reflects competence! One of my girls would do wonders with this unhealthy room. She would clean thoroughly, organize all. Will you consider hiring one? I am always looking to place a girl. One of my best is available starting immediately. Anna would—'

'Much as I enjoy appearing competent, no thank you, Lady Eleanor,' said Holmes with a small smile. 'Now if you will excuse us, please.'

'It is hard to take no for an answer, Mr Holmes. You say Heffie can do the job I require and have insisted, past my reservations. Yet you will not take my advice. Why not consider Anna? She would tidy up this mess in a day.'

'Thank you, madam,' said Holmes more firmly, 'but this room is exactly how I like it.'

'But it is very kind of you to suggest,' I offered.

She paused. 'I will expect your . . . Heffie, then. When exactly?'

'I will have her there by morning. In the meantime, place Judith temporarily in a new room with other girls. Please have an extra bed made ready in Judith's room for tomorrow.'

She nodded and departed without another word.

'What an extraordinary woman,' I exclaimed.

'In what way, Watson?'

'So elegant, so self-contained. And quite lovely for her age.'

'She is only a few years older than you. And she, or her girl, is lying, at least about a few things.'

'What? Seriously, Holmes?'

'The knife is suspect. It is too dull to have made a small wound. And when Lady Eleanor withdrew the knife, I also spotted a receipt dated today from Verrey's Restaurant.'

'What does that matter?'

'Odd to dine socially while on an errand such as this. Perhaps it is nothing. But you know me, Watson. I do not find most women all that trustworthy.'

'Well, I disagree. I think Lady Eleanor was simply upset. Anyone would be.'

'Let us drop the subject, Watson. We have more substantial work to do. It is now past five and already dark. I am going to fetch Heffie and set her on the job.'

'I shall go with you,' I said, curious about this girl whose description had frankly intrigued me.

'I have another task for you, Watson. As the Goodwins have not sent over the list of Luminarians which they promised, I would like for you to go to Mayfair and retrieve it from them. That should, at least, prove entertaining. Meanwhile, I shall be back for supper by eight, and will see you then.'

'Shall we dine at Simpson's, Holmes? You could do with a fine roast beef and Yorkshire pudding!'

'You persist, Watson! Yes, then. Eight o'clock? I look forward to it.'

CHAPTER 9

A Question of Taste

y career had taken me through challenging terrain on three continents, but I will admit that there were corners of London which could seem both foreign and unnerving to me. Mayfair was one.

Before departing, I sent over a quick note to the Goodwin brothers to politely warn of my impending visit and made an effort to elevate my appearance – a close shave, a fresh collar, and a quick change back to my 'ostentatious gold watch', as Holmes had called it. While he teased me about pretension, these touches added needed *gravitas*, or so I felt.

My curiosity rose as my cab drew near Grosvenor Square. I had long admired the grand houses nearby but had never set foot inside one. Thankfully, the rain had ceased, but the wet streets gleamed and a touch of frost appeared on the grass on the lawn in the centre of the square. The air had grown much colder and a further freeze during the night would turn the pavements treacherous.

We pulled up to an enormous home not far from the square. The Goodwins' residence was startling in its grandeur. Three storeys high, gleaming in marble and masterful plaster, a frieze of cavorting ancients across the portico, it was a remarkable edifice. Set back from the street, and fronted with a half-moon of private driveway, the enormous house buzzed with activity and glowed with numerous outdoor electrified lights.

Bathed under this bright glow, the Goodwins' own carriage, shining black with a gilded coat of arms painted discreetly on the doors, stood at the entrance. It had recently arrived, for a glossy matched pair of chestnut beauties stamped and snorted, their breaths showing as white puffs in the frigid air.

A driver sat atop, rubbing his gloved hands for warmth, while two servants, sporting powdered wigs and velvet coats adorned with gold lace and buttons, ran to and fro with packages from expensive grocers and specialty shops. Servants costumed in anachronistic livery was something I had read about but never seen. A strange conceit, I thought!

Boxes from Fortnum and Mason appeared in one of the servant's hands, and their delicious Scotch Eggs came to mind. They were a favourite of Holmes's as he could stash them in his pockets while on a case. Unless Fortnum and Mason's extravagant delicacies were daily fare for the Goodwins, some kind of party was being prepared.

A servant took my hat, coat and cane, and I was happy that I had transformed myself, even modestly, for this visit. I was asked to wait in a salon which was, by itself, nearly twice the size of all the rooms at 221B taken together. The decor was ornate – Regency, perhaps – with baroque touches, hand-painted cabinets with cherubs madly cavorting, and much of the furniture edged in gold.

The chairs and settees were upholstered in subtle satin stripes, and delicate and complicated china figurines dotted every available surface. I was afraid to move, lest I should knock over one of these costly items, and so stood rather uncomfortably in the centre of the room.

I heard voices in the hallway just outside. I recognized one as Andrew Goodwin, he of the Byronic look. 'She is simply the best pastry chef we have ever had, Billings,' he said. 'I will not let her go over gossip and rumour.'

Billings! Could he be referring to Titus Billings, the new man in charge of the Metropolitan Police? I moved closer to the door and secreted myself behind it so I could see them near the entry through the crack while remaining hidden from their view.

I recognized Titus Billings from the newspaper. He was a huge man, taller even than Andrew Goodwin. Broad of shoulder, he was muscular, with thick, wavy black hair and beetle brows. He had a military moustache and bearing. Late of the army, I thought, just as Holmes had judged me in those first moments of our meeting at Bart's.

'My dear Lord Goodwin, this does not come from me. But from the . . . er, Royal cousin himself,' Billings said, his booming voice lacking discretion. 'The French are a rising menace. It would be to your own interest to replace your French staff – and the Italians, too while you are at it – with good British stock. Those Frogs in particular are not to be trusted.' Billings dropped his voice, and continued confidentially, 'The unnamed Royal gentleman to whom I refer purged his own kitchen of all the dirty foreigners, and good riddance to them all. The theft of his treasured silver stopped at once.'

True story or not, I was horrified to hear this blatant prejudice spilling from a man so highly placed in law enforcement. I was no naïf on the subject and had encountered deeply prejudiced men in all ranks of the military. But in this context, and so vehemently spoken by a man in his position, it was nothing short of shocking.

'Oh,' said Goodwin, 'are you going about London, warning us all from door to door?'

'Sir!' said Billings, affronted. 'I am attempting to do you a favour.'

'Surely you cannot dismiss an entire nationality on the basis of a few anarchists and the theft of three forks? Nor will you succeed in eliminating the French from our shores. Besides, how then, shall we dine?' he added with a smile.

'Heed me, Lord Goodwin,' said Billings. 'If I could stop every Frenchman from entering Britain, I would. The dirty, lying—'

'My mother's family were French, Mr Billings.'

Billings was taken aback, but only for a moment. 'The

Royal cousin himself has given me leave to act on his preferences. Of course, I—'

'The Royal cousin who himself is not English?'

'Sir, you do not take my point. I speak of the criminals among those who flood our shores. Not your relations. But bombers, thieves, murderers! We should be more selective. You would be wise to—'

'Let me stop you, Mr Billings, before you place both feet in your mouth and have trouble making it out the door.'

'But the Royal personage himself—'

'Our cousin as well. Oh, did you not know? I suggest you take your theories and trot on home with them where you can commiserate with others who share your views. Perhaps over a good Beaujolais. Good day, Mr Billings.'

Billings left abruptly. I thought that whoever was working closely with that blustering man ought to watch his back, for when a bully like that is chastised, others will be made to pay.

I stepped back from the door, and just in time, as Lord Andrew Goodwin bounded in. I now got a good look at his at-home loungewear: a black velvet dressing gown with blue silk quilted lapels, fine embroidery all down the front and sleeves, and carpet slippers which were worked in the finest needlepoint shot with gold. He was otherwise as impeccably groomed as he had been earlier that day. What an enormous amount of upkeep went into this young gentleman's appearance, I thought.

But I quite admired him for standing up to Billings.

'Dr Watson, how good of you to come out of your way

in this terrible weather,' he said amiably. 'So chilly out! I've just had all the fires lit. Twenty-three of them, including the servants'. I am so sorry that we have neglected to send you the list as promised. We are entertaining tonight, and the thought just flew from my head.'

I wondered that someone might be murdering members of the society he had founded and yet this 'flew from his head'.

'Please, let us come away from this stifling room. This home has been in the family a long time, and this room was my grandmother's favourite, and remains pleasing to our lady guests. I cannot fathom why they placed you here. Follow me to our study and see if James and I can't come up with another name or two for you.'

As we moved quickly through the ground floor of the house, I was aware of many rooms through which a seemingly endless supply of liveried servants scurried, carrying vases of fresh flowers, trays of champagne flutes, soft lap blankets of what looked to be cashmere, silver bowls of nuts, candied fruits, and small cakes, in preparation for what were most likely distinguished guests. As they passed us in the spacious hallways, each servant stepped aside deferentially with a small bow of the head. Andrew Goodwin appeared not to notice they were there.

We eventually reached a large, wood-panelled chamber, as equally sumptuous as the original room, and perhaps just as pretentious, but of an entirely masculine character. Darkly panelled, it sported heavily framed seascapes. A vast bookcase covered one long wall, filled with gilded books and a collection of astrolabes and sextants.

On one wall was an artfully arranged collection of seafaring memorabilia – an anchor, a harpoon, a fragment of heavy netting, with a brass diver's helmet on a table before it. Andrew Goodwin noted my keen interest and said, simply, 'Our grand uncle was a ship's captain at only twenty-five, but left the Navy to become an explorer. Remarkable fellow. Naturalist. Anthropologist. Lost off the coast of Japan at the age of sixty-two. Have you been to sea?'

'I am no sailor, but I do enjoy reading about the sea,' said I.

'I'm a Jules Verne man, myself,' murmured a voice behind me. I turned to see James Goodwin reclining on a tufted leather sofa, similarly attired to his brother, in a dark green velvet dressing gown, smoking a cigarette with a particularly pungent odour.

Ganja! I recognized the distinctive reeking scent of his cannabis cigarette from my time in India. I was familiar with its effects and knew, of course, that it had its enthusiasts in London – but I had presumed them to be of an artistic bent, rather than James Goodwin, the young aristocrat and statesman who lounged before me.

This younger man, who had struck me as the more jittery of the two brothers, now lolled about, regarding me with drooping lids and a beatific expression. His patent leather coiffure was slightly awry, a black comma of glistening hair escaping onto his forehead.

'Oh, it's the doctor. Sorry, old man. Preparing for guests, what?' he drawled. 'So much work, so much hustle and bustle.'

But not for you, I thought.

'James,' said Andrew Goodwin, 'at least offer our guest some refreshment.'

I noticed a sideboard on which stood several crystal decanters of citrine, topaz and ruby coloured libations, but instead James raised the lid of a carved wooden box and offered me one of the strangely shaped cigarettes from within. He giggled as he did so. 'Very nice stuff, old man,' said he.

'No, thank you,' I replied. I hold the medical opinion that recreational use of powerful intoxicants like cannabis, morphine and cocaine endanger those who indulge in them, hence my concern over my dear friend and his all too frequent use of the latter two. At least Holmes had never, to my knowledge, indulged in cannabis. James Goodwin's groggy state suggested it would not suit my friend. Holmes chose either to dull his senses or to sharpen them, never to twist them like a corkscrew.

Noticing my disapproval, Andrew Goodwin moved between us, offering me a whisky, which he had poured for me, unasked. I took it.

'We are about to entertain a group of James's university friends whose varying degrees of professional and social success make them a very mismatched crew,' he said. 'We are always challenged to integrate these friends in a harmonious fashion. This is enervating to my dear brother – unless he is suitably inured to the proceedings by his favourite smoke.' Andrew Goodwin's discourse seemed more for his own amusement than my edification. Both young men grinned at me.

I took a sip of exceedingly tasty whisky and gathered my thoughts. I was here, after all, on a mission from Holmes.

'An excellent whisky, thank you,' I said. 'Now, sirs, let me not keep you from your preparations. The additional names of Luminarians, if you would be so kind? Mr Holmes would be most appreciative.' I set my whisky down on a polished table.

'Ah, have you thought of any more, James?'

'Wrote them down,' murmured James, his eyes closed. 'Desk there.'

The top of the massive campaign desk was bare. The older brother sighed, then proceeded to open first one drawer than another. 'James is known to stash things willy-nilly when receiving certain . . . er . . . visitors,' said he.

The younger brother grinned, sleepily. 'Well, one can't have Tillie seeing all our private information, can one?'

Whoever Tillie might be, or what she had been doing in this room, I did not care to know, but I was determined in my mission.

I cleared my throat.

'Ah, yes, Dr Watson. Forgive me. Here it is.' Andrew had located a sheet of paper and looked it over. 'Hmm. I can think of only one or two more,' said he, sitting down at the desk, and picking up a pen.

His brother grinned up at me from his settee. 'As you can see, we are not terribly organized. We are, perhaps, a bit spoiled in that regard.'

In every regard, I thought.

'I am quite hungry, I find,' said James, suddenly rising unsteadily to his feet.

'Go, then! Go, James!' said Andrew, shooing away his brother, who slithered from the room, trailing a perfume of *ganja* behind him. I glanced at my watch. It was after seven-thirty, and I was to meet Holmes at Simpson's at eight. I hated to keep my friend waiting.

'Thank you, but I must be off, Lord Goodwin,' said I.

'Here,' said Andrew Goodwin, handing me a single sheet of paper. 'Let me not detain you. Confidential, please. We have given our word of honour to keep the membership private.'

'Why, sir, if you don't mind my asking?'

'Some of them prefer to keep their philanthropy secret,' he said with a shrug.

Thanking him, I folded the list into a small square, and placed it in my waistcoat pocket for safekeeping.

I arrived at Simpson's on the Strand only five minutes late and was relieved when the *maître d'* informed me that Mr Sherlock Holmes had not yet arrived. Unfortunately, the preferred private booths at the edge of the large dining-room were completely occupied and I was shown to a table in the centre of the room, very much on display to the other diners.

As I waited for Holmes, I was eager to peruse the list, but did not feel comfortable consulting it in such a public place. Simpson's, originally a chess club, now offered the finest roast beef in London, and as such, attracted a notable clientele. Absolutely anyone in the city could be seated next to me, and the room was filled to capacity. I sat for a time, nursing an *aperitif*. At last I could not resist, and I pulled it from my pocket for a quick peek. Almost immediately I felt the eyes of a man on me from at a neighbouring table and quickly tucked it back into my pocket.

I awaited Holmes for nearly an hour, ordering first one, then a second glass of wine, and eventually gave in to ordering dinner. I enjoyed a wonderful roast beef from the silver trolley, which carvers in elegant uniforms rolled through the dining-room.

I took my time, but still no Holmes. As it got on to nine, then ten, and finally ten-thirty, and I was finishing dessert and an after-dinner port, I could not shake my vague sense of foreboding. Holmes frequently went missing for hours at a time while on a case. But he would not make such a specific appointment for a dinner in his favourite restaurant and not show up without sending word.

I paid and left. A slow dread had crept over me.

CHAPTER 10

The Snake and Drum

passed by 221B and ascertained that Holmes had not returned. I began to worry in earnest. I knew only that he had gone to fetch Hephzibah O'Malley, called Heffie, and that she could be found round about Spitalfields. Even the police refused to venture alone into some of that London neighbourhood's darker alleyways and rookeries. Though I knew first hand of Holmes's prodigious boxing and singlestick skills, I nevertheless worried.

I regretted now that I had not insisted on accompanying him. How would I trace his movements? Perhaps it was the good French wine I had enjoyed at dinner in combination with the other libations of the late afternoon that emboldened my next choice.

I remembered that he had said the police made regular use of Heffie's talents. But with the late hour and what I knew of the changes afoot at Scotland Yard, it was to Inspector Lestrade's own home that I decided to pursue the question.

I arrived in a small street in Pimlico and knocked at the door of a two-storey older structure, modest but in good repair, as sturdy as its occupant. In a moment, Lestrade, groggy and in nightclothes, faced me blearily at his front door.

Alarm flashed across his sharp features as he recognized me. 'Dr Watson! What brings you at this hour?'

'Terribly sorry to disturb you but I need some information from you, Lestrade.'

'Nothing has happened to Mr Holmes, has it?' His concern was genuine, and I liked the man for it.

'He left some time ago on an errand and has not returned as promised. I need an address.'

Lestrade was now fully awake and charged with energy. 'I shall do my best!'

'He went to retrieve Hephzibah O'Malley. I need to know where you think she may be found.'

'Heffie! Why the girl is almost always at the Snake and Drum, down Spitalfields way. She sleeps in a rented room at a brothel close by. You're not thinking of going there now?'

'Yes.'

'I would not send a man alone there, especially this time o' night. And certainly not dressed as you are, Doctor.'

I felt a flash of embarrassment. I was still in my best clothes for my visit to the Goodwins, including the gold watch Holmes had found so pretentious.

'Please, the address, Lestrade?'

He wrote it down for me, then with further warnings offered, bless him, to accompany me. I refused. He did not realize that the more fearsome he made the place sound, all the more was I in a rush to get there.

It took three tries before I could find a driver who agreed to take me to the Snake and Drum, and he demanded payment in advance. En route, I removed my new watch from my waistcoat and stashed it in an inner pocket.

As we approached our destination, the streets became narrower and darker, streetlights shattered or missing, and tall, tilted houses crowded together, with broken windows covered only by fabric. Derelict creatures dressed in rags sat shivering on the pavement in the freezing cold. Just as the grand champagne party going on at this moment near Grosvenor Square was not a London I knew well, neither was this sad and extreme opposite.

Eventually the driver let me off in front of the Snake and Drum, which had once been, if not grand, at least respectable. Its ancient sign had traces of gold on it, long since given over to the elements, and it creaked on rusty chains in the chill wind that had come up. Refuse and soaked rags littered the wet street, and I became aware of the sounds of shouting from one house, and a baby crying from another. These sounds blended with the whistle of the wind through the narrow streets and the dull drip of water on tin lean-tos that had been added on in various yards and alleys.

I shuddered with a combination of cold and dread, my

woollen overcoat failing to cut out the dampness that somehow seemed worse in this dark street than it had on Baker Street and in Mayfair. Through the pub's thick windows, I saw nothing like the cheery glow of the establishments near us in Marylebone, but rather dim pools of light from oil lamps and candles. I could make out dark figures within, and hoped Holmes was there.

The sound of drunken laughter suddenly poured from the door as two inebriated roughs spilled from it and onto the street, where one of them retched and vomited into the gutter. His battered hat fell off his head into the filthy stream, as his companion barely managed to hold him from falling into it himself. I moved past them and entered.

I found myself in a foul den populated by perhaps thirty ragged figures. A quick glance around revealed neither my friend nor any female at all. An ominous silence fell over the bleary and lank-haired patrons who all looked up from their drinks and their cards and their drunken *tête-à-têtes* to regard with hostility this vastly overdressed interloper. For the second time today, it was as though I had stepped into another city altogether. Even the names of London's varied locales were evocative of their character – Mayfair, with its lightness and beauty, and Spitalfields, where men vomited and fought and shouted at each other in the rank and filthy streets.

I knew at once I had better make my move and do so confidently. I strode to the bar and stood next to a very old man whose long white hair, enormous nose and bent, thin frame slumped over a small glass of half-drunk beer made it seem like he had sat there for a lifetime nursing his one drink.

I attempted to get the barman's attention with no luck. I took a half shilling from my pocket and rapped it sharply upon the oak bar. The entire room went silent. That was my first mistake.

'Glass of, er, what do you have?' I asked. There were guffaws all around.

With a sneer, the barman informed me I could have 'Ale or beer. Or, beer or ale. Take yer pick. Or gin.' He then moved away.

Irritated, I signalled again with my coin.

The old man leaned in close to me. 'Not 'ere, matey. Joe'll 'ave you for breakfast if ye try to hurry 'im along.' I turned for an uncomfortably close view of the wizened old man with his enormous nose reddened by drink, yellowed teeth, and a jacket patched of rags and rough wool.

'Holmes?' I said, softly.

The man's mouth widened into a clown-like grin. What a remarkable set of false teeth, I thought, wondering where Holmes had procured them.

'All right, enough,' I whispered. 'Have you had no luck here? No sign of Heffie?'

He stared at me, then his eyes appeared to roll back in his head and he suddenly pitched forward, landing in my arms. I just caught him before his head hit the bar. What could my friend intend with this strange show?

A moment later, his tall, inert form was stretched upon

the floor. An excellent simulation, I thought, of someone who had been drinking for days. I leaned in close to whisper something but there was no response. I touched his face and to my surprise, I discovered that the nose was real.

This was not Sherlock Holmes.

I backed away from him as his friends gathered round, laughing, to lift him up and ply him with hot water and gin. Apparently this was an oft-repeated event.

My stomach lurched. Where was Holmes, then? I turned again to my task. Finally capturing the barman's attention, I paid for an ale, and tipped generously. I asked after Heffie.

'Left here two hours ago with a tall gentl'man,' said he, friendlier now that his palm had been greased and he had witnessed me save a regular customer from a concussion.

I took a sip of my drink, thanked him and turned to leave.

'Jest a wee minute, sir. 'Tain't the part o' London to be wanderin' alone 'ere. You'll be needing protection. Yer friend declined it, much to 'is sorrow.'

'What do you mean?'

''E were set upon jus' outside by a gang o' four. Armed wi' sticks and a chain, mean 'uns. After 'is wallet, I s'pose.'

'What happened? Was he . . . were they hurt?'

The men around me guffawed. 'Naw, he 'ad protection. Heffie!' one said.

'She's a little hellfire, she is,' said another.

More laughter. I was not sure of their meaning.

'The two of 'em took on the four,' said the barman. 'Beat 'em sound, they did. Though they took something for their pains. 'E got knocked about a bit, savin' 'er. Poor gentl'man. There were blood.'

'I think 'e kept 'is wallet, though,' said another.

''Less Heffie took it off 'im later,' said a third, and everyone laughed.

I got up to leave.

The barman cleared his throat and, catching my eye, nodded to my left. I followed his gaze and noticed that several large and dangerous-looking men stood between me and the door and were staring at me with less than friendly interest.

'A shilling will see you to your cab safely,' he whispered. 'Be smarter than your friend.' He grinned, showing a horror of rotten and missing teeth. 'You ain't got Heffie to proteck you.'

I spent no time ruminating and duly paid the barman. On his signal, two of the intimidating thugs relaxed their menacing stares, broke into smiles, and proceeded to convey me safely to a cab.

As it transpired, it was a costly evening. In the cab, I discovered that my new watch was missing from my inner pocket.

The old man, of course. Damn me for a fool.

PART THREE

ALLIES AND OTHERS

'Let's plunge ourselves into the roar of time, the
whirl of accident; may pain and pleasure, success
and failure, shift as they will – it's only action that
can make a man.'
—Johann Wolfgang von Goethe, *Faust*

CHAPTER 11

Heffie

t was nearly one in the morning by the time I returned to 221B, and with great relief I saw the lights on upstairs and the silhouette of my friend in the window. Feeling chagrined for my fool's errand and for the utter naïveté that lost me my watch, I was nevertheless glad to find my keenest worries unfounded.

Holmes, clothed in his dressing gown and with pipe in hand, paced back and forth in front of the fire as I entered the room. I immediately noticed a swelling and small cut on his forehead with several stitches in it.

'Holmes! What happened to you?'

He glanced up at me, frowned and said, 'Watson, you really should have more faith in me! Spitalfields, alone at midnight? And dressed like that? You are a stalwart fellow but even so, that was foolish.'

'Says the man with a cut on his forehead! Let me see that wound!'

'What did you mean by going to the Snake and Drum by yourself? And how did you know to go there?'

'Lestrade. I was worried – and apparently with reason! Who attacked you?'

'Common thugs, Watson. Heffie and I prevailed, obviously. But, dear fellow, you should not have gone alone. Surely, Lestrade warned you?'

'He did.' I had moved closer and was taken aback at what I saw. 'Whoever did these stitches, Holmes, was a rank amateur, ' I exclaimed.

'I did 'em,' said a female voice with a distinct East End accent.

I turned and was astonished to see, settled cross-legged in front of the fire, what first appeared to be a bundle of rags, at the top of which emerged the round, freckled face of a girl. Brow furrowed, with a face smudged with dirt and a halo of frizzled blondish red curls frothing out in a circle all around it, she resembled a small lion. I guessed her to be around fifteen.

She stared up at me with frank resentment.

'Hephzibah O'Malley. Dr John Watson,' said Holmes, formally.

The filthy creature took a noisy sip from one of Holmes's cut crystal whisky glasses, and peered at me over its gleaming facets, her pale green eyes fixed in a challenging stare. Despite her slovenliness, I could see the pretty young woman this urchin could become, and the spirit underneath.

'S'wrong wit' them stitches?' she demanded to know.

'They are too big, too few, and uneven,' I said.

'So?' said she.

Those eyes were older than her years. Despite her rudeness, I read into them a keen intelligence and sensitivity.

Holmes intervened. 'Heffie, Dr Watson is an army surgeon.'

She shrugged, unimpressed. 'I done stitches dozens o'times,' she declared.

I sighed. Holmes had been regarding all this with amusement. 'Ah, you are jealous, Watson. I am sorry, for all of it. A trifling wound, but you know how minor cuts on the head will bleed. I hope you at least enjoyed your roast beef at Simpson's?'

I removed my scarf and hung up my coat.

'You missed an excellent meal,' I said. 'But . . . how did you instantly know I came from the Snake and Drum?'

'Hmm, let's see. The tilt of your hat. That speck of mud on your instep. The fading curl of your left moustache.'

Heffie laughed.

'I am too tired for this, Holmes,' said I.

'All right. How about this? I can *smell* that you have been to the Snake and Drum. Your coat bears the distinctive odour of wood-fire, kerosene, cheap gin, and terrible shag, of which the Snake and Drum is redolent. And there is something else on your fine jacket here.' He moved closer and sniffed the air near me. 'Hmm . . . cannabis. Very faint.'

'That . . . is remarkable!'

'Can o' what?' wondered the girl.

'*Ganja*,' said Holmes.

'Ewwww, nice!'

'Heffie, you must excuse us now. Please go downstairs. Mrs Hudson has drawn you a bath and there is a bed for you there. I'll see you get to your assignment in the morning.'

She finished her whisky, set down the glass and left the room, pausing at the door to give me a final, rude appraisal. 'Doctor, eh? Useful, I s'pose. I got a toe—'

'Good *night*, Heffie!' said Holmes. She departed.

He turned to me. 'Watson, I apologize. It was unforgivable of me not to have sent word. Halloa! What's this? Had I looked closer I would have been able to deduce where you had been by an even more obvious sign!'

He was staring at my waistcoat. 'Tell me you were not robbed of that fine watch, Watson?'

I sighed. There was no fooling the man. 'Yes, I was.' But I would never admit that it was by someone whom I mistook for him.

'Let me guess: it was a tall, elderly derelict with a red nose who – Oh! I see there is more to that story! Ha! But I shall leave it. You ventured to that terrible place out of concern for my welfare, and it is churlish of me to give you grief. Sorry, dear friend. Let us attend to more important matters. The list of Luminarians. Mayfair. Did our friendly viscounts provide?'

'There really is no official list. They remembered a few more names, and wrote them down,' said I, reaching into my pocket and finding . . . nothing! I began feeling in all of my pockets, with increasing panic. The folded-up list was gone.

It had vanished along with my new watch!

Holmes sighed. 'Bad luck! Watson I am sorry about your experience at the Snake and Drum. But surely you looked at the list? How many names can you recall?'

'I only glanced at it. There were six or eight names on it.'

'Yes?'

'Er, well. Mycroft was definitely on the list. I looked for him.'

'Fine. What of the others?'

'I really did not study it.'

'But later, at Simpson's. Were you not curious?'

'I was not in a booth. It felt conspicuous, Holmes.'

'Come on, Watson! Were the names in alphabetical order by chance?'

'No.'

'Any names beginning with B?'

'I am exhausted, Holmes, perhaps in the morning.'

He growled in frustration. 'Names, Watson, think!'

'I . . . yes, there was a Benjamin, a John Benjamin. I don't know who that is, but that name is somehow familiar.'

'Benjamin! Double suicide. Three weeks ago. Wealthy cloth merchant famous for some very generous pensions he gave to his employees. Hanged himself with a bolt of his own cloth. His wife did the same. It fits. It fits! If it is murder, there is our B!' He clapped his hands in delight.

'Holmes!'

'A bolt of his own cloth. A playful touch!'

'*Playful*, Holmes? Sometimes I sense you have a heart

of stone.' Wearily, I took off my jacket. 'Good night. I am about to fall asleep standing up.'

But for Holmes, it was as if it were bright morning after a good sleep. Energised, he resumed his pacing.

'Yes, of course. We must get an early start, Watson. Tomorrow I shall deposit Heffie with the headmistress at Lady Eleanor's school, where she will begin her assignment.'

'Good night.'

'I have every confidence that Lady Eleanor's young charge Judith will be well looked after. And then we can concentrate on more important things. This is a deadly game for someone. Fascinating!'

'*Good night,* Holmes. You really should rest.'

A timid knock came at the door, and Mrs Hudson peeked in, wearing a dressing gown over her nightclothes, her sleeping cap atop her grey curls.

'Mr Holmes? The girl is fast asleep. Couldn't get her near the bath. But I almost forgot. This letter was dropped off for you late this afternoon by Mr Lestrade. It is Mrs Danforth's farewell note, which he said you requested?'

Holmes took it with a quick thanks to Mrs Hudson, shut the door and sat by the fire to read. His face, so animated a moment ago, grew grave. He handed the note to me.

'Before you retire, Watson, take a look at this sad note from the late Mrs Danforth, and tell me if you think it is genuine. I must know if she was a suicide or was murdered.'

Wearily, I took from him a small, pale pink envelope

which was addressed on the outside '*To whom it may concern*' in a shaky, feminine hand. It read:

To my friends, family, and to Mr Sherlock Holmes, .

I have just heard that Charles has been released from gaol and knowing him as I do, I beg you to forgive me for choosing this sad way to depart this earth. I cannot prove it but know it was he who killed his father. I have lived with a monster these twelve years and can bear it no longer. My end is unquestionably nigh, be it by his violent hand or my own gentler one. Please forgive me the cowardice for choosing the latter.

Sincerely,

Constance Danforth.

I put the note down. 'You say she took poison, Holmes? We certainly met up with the fiend she describes. I believe this note is genuine.'

Holmes nodded and stared into the fire, thinking.

'Mrs Danforth, then, was not murdered. And yet . . .' He stood suddenly. 'Well, dear friend, it has been a long day. I hope you do not regret your choice to visit me while Mary is away. You may be worn to sawdust soon. I wish you good night.' He smiled.

As I lay in my bed moments later, I reflected on the wild ride of this visit. In the course of a mere eighteen hours, I'd witnessed an attack, visited St James's, Fitzrovia, Mayfair and Spitalfields, in audience with the richest, the most connected, and the lowliest that London has to offer. I had already been to places and seen people far from my normal purview. It had been many leagues distant from the routine of examining babies with coughs and bricklayers with cut fingers.

But despite my utter failure at the Snake and Drum, I felt happier than I had been in more than a year. Mary was right. I had needed a dose of Sherlock Holmes.

CHAPTER 12

The Dogged Detective

 awoke in the morning with the cold November light dimly glowing through the brown striped curtains I remembered so well. Peering out, I saw that it had snowed while I slept, and there was a fine coating of white spread thinly across the yard and clinging to the remaining brown leaves of the plane tree which stood forlornly in the centre. I could feel the deep chill seeping in through the window joints and along the floor. It was unseasonably early for this wintry weather. Dressing quickly, I added my familiar old brown dressing gown which I had neglected to take with me and was still hanging in the armoire.

Downstairs in our sitting-room, Holmes sat by the fire, a coffee in hand, poring over the newspaper. Except for the cut on his forehead, he was as fresh and relaxed as though he had just enjoyed a week's holiday. I poured myself a cup of coffee from the silver pot left by Mrs Hudson, then gasped, nearly dropping it in surprise.

For there, stretched out in front of the fire at Holmes's feet, was an enormous mound of a black, shaggy dog. It was as though the bearskin rug on which the creature rested had suddenly come to life.

At my exclamation, the dog lifted a head the size of two human skulls to regard me alertly with rheumy brown eyes. Its long pink tongue lolled from an open mouth, and I apparently met with its approval, for the tattered flag of a tail beat the floor twice, then sank down again onto the rug beneath it. It lowered its head and shut its eyes once more.

Holmes looked up at me, enjoying my reaction.

'What the devil is this creature doing here, Holmes?'

'He followed me home last night. Or rather early this morning. It had begun to snow, and I took pity on him.'

'You went out *again* last night?'

'Mrs Danforth's suicide note. I agree that it seemed genuine, but there was a small detail that troubled me. Last night, in a brief visit below stairs in the Danforth home, I ascertained with relative ease that the poison Constance Danforth took was supplied unwittingly by a maid, who is now consumed with remorse. The girl related that her mistress insisted on being supplied with a box of rat poison, discreetly, for "a friend's use". A second servant corroborated this. I have sadly confirmed that her death was a suicide and not a murder. It was tangentially related to her father-in-law's murder, but not directly.'

'A terrible way to die. But you have had little sleep, then, for a second night! Let me take a look at that cut.'

Holmes waved me off. From my vantage point it looked no worse than the night before. 'What has become of Heffie?'

'I deposited her at the school about an hour ago.'

'Then Holmes, you have had no sleep at all!'

'I am quite invigorated, dear boy! There is something connecting these disparate deaths, and I will find out what it is.'

He bounded from the chair and over to a large black-board on wheels, which I had not seen in some time, and which I knew he kept stored in the attic. 'Look at this!'

Across the top had been chalked the letters A–H. Below A, C, and D, were the names Anson, Clammory and Danforth, and the words 'Murder', 'Suicides' and more names. Underneath B was Benjamin with a large '?' below it. E and its successors loomed empty.

A rectangle inscribed with a D was present on the Anson column and none of the others. It was connected with an arrow to a circle containing my name.

I pointed. 'What is that?'

'A Devil Tarot card was found next to Anson's body. The same as the one handed to you in Hyde Park.'

'A warning, do you think?' I said. 'And of what?'

'Possibly a warning. Possibly a tease. Possibly unrelated, though that last is unlikely. It would be advisable to locate the young lady who handed it to you. But in the meantime, I think it means that you and I should be on the alert. No more wandering alone to Spitalfields, Watson.'

'As you did?'

He smiled at me.

'Holmes, this alphabet theory is not compelling,' I said. At his sharp look, I regretted the force of this statement. 'Well, not to me. I mean, how would the killer, if it is the same person, know who all of the Luminarians are? There seems to be no list.'

'Excellent question, Watson, and one I am pondering. Perhaps the killer is a Luminarian himself. And upon receiving this honour, he then asked for or otherwise found out the names of others. Perhaps not *all* the others, as there is no list, but enough to act upon.'

'I suppose so.'

'Alternately, the person is a friend or acquaintance of one or more of them, and through gossip or casual social contact – perhaps at the Goodwins' famous parties – has learned some names. Speaking of which, after your sleep Watson, have you perchance been able to remember any other names you saw on the short list you had in hand?'

I shook my head, ashamed that I had not committed the list to memory and had allowed a fine meal followed by the evening's adventure to distract me. Perhaps marriage *had* dulled my faculties.

'I am sorry, Holmes. I suppose I could return there and ask for it again.' I would certainly feel a fool, but I would do what was necessary to make up for my carelessness with the list.

'No need. I have sent word to them to send it to us again. Any further impressions gleaned from your visit to the Goodwins?'

'Well, the entire Luminarian business seems like something they regard lightly. They were getting ready for a grand party while I was there yesterday, and despite the imminent threat, they seemed far more concerned with the festivities.'

'Their social life is more than it seems, Watson, and those two cultivate being underestimated. Trust me. The most illustrious and moneyed characters of the capital are counted among their close friends. While they may appear frivolous, they are not. Mycroft informs me that some remarkable back-door political transactions spring from those parties, Watson.'

'Really, Holmes! James Goodwin was smoking cannabis.'

'And I occasionally partake of cocaine. I said, do not underestimate them. Of course, most of London lives in hope for an invitation. Their good will confers instant status.'

'I suppose that being chosen as a Luminarian is regarded as quite an honour. But, by heavens, the hubris of it all! But why would someone want to kill this group? Jealousy?'

Holmes smiled, and sitting back down, took up his pipe.

'That is what I must discover.'

'Holmes, what good is an honour unless it is made public? I mean, is that not the very definition of an honour?'

'To some, I suppose. Not to me, Watson. The satisfaction of a job well done, the solution of a pretty little puzzle. For me, the game is all, and I do not require public approval.'

'Holmes, you have said this before, and I must disagree. For you, I would say that your work is in the service of justice. And perhaps art. But it is hardly a game.'

'You are partly right, my friend. But the solving of a crime must be, to me, like a game. If I allow my feelings to engage, I lose the edge I need to find the solution. No, it must remain a game.'

He smiled at my raised eyebrow, then turned serious once more.

'Watson, let us try an experiment. A game if you will. Close your eyes. Try to bring up a clear image of that sheet of paper in your mind's eye.'

I did so. The image did not come. 'I am trying, Holmes,' I said.

'No, quite literally. Picture it in detail. What colour was the paper? Was it folded? How many times?'

As a writer, I had trained myself to visualize people, places and events. Some came more clearly than others, of course. But some were blurred as if by a London fog – by time, emotion, or the mysterious workings of the human brain.

The list remained a blur. I struggled. Finally, I said, 'The paper was cream coloured with the Goodwin family crest, or what I believe to be the family crest, stamped in gold at the top. The list was written in black ink. There was more than one hand in the list, for some of the names were written by James and some by Andrew Goodwin.'

'Do you know, or can you *see* the two handwritings?'

'See.'

'Good. Keep your eyes closed, Watson. Now scan down the page. Is Mycroft's name there?'

'Yes. Actually, I noticed that straight away. I was looking for it.'

'And any other names? Besides Benjamin.'

I closed my eyes trying again to bring forth the image of that slip of paper, but I simply could not. I shook my head. 'Too much has happened, Holmes. I am out of practice for this kind of work.'

The previous day was a tumult of activity, and I had not had my coffee. I stepped carefully around the enormous dog and sat down in the basket chair. A few minutes passed as we drank our coffee in silence, Holmes's smoke curling around him like a dog circling round its bed.

A snore came from the living bearskin rug between us. 'You do not plan to keep this dog, do you, Holmes?'

'No, Watson, in fact I have sent Billy to old Sherman in Lambeth.'

'Oh yes! The man who provided us with Toby, that mongrel with the excellent tracking nose. The very case where I had met my—'

'—your dear Mary. Yes, Watson.' Holmes sighed. He was happy for my marriage, or professed to be. 'Sherman will no doubt take in the dog, or he will know someone who would. This is a valuable animal. A Belgian herding breed, if I am not mistaken.'

The dog snuffled loudly, sneezed, then hauled his ragged and enormous frame clumsily to his feet. He moved in the direction of Holmes, then placed his large head in my friend's lap. Holmes looked surprised only for a moment, then, pipe in mouth, began to idly scratch the dog behind the ears.

The dog raised his gigantic head and gave a deep bark

so loud the drinks tray rattled on the sideboard. This was followed by the doorbell ringing and an anxious and furious knocking. Mrs Hudson's alarmed voice was heard and then a pounding of footsteps up the stairs.

Holmes and I were on our feet in an instant to see the figure of a cloaked man, hat low over his brow, burst into the room in a dead run. He flung the hat from his head and shouted, 'Hide me!'

The dog growled and barked again, and the man jumped backward, nearly stumbling over the low Moroccan table by Holmes's favourite chair. He caught himself before falling and turned to face Holmes. 'They are coming! Hide me!'

I regarded with surprise the handsome, tanned face with the trimmed moustache and mocking eyes, now widened in panic. A dubious character, indeed. It was the French detective Jean Vidocq!

CHAPTER 13

The Baguette Brigade

ean Vidocq was never particularly trustworthy, and wherever this con artist appeared trouble generally followed. But he and Holmes shared a peculiar, wary bond which I did not fully understand.

'Who is after you, Vidocq?' asked my friend, with a calm bordering on insolence.

'Victor Richard and his gang. The anarchists.' Vidocq smoothed his hair nervously.

'You know full well that I am working on the case as well.'

'I am so close to learning their plans. I know the time of their next bombing but not the location. But, *hélas*, they have discovered me!'

The dog barked again, and afterwards there was more pounding at the door.

'What a reckless choice you have made, leading them here!' cried Holmes.

More pounding below us.

'Please. They might kill me. I must hide!' said the Frenchman. Handsome, cocky, and the consummate ladies' man, Vidocq was at this moment at his most vulnerable. For once he did not have a sarcastic word to fling at me.

'All right,' said Holmes. 'You can go into—'

Just then the door opened below. We heard the strident French voices of several men, one apologizing to Mrs Hudson in heavily accented English and the others evidently encouraging each other to '*Allez-y*' or 'Go there!'

'Quick, behind the sofa!' whispered Holmes.

As more words floated up from below, Vidocq dived behind the settee.

Holmes rushed to the landing, and despite the cold he opened a window a crack. He then returned to the sitting-room, closing the door after him as Vidocq compressed his large form into the small space with difficulty.

Thunderous tramping of boots on the stairs followed, and despite my feeling of resentment for this intrusive Frenchman, I positioned myself next to the settee to block anyone from standing where they could see Vidocq. At the very least, his discovery could harm Holmes's investigation.

What a precarious position this man had put us in!

Vidocq peered up at me, signalling '*Merci*'. I turned. Holmes had vanished into his bedroom, closing the door.

In a moment there came a pounding on the sitting-room door, and without waiting for a response, an intruder flung it open and rushed into the room. It was the rotund, apple-cheeked grocer whom I had met yesterday, although so much had happened that it seemed a lifetime ago. The anarchist and coffee expert Victor Richard was followed by three men brandishing baguettes like clubs.

I almost burst out laughing.

'Ah, Mr Richard!' said Holmes pleasantly, emerging from his room, transformed once again to the slightly awkward Stephen Hollister. He eyed the three 'armed' men. 'To what do I owe this visit from the . . . er . . . Baggety Brigade?'

'*Mon Dieu*, it is Monsieur Stephen Hollister! I did not know you lived here!' Richard's angry expression dissolved into smiles.

'Really? I have been your customer for some time. Your coffee grinder, by the way, is as *mervy-you* as you say!'

'Ah, *bien sûr*! I am glad,' said Richard, his close-set brown eyes sweeping the room, looking for places one might hide. Noticing the bloodstained tusk, chemistry set and other odd items, he blinked, confused.

'What is it that you do, Mr Hollister?'

'I am a writer of adventure novels, sir. A work that requires a lot of coffee. What can I do for you, Mr Richard?' asked Holmes pleasantly. 'You seem distraught.'

Victor Richard noticed the settee and realized it was large enough to hide a man. He began to sidle off to his right to get a better angle. I moved slightly to block his view.

Suddenly our hairy visitor, forgotten for the moment, sprang to his feet and barked. Richard, noticing the animal for the first time, started as I had done and backed away.

'Lie down, Hector,' said Holmes. The dog glanced up at him, and then lay down.

Hector?

'The dog will not hurt you, as long as you make no sudden movements,' said Holmes.

Richard nodded and kept his distance. 'We have followed someone here. I did not at the time know it was your house, Mr Hollister. I must apologize to your housekeeper—'

'Mrs Hudson is our landlady, not our housekeeper, and I am certain that a jar of your wonderful Provence lavender honey will smooth things over.'

'*Mais, oui!* But our business is pressing. We, er . . . there is a French thief, a man well known to us – who is responsible for, how you say, making a great deal of trouble for the shop.'

'What kind of trouble?'

'He has been stealing our trade secrets! We followed him here. He is tall, your height, but how you say? More big, with a small black moustache.'

'Trade secrets?' murmured Holmes with a smile. He gestured at the three men brandishing the long loaves of French bread. 'And, er, this bread? Were you planning to beat him into submission?'

I looked again at the menacing three. The loaves did look, if somewhat ironically, like police truncheons. I put out a hand to touch one. 'Stale,' I said. 'Quite hard, in fact!'

The grocer smiled. 'Embarrass him enough and he will leave,' said he, and seizing one from the man standing closest to him, he wielded it like a club, ever so reminiscent of a policeman dealing with a dangerous crowd. He took a mock swing at Holmes, who put up a hand.

From near the fireplace, I heard a low growl. Victor Richard had momentarily forgotten the dog, who now stared at him, teeth bared. He backed away, returning the baguette to his man.

Holmes laughed. 'Well then, he should be very afraid.' He looked closer at Richard and pulled the man's lapel back, revealing a gun. This was no ordinary grocer. 'Although I see you are, in fact, quite serious,' he added.

Richard pulled away, covering up the gun and eyeing Holmes with sudden suspicion.

'We adventure writers notice such things!' said Holmes with a smile. 'So you intend to really frighten him off?'

'Only if he refuses to return to France,' said the grocer.

The dog growled again, louder. 'Hector!' Holmes said to the dog. The dog sat but kept a wary eye on Richard.

'Mr Richard, may I suggest you do not draw your gun? Hector is rather protective of me.'

It was true, Holmes had a remarkable rapport with animals. Horses and dogs alike seemed to take to my friend.

'I do not like . . . big dogs,' said Richard.

I took the next moment to glance down. From my vantage point I could see that Vidocq, tall and muscular as he was, and huddled behind the divan, was immensely uncomfortable. He looked up at me in genuine panic. I would be lying if I said I did not in some small way enjoy his discomfiture.

'I would swear the man we are following came inside

here,' said Richard, backing away ever so slightly from Holmes and the dog. 'Did you not see or hear anything?'

'Well, yes! A bang on the door below, I heard steps and then I heard someone open the window on the landing here. I simply presumed it was Mrs Hudson wishing to air out the place. My friend's coat smells strongly of woodsmoke and cheap shag, you see, from—'

Richard and his three men rushed out onto the landing and to the partly opened window. Holmes followed.

'Ah, it is freezing outside!' said the detective. He closed the windows. 'You say someone came in here? How odd. Perhaps Mrs Hudson had the door open for some reason and he simply took the chance. He must have exited this way. I have taken that escape route myself a few times.'

At Richard's look of puzzlement, Holmes added, 'The ladies, you know?' He winked. This was particularly humorous, given the awkward demeanour of his Stephen Hollister character, not to mention Holmes's own famous avoidance of female admirers.

The Frenchman nodded sympathetically. 'Where does this courtyard lead?' he asked.

'It connects to a mews back there, and eventually the next street.'

'*Allez-y!*' shouted Richard to his men. 'I am sorry to trouble you, Monsieur Hollister. Expect some honey for your landlady, and coffee for you. Our very great thanks. You should keep your door locked.'

The French cadre took their leave. With much grunting and a great show of discomfort, Vidocq unfurled himself from where he had been hidden. He noticed with horror some dust on his fine jacket and brushed at it furiously. 'Thank you,' he said, with a tinge of resentment. 'Have you a clothes brush?'

I handed him one from where it hung from the coat rack.

Holmes removed his glasses and teeth, then lit his pipe, pointedly ignoring Vidocq, who was indeed a sorry sight. The Frenchman appeared to be simultaneously embarrassed by the need for our help and disgruntled by the manner in which it had been given.

'Well, Vidocq, I suppose this ends your work here for the French government, for now,' said Holmes. 'What is the time of the next bombing that you claim to have discovered?'

'Ah, you have the location then,' said Vidocq, instantly alert to my companion's intent.

Holmes equally understood Vidocq. 'And you have the time. No matter. You can be the one to report. The location will be at Borough Market, at the northern end where Church and York meet. But heed me, Vidocq. Report our combined intelligence and then say goodbye to my brother as you leave for Paris. He will make sure that you do.'

'Mycroft Holmes! One day he is with me, the next against!' exclaimed the Frenchman, brushing the dust off his left sleeve in a fury.

Holmes shrugged. I rather thought the same of Mycroft Holmes myself.

'I have felt your intrusive presence in my work, Holmes.

I would think your brother would have prevented you from interfering.'

Holmes laughed sharply. Hector gave a low woof at this. 'My brother does not dictate my cases, Vidocq.'

'*Vraiment?* That is not my impression. Ah, well, I am now, how you say, an old duck.'

'Dead duck. If you don't mind, Vidocq, I have pressing business.'

He left, and I discovered one of the stale baguettes had been dropped in the corner of the room. 'Imagine Vidocq being frightened of a loaf of bread!' I said, wielding it.

'*And a gun*, Watson.'

Hector moved slowly to me and regarded me with sad eyes. I held out the baguette and the dog took it delicately into his mouth, then sat down with it in front of the fire and began gnawing on the thing like a bone. The whole event struck me as funny and I burst out laughing.

'Watson, you laugh, but do not underestimate Richard and his men. Earlier, another French government agent was sent to infiltrate Richard's group but was discovered. Shortly after, in a pub, this agent was surrounded by what seemed a drunken crowd of men, who sang him loudly all the way to the train station where he departed for France and never showed his face here again. The onlookers found it hilarious. The press made a meal of it.'

'Well, it is amusing,' said I.

Holmes stared at me pointedly. 'He was lucky. The agent sent before that one was found floating in the Thames.'

Hector looked up from his treasure and woofed softly,

and then came yet a third pounding at the door downstairs. It was not even ten in the morning! The dog dropped the baguette and leapt to his feet with a loud bark. Holmes silenced him with a point of his finger.

In bounded Inspector Lestrade.

'Ah, another murder! Where? Who?' said Holmes, with an eager smile.

'Holmes!' I remonstrated.

'It is Claudio Enrietti!' said Lestrade breathlessly. 'The opera star! Found dead this morning in his dressing-room!'

I do not follow opera but the name struck a chord. From the foggy image of the list of Luminarians, a name suddenly emerged.

'Holmes!' I cried. 'Enrietti was on the list!'

'E!' shouted my friend, leaping to his feet. 'Watson, we have our E!'

CHAPTER 14

Death at the Opera

 estrade dashed out to hail a cab as we donned our coats and ran for the door. The dog, suddenly animated with excitement, barrelled past me on the stairs and emerged next to Holmes onto the landing outside our front door, as if he were Holmes's newest partner. There was a sudden flash of light on the two of them – bright even in the glare of morning sunlight – followed by the sharp sound of sarcastic laughter.

I emerged to discover Gabriel Zanders, the feral-looking reporter with the tight suit and wispy moustache, whom I recognized from Speakers' Corner. He had a photographer in tow, and a wide grin on his insolent face as he regarded Holmes and the dog.

'I see you have a new friend on your investigations,' Zander taunted. 'Who's this fellow? Oh, it's Mephistopheles!'

What on earth was this man on about?

'Ah, Mr Zanders. How serendipitous. So now I'm Faust visited by Mephistopheles!' Holmes said, as if musing.

The reporter was grinning. 'Preee-cisely, Mr Holmes. The Devil in the form of a big black dog. A fitting image.'

'Hmm, it did not go so well for Faust,' said Holmes.

'By golly, you are a smart one! I can see the headline now. *'Detective sells his soul to the Devil!'*

'Few of your *Gazette* readers will appreciate the allusion,' said Holmes. 'How many do you expect know the Faust legend?'

'The Times' readers are a more literate crowd.'

'Ah, *The Times* has taken you back, then?'

'They enjoy selling papers, Holmes.'

'Kindly use the honorific when addressing me,' said Holmes coldly.

The dog suddenly left his side and sat down next to Zanders. He looked up at the reporter, mouth open, tail wagging.

'Ah, so he's *your* dog, Mr Zanders. A plant,' said Holmes. The dog leaned into Zanders' leg, confirming this.

From half a block away, Lestrade called out, 'Mr Holmes. Doctor! Cab! Down here!'

Holmes held up a hand. He turned back to the reporter. Zanders shrugged, patting the dog's head.

Holmes smiled pleasantly. 'If you applied this much effort to actual journalism, you could go far,' said Holmes. 'But, persist and I will see you brought up for slander. Good day.'

Moments later, our carriage thundered through the streets on the way to Covent Garden and the Royal Italian Opera.

'That was certainly odd, Holmes!' I ventured.

Holmes shook his head. 'He doesn't deserve his own dog.'

Heading towards the scene of the murder, our carriage careened recklessly from Baker Street south past the British Museum towards Covent Garden and a rather grimy section of town. Given the early hour, the streets were still littered with refuse from the nearby market. The light snowfall from the night before was already melting and tides of horse droppings and rotting produce eddied around the gutters. From this sordid base rose the imposing, columned edifice of the Opera House, home of the Royal Italian Opera. The building, though darkened by smoke and grime, greeted the thin morning sun with a certain grandeur.

I had accompanied Holmes here on several occasions but had never seen the place at this hour. Lestrade hoped to deliver us unobserved, and before Titus Billings might arrive. Holmes knew he would be barred from the scene if the acting head of the Metropolitan Police made it there first.

But, alas, we discovered the official police vehicle parked near the stage door entrance, the door propped open with an arrogant-looking young officer posted there whom Holmes did not recognize.

'No use, Mr Holmes,' said Lestrade. 'That's young Fleming. He's thrown his hat in with Mr Billings. Quite a few of the young ones have.'

'Follow me. I know another way!' Holmes cried, and leapt from our still moving carriage. Lestrade and I followed him through a door, around the corner, where a friendly stagehand, who recognized my friend, led us on an alternate route to the dressing-rooms – via the stage and into the wings.

I had never been backstage at a theatre of this size and even as we rushed through, I was astonished at the enormity of the scenic pieces, the tangle of cords, electric lights, and a myriad of unidentified objects. A rack held swords, another brightly coloured dressing gowns and feather boas. A table displayed pistols, ropes, angels' wings, a candelabrum and silver platters of food made of plaster.

We followed a set of darkened stairs leading down to a warren of corridors and the dressing-room area. Ahead of us was a door, and crowded at the entrance was a group of excited gawkers. These figures were silhouetted intermittently as the bright flashes of a photographer at work lit the room before them. More people rushed by us with whispers and squeals of horror. 'Murder! Last night! Did you see?'

Holmes stopped us, and asked Lestrade, 'Why have they not secured the murder site? It is a circus in here!'

'Mr Billings does not follow protocol,' the inspector whispered.

'At least the photos may prove useful – if they have not disturbed the scene,' said Holmes.

We pushed through the throng to Enrietti's dressing-room. Nearly at the threshold, we heard the deep, strident baritone of Titus Billings's voice cut through the clamour, coming from somewhere off to the side.

There, down an adjacent corridor and thirty yards away, with Billings presiding, several policemen surrounded a colourful individual wearing an expensive top hat and red cravat. This man – whom I took to be the theatre manager – stood his ground, unafraid of the bullying Chief Commissioner.

Billings thrust a beefy finger into the chest of this stalwart figure. 'Theft! Crime! And now murder!' rasped Billings. '*Foreigners* everywhere in your theatre. What do you expect?'

'I expect to put on a show,' replied his opponent. 'With the greatest artists in the world! From France! From Italy! From . . . Timbuktu! I will hire whom I please!'

'Quick, Watson, now is our chance,' Holmes intoned. He and Lestrade pushed through the crowd at the dressing-room door and ducked inside, Lestrade blocking others from entering with one strong arm.

'I'll try to hold him off,' he said, then turned to the gawkers. 'Stand back! Police business.'

With difficulty, Holmes pushed the door closed on the curious onlookers. We turned, facing into the dressing-room. A photographer was bent over, blocking the corpse. Another man, small, with dark, curly hair and a green kerchief around his neck, sat sobbing at a dressing table.

The photographer rose. We got our first good look at Enrietti. The expression on the dead man's face is one I shall never forget.

CHAPTER 15

A Voice Stilled

laudio Enrietti's mouth was wide open, as if he were delivering the climactic notes of his most famous opera. The eyes were wild, nearly popping from their sockets – brown marbles surrounded by the whites stained red with blood. It was the face of a nightmare. The world famous baritone and notorious ladies' man now lay prostrate on the floor, clad in a velvet dressing gown which gaped open immodestly, revealing long woollen underwear.

Enrietti had been a tall, barrel-chested man in his sixties, with hair dyed an artificially brilliant bronze. His body lay sprawled underneath a closed window, hands clutching his own neck, his face faintly blue.

The photographer turned and smiled upon seeing my friend. 'Mr Holmes!'

'Ah, Windy! Glad it's you!' said Holmes. 'You've captured

all angles on the body? Good, then. Be sure to miss nothing – the table, the food, the hanging rack.' The photographer set to it. 'Watson, cause of death?'

I was already kneeling by the corpse, starting my investigation.

'Who are you?' Holmes demanded of the seated man. I glanced up to see the small fellow shrink back towards the dressing table crowded with potions, false hairpieces, stage makeup and photographs. He was dark-skinned with curly black hair, and now peeked from between his fingers to reveal a tear-stained face. 'I am Angelo. Dresser. Friend.' He had a thick Italian accent.

'Don't move from there,' ordered Holmes. He bent down to the corpse beside me. Even with luck, we'd have only a few minutes here.

'Asphyxiation?'

I nodded. 'Looks that way.'

Holmes leaned over and his long, slim fingers danced over the corpse – checking the eyes, mouth, hands and fingernails, and then the pockets of the robe. He stood and examined the sill of the window with his travelling magnifying glass.

'Enrietti ran to the window for air,' he said. 'Clawed it open. Paint under the fingernails, and the marks here on the sill. He was successful, I think, for all the good it did him. The window is not latched. Odd. Someone closed it later. Carry on, Watson.' He turned to the dresser. 'Was it you who found the body?'

I kept my eyes on my work as they continued.

'*Sì*. I find *mi* Claudio. And I close the window.'

'Why?'

'He hated window open. Never he open the window.'

'Never? Until tonight. Why?' Holmes sighed. 'Watson, any progress?'

'Give me a moment!'

Enrietti's once handsome, chiselled face had contorted in his death struggle. The bloodstained eyes were telling. His tongue was swollen, though not enough to choke him. I examined the neck and chest for signs of bruising or compression. 'No evidence of manual strangulation,' I said.

Holmes turned back to the dresser. 'Why did Enrietti hate having a window open? Draughts? Protecting his voice?'

'He . . . he afraid.'

'Of what?'

'Of eh . . . eh . . .'

Holmes stamped in impatience. 'Watson, anything more?'

'Nothing obvious in the airway. No contusion on the neck or chest.'

'Keep looking.' He turned back to Angelo. '*When* did you find him?'

'This morning. I come to prepare the costume for tonight—' He sobbed. 'No sing. Ever again.'

'You usually sleep here?' said Holmes, and I looked up to follow his gaze to a pile of bedding and a pillow stashed into a corner. I had not noticed this. The man nodded. 'Why not last night?' asked Holmes.

'Claudio, he ask me to see young lady home. Was very

late. I had not money for cab back. I walk. Very far. I not know London and lost,' he wailed. 'If only I not lost!'

'What young lady?' said Holmes.

'Do not know. She come, like so many come because she love Claudio. Everybody love Claudio. Many women. This one bring flowers two times. Yesterday. Day before yesterday.'

'Where did you leave this young lady?'

'I . . . I could not say. She direct the cab.'

'But you returned from there! What part of town?'

Angelo shrugged. 'I very lost.'

'And drinking?'

'A little drinking.'

Holmes exhaled in exasperation. 'I see no flowers.'

'He *allergico*. Threw away always the flowers.'

'Can you describe her?'

'Ahhh, no. Sorry. The girls, they are all pretty. Dark hair, I think. '

'How old?'

'I do not notice. Young. It is possible fifteen, maybe twenty?'

'That is a wide range.' I heard the frustration in Holmes's voice.

'The girls, the women, they are all the same to me. So many. Every night.'

'Why did you see this one home in particular?'

'I do not know. Mr Enrietti, he ask me to. Maybe because she cry.'

'Cry?' exclaimed Holmes.

'I find her here hiding in the costumes. In that rack over there.'

Holmes grunted and moved to the rack of costumes. It was densely packed. I could see even from where I was crouched near the body that it could, in fact, hide someone. Holmes slid some of the costumes back and forth, looking behind them.

'Was that unusual, finding a girl hiding here?'

'Not essactly . . . One or two every season do this.'

I looked up from my examination of the corpse. 'I think I have gone into the wrong profession!'

'It is something to consider. What do you find, Watson?'

'Nothing blocking the airway. I am leaning towards poison.'

'Ah!' I heard Holmes move behind me and I turned to see him bending over a small table.

'His dinner here is untouched but for a single bite. Angelo, who brought in this tray?' he demanded.

Outside the door a commotion sounded and Billings's loud voice carried over the others, barking orders. We had moments, if that.

'The theatre provide. But food is no poison,' said Angelo, swallowing a sob. 'I always taste for him. Food is good! But he no eat, this bite is me. I do not know why no eat.'

'Because he died before he could. The food was brought in after the show? Come on, Angelo!'

'It brought in at intermission. But always, he eat after.'

'But he ate nothing last night. He must have been killed shortly after his perfor— Hullo! You always *taste for him*? You're his . . . *taster*?'

'*Si.*'

Something banged against the door. I heard Lestrade's voice. 'I think it is locked.'

'Since when?'

'Two years.'

'He kept the windows locked since then also?'

Angelo nodded.

'What happened two years ago?'

'Two years ago. Ah, so sad! His friend—'

But before the man could finish, the door flew open with a crash. The enormous form of Billings filled the entrance, flanked by two tall police officers I did not recognize. Both young men had some kind of gold braid on their uniforms. I had never seen that on a constable before.

'What is going on in here? Did I hear poison?' Billings cried out. 'Lestrade!' He called out over his shoulder, then turned to stare at Holmes in a cold fury. 'How dare you bring this amateur in here?'

Lestrade appeared in the doorway behind Billings. 'In cases of this kind, sir, Mr Holmes has been very—'

'Sherlock Holmes! I know of you! You're a charlatan. A devil. The papers have you right. Out of this room!' Billings ordered. He pointed to me. 'But you, Doctor, I know of you, too. You stay.'

One of the gold-trimmed policemen who entered with Billings tried to take Holmes by the arm to escort him from the room. Holmes stopped him with a glare and made his own way out – but turned to stand in the doorway. He was now officially out of the room, if barely.

Billings's eyes turned to Angelo, the dresser. 'Now, you,

you little Italian dog.' He approached the terrified man and, grasping him by the shirt, yanked him to his feet. 'I heard the word poison. Did you poison Claudio Enrietti?'

'N-no sir!'

Billings flung the man away and picked up the tray of food. From the doorway, Holmes murmured, 'I suggest you do not move the evidence, Mr Billings!'

'Quiet!' said Billings. Then, thrusting the tray at Angelo. 'What of this, then?'

'Is safe,' said the dresser. 'I taste for him the food. Is safe.'

'*Is safe?* Can you not *speaka da English*?' Billings grinned at his men and the two acolytes laughed.

Before anyone could move, Angelo scooped a piece of meat from the plate and into his mouth. The dresser swallowed the mouthful proudly, eyes shining. 'You see. All is well. I tol' you—'

In the doorway, Holmes whispered, 'Oh, no.'

Angelo stood still, triumphant. Then suddenly his expression changed to confusion. He gagged. Coughed. His eyes filled with terror. He coughed, again, choked, grabbed his throat, and then retched.

'Watson!'

I lunged forward and caught the man as his knees gave way. Angelo began to foam at the mouth, and his entire body spasmed. He crumpled and I eased him to the floor. I rolled him onto his back. His eyes were open and glazed over. Death had been nearly instantaneous.

I had seen this before. I stood up and smelled the food.

'Cyanide!' I said.

CHAPTER 16

Italian Air

or a moment, no one moved. Then Billings took up the plate and smelled it. 'I smell nothing!'

'Not everyone can smell cyanide,' I said. 'Believe me, it is there.'

'Why don't you try it if you don't believe him?' said Holmes calmly.

Billings dropped the tray onto the table and glared at him. 'Quiet, or be arrested.' He stepped forward to the dresser's body and gave it a sharp kick, presumably to ascertain for certain that he was dead.

'Lying little bastard. And cowardly, too. He chose to go this way instead of to gaol. The case is clear cut. This Angelo servant killed his employer, Claudio Enrietti. Poisoned his food. Then committed suicide in front of our eyes. Take that down,' he directed one man, who duly scribbled in his notebook. Billings waved to another, 'Clear these bodies away.' The men scurried to do his bidding.

Gold trim in exchange for servitude, I thought.

As they moved past Holmes, I saw him shake his head ruefully. His eyes met mine.

Billings turned to me. 'Probably some Italian thing. *La Famiglia*. They bring their troubles with them. You, Wilson, is it? Doctor, right? I have read of you.'

'Watson. Yes, I am a medical man.'

'The Enrietti death. It was poison, yes?'

'It looks to be poison. But certainly not the same that killed Angelo. Enrietti's was a case of compromised respiration.'

Billings said nothing, sizing me up with a fierce concentration. Then, 'It was poison. Poison is poison. We are finished here. Make your report at Scotland Yard to back up my own officers' reports. Match it, if you expect to be paid. Work well for me and I will have use for you.'

I was speechless. The man was trying to hire me!

Ten minutes later the police, including Lestrade, had departed, locking the dressing-room after them. I doubted they would pursue the case further and wondered why they bothered. We lingered in the hall outside the locked door.

'The man is not precisely an idiot, but he is more interested in closing cases than solving them,' said Holmes.

'Agreed. They were not poisoned by the same substance. But what happened to that food?' I wondered. 'Angelo tasted it before he left to see the girl home.'

'The murderer was taking no chances,' said Holmes.

'Perhaps they knew of the tasting routine, and when Enrietti ate. Must have poisoned the food during the performance, in case . . . in case whatever else it was that killed Enrietti did not work. I need to know how Enrietti was poisoned.'

'How odd that they have not secured the crime scene,' I remarked.

'Billings does not care, Watson.' We looked about us. The corridor was dark and empty. Holmes pulled out his small lock-picking kit and, in a moment, we were back in the room.

Now that it was empty, I became aware of that particular dank smell of death. Holmes and I began to root systematically through the detritus of a theatrical life that had, until mere hours ago, flourished in this room. We looked for signs of a struggle, an intruder, or some method of delivering an inhaled poison. 'Search also for anything which might reveal why Enrietti feared murder for the past two years,' Holmes instructed. 'Private papers, letters.'

As he rifled the pockets of costumes and several sets of elegantly tailored street clothes on hangers, I examined a row of men's soft dancing shoes and the neat array of bottles and potions on the dressing-table. Tucked into a corner of the mirror was the photograph of a startlingly beautiful young woman. I removed it from the mirror and turned it over. It said, '*Mi Papa, t'amo. Giulia.*' A loving note from Enrietti's daughter. At least there was someone left to mourn the dead man. There were no papers, however.

The door clicked open. It was the manager we had seen before.

'Mr Holmes! Ah, good,' he said. 'Ugh, this room. The barbarians have departed. Do you know what happened?'

'No, Mr Bellagio. But I intend to discover it.'

At my puzzled look, Holmes explained. 'I solved a case of backstage theft last year for Mr Bellagio.'

The man sighed. 'Poor Claudio. And shame about this,' said he, stroking his moustache. 'Our best dressing-room. No performer will ever use it again.'

'Why not?' I blurted.

'No one is more superstitious than an actor, Watson,' said Holmes. 'Just as, backstage, no performer will utter the name of Shakespeare's, Mac—'

'No!' cried Mr Bellagio.

Holmes sighed. He was never one for superstition. 'One question before you go, Mr Bellagio. Did you notice any young women visiting Mr Enrietti in his dressing-room the last two or three nights? Perhaps bearing flowers. Roses, most likely?'

He shrugged. 'There were many, every night for Mr Enrietti. I did not notice one in particular. '

Holmes thanked him and the manager left us to complete our task.

'You're sure it was cyanide for Angelo, Watson?'

'Yes.'

'Obviously placed after the tasting,' said Holmes. 'But the question is, who put it there, and when?'

I continued my search.

'That person may or may not have known of Angelo's role of taster. Although . . . you thought an inhalant, Watson?'

'I saw nothing in Enrietti's mouth or back of his throat. And he was going for air, so his lungs must have stopped working. No inflammation in the throat. I am nearly certain the poison was not ingested but inhaled.'

'So presumably the murderer planned that if the either the food or the inhalant did not work, the other would.' Holmes stared around the cluttered room. 'If an inhalant . . . then what was the delivery mechanism?' he mused, sitting at Enrietti's dressing table. He began to pick up and examine each item there. 'And how did he alone breathe it in, and not Angelo, the dresser? A handkerchief? But I see none. Flowers which he might have sniffed? None, he was allergic. The girl tried to give him flowers but apparently that was a common occurrence. And they did not remain in the room.'

He pawed through a stack of sheet music and came upon something underneath. It was a long, slim cardboard box with some black and white print and a picture of an oddly shaped instrument that looked like a recorder with a bulge at each end.

'Hullo, what's this?' He held it up and I read aloud the text on the box. '*Dr Carter Moffat's Ammoniaphone. Artificial Italian Air. It Strengthens the Voice and Enriches the Tone.*' He laughed. 'Yes! Oh, yes! This fits the bill perfectly! I believe we've found our murder weapon!'

'What is that thing, Holmes?'

'It is a device that singers – or at least the gullible among them – have been using of late. I saw a demonstration some time ago at St James's Hall. A Glaswegian professor – a quack, frankly. His theory: Italy has produced many opera stars. The reason: Italian air! Read!'

I took up the box and read: '*The ammoniaphone is invaluable in all pulmonary affectations. It is charged with a chemical compound, combined so as to resemble in effect that which is produced by the* soft balmy *air of the Italian Peninsula* when inhaled into the lungs, *hence the term "Artificial Italian Air".*'

He took out a handkerchief and carefully lifted out the device and regarded it.

He coughed sharply.

'Careful, Holmes! Don't breathe it in!'

'A residue of white powder is in the box. Give me your handkerchief.'

He replaced the peculiar instrument into the box and wrapped it in both our handkerchiefs. I ran to the window and thrust it open. Holmes carefully set the box down, binding it further with a dark blue scarf unwound from his neck. He coughed again, then joined me at the window.

We both breathed in fresh, icy air.

'Watson, this killer is remarkably creative,' said Holmes, breathing heavily. 'The methods are *outré* yet well-conceived. We must discover what happened to Enrietti two years ago.'

'Perhaps Giulia, the daughter in the photograph, will

know? Or the newspapers,' said I, anticipating a visit to their archives.

Holmes stared out at cold light and the snowflakes that had begun to drift past the window. His face was eager, and he nearly vibrated with excitement. 'This case grows more complex daily! Anomalous murders. Eminent victims. And then there are peripheral deaths! They seem randomly occurring, perhaps not part of the master plan. And yet—'

'Are you sure these connect, Holmes? Each victim is famous but . . . the methods are so varied. Can you be certain all this is the work of a single person?'

Holmes removed from his pocket a small card and held it up by his face with an impish smile. It bore a blue pattern on the back. He turned it over to face me. The Devil. Exactly as the one planted on me at Speakers' Corner. And probably the same as at the murder site of Horatio Anson, whom Holmes believed was the first victim.

'My God, Holmes? You found that here?'

'Mixed in with the sheet music, near the ammoniaphone.'

'This killer taunts us. And the police. Is that not rather stupid?'

'Apparently not, Watson. Billings missed it.'

'But he is a fool!'

'Not a fool, Watson, something much more dangerous. Billings is a man bent on closing cases quickly and consolidating power. There is an agenda in play.'

I took the card and stared at it. 'Certainly, these deaths are the work of the same person, then.'

'Only death and taxes are certain, as Benjamin Franklin said. The cases are uniquely creative, and devious – but yes, Watson, I believe it is likely we are dealing with a single killer. At last, one with whom it is an honour to match wits!' His eyes shone with excitement.

Neither he nor I could have possibly anticipated the next bump in the road.

PART FOUR

SETBACK

'No pressure, no diamonds.'

—Thomas Carlisle

CHAPTER 17

Snap

olmes directed our cab first to the address of Mr Ambrose Kepler in Holborn, a renowned toxicologist. There he deposited the curious ammoniaphone. He returned to our cab with the blue scarf he had used as an additional wrapping, which alarmed me. I was wary of possible contamination and said so.

'Kepler was not bothered by it, and he would not last long in his business if not sufficiently cautious,' said Holmes. 'But dispose of it, if you must.'

We proceeded towards Victoria Embankment and the new location of Scotland Yard. I would have preferred to keep our distance from Titus Billings, but Holmes insisted, as Lestrade had promised to provide us with police files on Anson, Benjamin and Clammory. Holmes was on fire about the case.

'Will they not miss the files?' I wondered.

'Do you think they are poring over them? You noted the rigour of this morning's investigation. No. We must press on, as the murderer surely will.'

'Your brother warned against confronting Billings until he can discover a way to loosen this fellow's grip.'

'I cannot wait for those wheels to turn.'

'That was only yesterday, Holmes!'

'Yes, and two more have died since, one in front of our eyes. Watson, we must not delay.'

At New Scotland Yard, I satisfied myself by disposing of Holmes's blue scarf deep in a bin at the side of the building where no one was likely to come upon it. We entered, unimpeded, through the front doors, and to my relief, were guided down the freshly painted hallways to Lestrade's new office.

While most of the police respected and even admired Holmes, some resented him, and he was not universally welcomed. Past visits to Scotland Yard had occasionally made me uncomfortable, but Holmes did not seem to care.

At last we entered Lestrade's new office, but he was not to be found. The office was less than impressive. There were no windows or bookcases – only a desk, three plain chairs – but there was a telephone at a reception desk down the hall from his door. That, at least, was progress, I supposed, although there were so few telephones in the city as of yet, I wondered who he could be calling.

'There is a telephone in our future at Baker Street,' remarked Holmes. 'Imagine the time it will save! We might have beaten Billings to the opera this morning had not Lestrade been obliged to collect us first!'

We sat down. Holmes took an interest in a strange handcuff device on Lestrade's desk. It had a single opening for a wrist, and a kind of handle on one end. He handed it to me.

I twisted the handle and the opening widened, then retracted. 'That is odd!'

'Have you never seen one of these, Watson? It's a nipper. Also called a "come along". Used to transport recalcitrant prisoners.' He plunged the thing down on an imaginary wrist and twisted. 'I haven't seen one of these in years. Most departments gave them up. Too dangerous.'

'Too many broken bones, I would imagine.'

'Exactly.'

Lestrade joined us in a moment, with apologies. 'The files are being reorganized from the move, under one of Billings's men. I can get them for you shortly, while he is at lunch, Mr Holmes. Meanwhile, it would be best if you stay undiscovered. At least take off your coats, gentlemen.'

As we removed our wraps, he took up the nippers from his desk, and with a frown tossed them in a drawer. 'New issue,' he said in disgust. 'Billings's idea. I would no sooner use these than a bullwhip or a brass knuckle. The man is uncivilized.' We heard a sharp knock on the door of Lestrade's office, and without waiting for a reply in strode Constable Fleming, the young officer whom we had been obliged to circumvent at the stage door that morning.

He projected all the authoritarian dignity he could muster

as one barely out of his teens. 'Mr Lestrade, Mr Billings has been informed of your visitors and will deal with you later. Everyone on the force is to read this.' He handed Lestrade a pamphlet, on which I glimpsed a title: '*Might Is Right*'. Lestrade glanced at it and tossed it carelessly on his desk, an action not lost on Fleming.

'He would now like to see Dr Watson in his office. Mr Holmes, you may tag along if you wish.'

Holmes laughed. Lestrade shook his head in disgust.

'I suggest you do not keep him waiting,' said Fleming, perceiving the slight. Holmes shrugged and made a show of deferring to me. There seemed no point in refusing, if we were to have any further hope of obtaining the desired files.

I could not have anticipated the horrifying direction this ill-considered visit would take.

As we proceeded towards Billings's office, Fleming handed two more men copies of this curious pamphlet, placing the rest in his pocket. As we rounded a corner, Holmes pretended to bump into Fleming, but I observed that he pickpocketed a pamphlet and with a wink to me placed it, folded, in his own pocket.

In a moment or two, we faced Billings in his cavernous office, seated at an enormous, leather-topped desk, in front of windows with a panoramic view of the Thames gleaming in the blue snowy light.

'Dr Watson! I presume you are here to file your expert witness report on the poisoning of Mr Claudio Enrietti by his dresser – what's his name, Arturo? Angelino? No matter.

Good of you to be so diligent.' His words were polite, but his tone held a menace that was not lost on me.

Holmes ignored Billings and had meandered across the room to get a closer look at a wall of framed photographs and certificates, as well as a few knives and weapons I recognized from my own tour of India and Afghanistan.

'A distinguished military career, I see, Billings,' he remarked. 'Certificate commending your bravery. A newspaper clipping. A weapon with dried blood, I presume used by you to quell some rebel individual threatening the Empire.' There was the slightest hint of sarcasm. 'And a portrait of General Gordon. Your admiration for that warlike gentleman is shared by Watson, here.'

I cleared my throat. 'Yes, indeed.'

'But no medals? I presume you have those in your study at home?' said Holmes.

I thought it unwise for my friend to bait the bull who sat before us.

But Titus Billings did not rise to the bait. 'Dr Watson,' he said, his voice friendly. 'In reading the accounts of your adventures with your friend here, I sense that you have been modest about your own contributions to the cases the two of you have solved. I rather think, from my observations this morning, that you provide the actual intelligence behind the partnership. Let me have your report, please. Poison killed both singer and servant, would you not say? In the same room. Within six feet of each other. The servant poisoning the master, then committing suicide to avoid gaol. I have seen it before.'

'The poisons were not the same,' I said.

There was a click behind us. We turned and saw that two tall policemen with gold braid on their uniforms had entered the room in silence and closed the door behind them. Without speaking, they took up places on either side of the door. Billings had summoned them, somehow.

From across the room, Holmes shot me a warning glance.

Billings continued in his pleasant voice, 'Nevertheless, Dr Watson . . .' He turned to Holmes. 'I presume you have come with Dr Watson as a friendly gesture of support. No? Then why are you here, Mr Holmes?'

'I'll wager you know precisely why I am here,' said Holmes quietly.

'You think that London is menaced by some heinous murdering mastermind.'

'Well, yes. There are several murders which I believe are connected. Enrietti's appears to be the latest in a series. As acting head of the police, it is your duty to follow up on this clear pattern, and to keep London safe from this murderous spree.'

'You presume to advise me of my job, Holmes?'

Holmes pondered a moment, debating whether to show his hand. I was puzzled that he chose to do so.

'The killings, I believe, are being committed alphabetically,' he said. 'A–Anson, B–Benjamin, C–Clammory, D–Danforth, and today, E–Enrietti. All are members of a secret group called the Luminarians. All are philanthropists. And in most cases, there have been attendant deaths. Suicides, or other murders.'

'Those you name have all been cleared. I know about that "Luminary theory",' said Billings dismissively. 'We examined and discarded it. It is a fictional society concocted by two egotistical brothers who go to great lengths to amuse themselves. There is absolutely nothing in what you say.'

'This killer is highly creative. The series of murders will continue under your watch unless you—'

'You are misinformed! And simply wrong. Sebastian Danforth? You know full well that *his own son* killed him. And the Benjamin case was a double suicide. There is no *series* of murders.'

'You are mistaken,' said Holmes.

'Yes? Where is the connecting evidence? Where is the key to tie these together? Have you any? Have you?' Billings's face had flushed a deep red. It was an extreme reaction, I thought, even for the bully he had revealed himself to be.

Holmes paused. 'A Tarot card was placed at the scene of Horatio Anson's death. The Devil. I believe it may be the killer's signature,' he said.

'You did not investigate that case.'

'True, but that detail was in the papers.'

'Cards were found nowhere else,' said Billings.

'Perhaps you missed it. As you did this one, today.'

Holmes revealed the Tarot card from his pocket. 'Found in Enrietti's dressing-room.'

Billings coughed and poured himself water from a carafe. He took a sip.

'I missed nothing. I suggest you planted this card. I have

long suspected that you have directed, perhaps even perpetrated, crimes for your own amusement and to create a hero of yourself. You are nothing but an attention-seeking waste of police time. Your friend is wiser.'

'Billings, there will be more deaths if this killer is not stopped.'

Titus Billings smiled at Holmes. It sent a chill down my spine.

'What is that card, *The Devil*? We are not superstitious here. But there is a kind of strange darkness about *you*, Sherlock Holmes. Even the public begins to notice it.' He picked up a newspaper from his desk. On the front page was an image of Holmes holding up a hand as two women swung at him with their handbags in Hyde Park.

'*The Devil Runs from Speakers' Corner Faithful in Hyde Park!*' Billings read and laughed.

Holmes ignored this. 'I believe Oliver Flynn will be targeted next,' said he. 'The "F" in the alphabet. You would be wise to keep watch.'

Billings laughed. 'Oliver Flynn! That effete excuse for a man! Let me tell you something, Holmes. Flynn is under the covers with the French anarchists. His are Irish terrorist sympathies. I'll have him in my grip before the month is out. You would better apply your skills against the tide of scheming foreigners who threaten our dear nation, rather than concocting half-baked theories about alphabet murderers.'

Billings stood from his desk and came round to face me. Holmes remained across the room, but I sensed him go on the alert.

'Dr Watson, I will expect your report before you leave the building. Confirm that the same poison killed Enrietti and his little man.'

'I do not concur, sir, and I will not perjure myself.'

'Why, I am surprised, Doctor! You are a gifted doctor. Or so everyone says.' In a sudden peculiar gesture of good will, Billings grabbed my right hand and pumped it in a vigorous handshake while reaching around with his left hand to grip me on my right shoulder. I felt a searing pain.

It was precisely the spot where a Jezail bullet had shattered the bone at Maiwand. I did not know how, but Billings knew exactly where I'd received that injury.

I gasped. Holmes was instantly at my side.

Billings released my shoulder and my hand and delivered this next to both of us. 'And of course, behind every great man, there is often the little woman whose support and love make great deeds possible.'

A ripple of unease flowed through me, at the same time as I thought how my sweet Mary would feel being called the 'little woman'.

'Let's see. Watson's wife – Mary, I think her name is,' Billings continued. 'Formerly Mary Morstan. Currently on holiday in the Cotswolds, is she? At a private home with some people called . . . the Trowbridges. Am I correct?'

My insides turned to ice. It was all I could do to keep from leaping on the man and throttling him. Holmes placed his hand on my arm to calm me and replied, in a voice like steel, 'Harm a single hair on Mary Watson's head and you will have more than the two of us to contend with.'

'My, my Mr Holmes, but you are excitable! Isn't he, gentlemen?'

The two men by the door spoke up.

'Yes, sir. Both of them, sir.'

'Very excitable, sir.'

'In fact, I feel threatened. Was that a threat?' said Billings.

'Come, Watson,' said Holmes, gripping my arm and pulling me towards the door.

But Billings moved quickly to block our exit, with his two men now flanking him.

'Which of these men just threatened me?' Billings said. He looked from Holmes to me and settled back on Holmes. 'This one, I think.'

'Step aside, Billings,' said Holmes quietly. 'You really don't want to rile Dr Watson.'

Billings raised his hand as if to backhand me, and Holmes blocked it with his own. In an instant, Billings's two men were on Holmes, each taking an arm. I tackled one of the men, but a flash of steel appeared in Billings's hand and he lunged at Holmes's wrist, clamped on the nippers and twisted them.

The two men released him, and with a gasp Holmes spiralled down onto the floor, his left arm extended behind him in a crazy angle, the nippers encircling his thin wrist. He writhed soundlessly in pain.

'Back away, Dr Watson,' commanded Billings. 'Now.'

I complied, thinking he would release Holmes. But instead, Billings gave the cuff a sharp twist and a crack sounded in the room.

Holmes gasped.

No one moved for a moment. Silence except for the sound of Holmes's ragged breathing. I could see his wrist was broken. A bone nearly protruded from the skin.

'My God, what have you done?' I cried.

With a flick of his own wrist, Billings undid the nippers, and replaced them in his pocket. He and his two men stood back, smiling at us. 'Handy little device,' Billings remarked.

Holmes, on his knees, cradled his wrist, which was ballooning before my eyes. His face went white. Shock was a real danger. I had to get him out of there.

I gripped him by the uninjured arm and hauled him to his feet. He said nothing but his eyes were glassy, his breathing shallow. We exited in a rush, but Billings's voice followed.

'When I see you next, I'll lock you up, Holmes!' he called out. 'Who knows what might happen when you attack your gaoler there?'

Moments later, as sudden flurry of snow descended around us, we were escorted out of the building. A sympathetic young constable hailed us a four-wheeler. I bundled Holmes into the carriage as Lestrade ran up to us, his face a mask of concern. He handed me our coats. Underneath was concealed a thick packet of papers bound in an oilskin envelope.

'Take these,' he whispered. He peered in at Holmes who was slumped against the window. 'My God, I just heard. Are you all right, Mr Holmes?'

Holmes opened his eyes. 'The files?' he murmured, barely audible.

'Anson, Benjamin, Clammory,' whispered Lestrade, handing me the packet. 'All there.' Holmes nodded and collapsed back in the seat.

'The nippers,' I said. 'Those things should be outlawed.' I climbed in next to Holmes.

Lestrade nodded gravely. 'Will he be all right, Doctor?'

'I will make sure of it,' I said, tapped the roof, and the carriage lurched into motion.

Holmes groaned and his eyes half opened. 'Your shoulder, Watson! Maiwand,' he mumbled. 'Are you all right?'

'Steady on, Holmes. No damage here.'

He nodded, relieved, then passed out.

CHAPTER 18

Helping Hands

s we raced across London to Baker Street, I splinted Holmes's wrist temporarily with my cane and cravat, which held until I settled him on the sofa in the sitting-room, arm elevated and iced. He lay there, eyes closed, pale and hovering on the edge of consciousness, as we awaited a response from a specialist on Harley Street whom I had summoned.

I prayed Dr Lunsford Meredith would be available, for he was renowned in London medical circles as the foremost expert on hand and wrist injuries. Indeed, the man was one of the pioneers of osteosynthesis – a method of stabilizing fractures with external braces bolted into the bone. I hoped that such an invasive remedy would not be needed, but whatever the case, there could be no better expert.

I dashed off a cable to Mary, tersely warning her of danger and urging her to remove herself to another place.

I received an answer soon thereafter. She and the Trowbridges would repair to Edinburgh and the home of Mrs Trowbridge's brother, careful to leave no trail. Not every wife would heed such a request without long explanation, and I counted my blessings that Mary did, acquainted as she was with Sherlock Holmes and the danger of our adventures together.

Thankfully Dr Meredith was free and forty minutes later Mrs Hudson, with a worried look, ushered the renowned specialist into the sitting-room.

Meredith was a stocky, broad-shouldered man of fifty, balding but with a ring of black curls and neatly trimmed mutton-chop whiskers. His conservative grey suit and calm manner inspired confidence, as did his large bag of very particular equipment and supplies. 'You caught me at a good time, Dr Watson. I had planned a matinee at the opera, but the performance was cancelled,' said he. Glancing at Holmes, who lay, eyes closed and apparently unconscious, he asked, 'Have you given morphine?'

I related the dosage I had administered but warned him that it was not all that effective with Holmes. The detective now rested in a kind of twilight state, fighting the drug, to which he'd objected. The files from Lestrade were spread in a jumble on his lap.

I removed them as Meredith cut off the sleeve of Holmes's shirt, and carefully extended the arm. He noted old needle marks and glanced at me but said nothing. Holmes's habitual use of cocaine and morphine as a means to soothe or distract himself made sedating him when urgently needed, such as in this moment, a dangerous proposition.

Meredith took up the arm gently and began a detailed examination. He asked how the break happened. I recounted our adventure, describing the details of the diabolical handcuffs, the 'nippers'.

Dr Meredith shook his head in disgust. 'I am familiar with those restraints. I campaigned to have them outlawed. It is outrageous that our own English police would resort to such brutality.'

Meredith laid out his tools and began a meticulous examination quite reminiscent of Holmes's own at a crime scene. This doctor's genius was soon evident. At times, his eyes were closed in concentration, and like a blind savant mapping a strange and complex piece of machinery in order to repair it, the fingers of one hand traced gently over Holmes's wrist, top and then bottom, as the other hand slowly raised and lowered each of Holmes's digits to feel the connecting movement. Intermittently, the doctor opened his eyes to make a small mark in ink on various places on the wrist.

I knew he was mapping the carpals – an intricate constellation of tiny bones connected via ligaments and muscle to the metacarpals and phalanges which made up the fingers. Although these structures were echoed in other mammals, this abstruse but brilliant design was what, in combination with a rich concentration of nerve endings, enabled our uniquely human dexterity, and ultimately writing, art, surgery, and the playing of musical instruments. I recalled being filled with awe in medical school at the ingenious design of the human hand. What a piece of work is a man!

'Callouses on the left hand,' noted Meredith. 'He is a string player, then?'

I nodded. 'The violin.'

'I have dabbled on the instrument.' Meredith looked up, his eyes landing on Holmes's violin in a corner of the room near the window. 'Oh, my. Is that a Stradivarius?'

'Yes,' murmured Holmes. Meredith glanced at him in surprise.

'You are awake! You must be a serious player, then.'

'Was.'

'Was what, Mr Holmes?' asked the doctor.

'A serious player.'

'Ah, yes. Well, the question is, will you play again? And my answer is this. It is uncertain but will depend partly on you. I am going to do a reduction with the help of Dr Watson, then set the bone. We will need for you to sleep through this.'

'No more morphine. Urgent case,' said Holmes, his voice slurred.

Meredith looked at him. 'Right now, you are not on a case. If you want to return to work, if you want to play the violin again, you will cooperate.'

Holmes hesitated but I grasped his other arm, and without preamble dosed him further with a substantial amount of morphine. He grimaced in frustration, then went limp shortly after. I watched him carefully, taking his pulse. Slow, steady.

'Is he under?' asked Meredith.

'I think so.'

Meredith led as the two of us performed the reduction, which required me to pull on the forearm so Meredith could push the bones back into place. This took more than ten minutes. At one point, Holmes groaned. I mopped his forehead, which was streaming with sweat.

'The violin. Is it important to him?' asked Meredith.

'Very. He says it helps him think. But I believe it is solace as well.'

'Has he any other routes to music?'

'He enjoys concerts. The opera.'

'Ah, as do I. The opera especially! Do you like opera, Dr Watson?'

'Sadly, it is just so much shouting to my ears.'

Meredith smiled. 'Give it time.' He continued to manipulate Holmes's wrist. 'Did you hear of the singer who just died?'

'Enrietti? Oh, yes!'

'Terrible loss. Magnificent voice. I was to hear his *Orfeo* this afternoon.'

'Sad, yes. In fact, that is our case.'

'Murder, then,' wondered Meredith. 'Foul play?'

'Yes,' murmured Holmes. His eyes remained shut as we both looked down at him in surprise.

'Well, I suppose Enrietti's past finally caught up with him,' said the doctor.

Holmes's eyes flew open. 'What past?'

Meredith looked at me. I shrugged. The doctor leaned in to Holmes. 'If you keep still, I will tell you.'

Holmes nodded, and Meredith continued his painstaking

work. 'It must have been two or three years ago. A restaurant in Venice. Enrietti was dining alone in a private room there with his best friend and rival, Calvari. They had been friends since childhood. Studied together. They had shared many bottles of wine. The waiters had been directed to leave them alone. Some time later . . . only Enrietti left the room alive.'

Holmes eyes were wide open and trained on Meredith. 'What happened?'

'Calvari was believed to have choked on his food. There were signs of a struggle, but this could have been the death throes of a man suffocating. Enrietti seemed devastated. But a week later, he was given a role promised to Calvari, and it made his fortune.'

'Hence the taster, Watson!' Holmes cried. 'Enrietti feared revenge!'

'Stay still,' said Meredith.

'The police concluded . . . what?' asked Holmes.

'It was deemed an accident.' Meredith was cutting small pieces of padding and inserting them into the splint, customizing the shape with precision. I had never seen this before.

'How do you know this, Doctor?' I asked.

'My wife and I follow opera. I love the music; she loves the personalities.' He smiled at the two of us. He took out gauze and what looked like piano wire and laid it all out on a table. 'Now sit back and do not move, Mr Holmes. I am going to do something unusual – for the detective on a case, and for the violin player you wish to remain. I must ask you, how likely *are* you to rest and keep this arm quite still over the upcoming days?'

'I will be careful,' said Holmes.

Behind him, I shook my head a vehement 'No' at the doctor. He caught this and smiled.

'As I thought. This will be uncomfortable, but you must keep this wrist and your fingers quite still until the swelling goes down and I can further map this break. I will immobilize your fingers in a neutral position, temporarily, and you can hide all with a glove.' He began cutting the wires into small pieces. From downstairs I heard the sound of a bell and Mrs Hudson answering the door. 'But – and this is important – it is for a short time only.'

A moment later, in bounded the two Goodwin brothers, now attired in the latest Savile Row fashions, Andrew in deep burgundy, and James in marine blue. *Soigné* as usual, shoes shined, the two gentlemen gave no evidence of weather, or of care. But they were excited about something.

'Mr Holmes!' cried James. 'Doctor Watson! Look what just arrived!' James waved a letter in one hand.

All in a tumult, they pulled up chairs close to where Dr Meredith and I clustered around the patient, drawing in to form an intimate circle. Only then did they notice what was transpiring.

'Jove's breakfast! What has happened to your arm, Mr Holmes?' asked James.

Andrew extended a hand to Dr Meredith, who was wrapping the brace carefully with gauze. 'Andrew Goodwin. My brother James.'

Meredith looked at the outstretched hand but continued

tending to Holmes. 'Busy here,' he said. 'Sit back, gentlemen, and give us room, please.'

Only slightly abashed, the Goodwins backed their chairs away an inch or so.

'Mr Holmes, we thought you might like to see this letter.'

Holmes appraised them through the fog of pain and morphine. 'Read it to me, Watson, would you please?'

Andrew Goodwin hesitated. 'Perhaps we should do this privately,' said he.

'Yes. Can this wait?' asked James, waving at the doctor.

Meredith threw them a stern look. 'No,' said he and turned back to his painstaking work

'This is private enough. Read it aloud, would you please, Watson?' said Holmes.

I took the letter. It was written in black ink, on cream parchment, with a matching envelope, addressed to Messrs James/Andrew Goodwin. Expensive paper, but not uncommon in fine stationery shops was my guess. I read:

Messieurs Goodwin and Goodwin—

Do you think you have slipped unnoticed into the pantheon of angelic Samaritans who live and strive for the benefit of society? You have not. I see you.

I see you and your self-congratulating group of reprehensible, hypocritical do-gooders who aim to cover your own sins with a camouflage of good works. It is time to face the consequences of the acts for which you strive so desperately to atone.

I alone call you to task for the very acts which fill

you with guilt and compel your pathetic efforts to remedy. You and every one of the Luminarians will die a spectacular and well-deserved death corresponding precisely to the sin which helped you to your exalted position.

Liars, murderers, cheaters, thieves, blackmailers, philanderers – sinners of all sort, every one of you. Your days are numbered. You shall reap what you sow, when the Devil calls for his due. And indeed, sir, I am en route.

Yours with a promise,

Lucifer.

I finished reading. A chill descended on the room. The Goodwins, for the first time since I had met them, seemed uncomfortable. Only Meredith, who had now taken up the first of his many pieces of wire and was spiralling it around Holmes's index finger, seemed untouched.

Holmes grimaced briefly in pain. 'Let me see the letter,' he said, and taking it up with his free right hand began to inspect it. 'Hold the light here, Watson.' I did so. 'And now the envelope. Hand me my magnifier, please.' I retrieved the glass and he placed the envelope on the back of the sofa, peering at it closely. He smelled the letter, then put it down. He sighed in frustration, then turned to the two visitors.

'Why did you wait to bring me this?' he demanded.

James and Andrew Goodwin shifted uncomfortably.

'You know of Enrietti's death?' said Holmes.

'Word travels,' said Andrew. The singer had only been found that morning. But murders sold papers.

'Shame,' said James. 'That is why . . . that is what . . .'

'A–B–C–D, and now E. I see. The clock is ticking towards the F. When did this letter come into your possession?'

'It just came,' said Andrew.

'No. It's been handled considerably, at the dinner table, and under a candle at night. It smells of the cologne your brother wore yesterday, but not today. I presume he has not touched it today. Do not play games with me. *When did it come?*'

Dr Meredith paused, staring at Holmes in frank admiration. I waved my fingers at him to continue, and he returned to his work.

'We really cannot say,' said Andrew.

'Not in front of strangers,' said James.

'Tell me now, or get out!' shouted Holmes, the force of his anger stunning everyone in the room.

'All right. The day before yesterday.'

'You had it when we first met you!'

'Er, yes. Well, you can see it implies criminal behaviour. We didn't want you to think that we were in some way involved with anything of a . . . *sordid* nature,' said Andrew.

'You two defy belief! Afraid I would think ill of you if it came out that every Luminarian had a dark past? This is critical! It is not a random honour you bestow. It is not merely success and philanthropy linking these Luminarians, these *victims*, together. It is a shared vulnerability. A shared past crime, or a mistake – *Ahhh!*' Tears sprang into his eyes.

Meredith wired one of the fingers into place. 'Sorry. Easy now. Just two more.' I offered Holmes my handkerchief; he waved it away.

'Oh, much more than mistakes. Crimes,' said Andrew. 'All our honourees.'

'Some of them, very bad crimes,' said James.

'I have often thought that philanthropy was motivated by guilt,' said I. 'Some of the most ardent do-gooders I know have been rather heinous in reality. Their past mistakes compel them to atone for those transgressions. Sometimes at great cost.'

'Thank you for *that* clever insight, Watson,' snarled Holmes. It was the pain speaking. He turned back to the Goodwins. 'Did you show that letter to my brother?'

'No.'

'Why not?'

James and Andrew looked at each other and hesitated.

'Why not?' Holmes repeated.

'We . . . do not exactly *trust* Mycroft Holmes,' said Andrew at last.

This sentence hung in the air. In all frankness, I did not fully trust Holmes's older brother myself. I would have difficulty to articulate why, but it had partly to do with his willingness to cause his brother harm. Holmes, however, would not hear of it.

'Fools! You know what this letter refers to? I warrant you know the skeleton in their every closet. And that indeed this was a condition for being so . . . "honoured" as a Luminarian.'

'No. It is not the first thing we looked for in the candidates—' said Andrew.

'In fact, it was not something we even thought about.'

Holmes impaled them with a stare.

'Much,' added James.

'At all!' said Andrew.

'Oh, Andrew, yes, we did!'

'All right, we did.'

'But we don't actually know them all.'

'Just a hint of each story.'

'Stop it!' cried Holmes. 'It is unthinkable that you would withhold this information.'

'Why? These past acts don't point to the same person. How could that information help you?'

'Cease your moving,' said Meredith to my friend, 'or we will be here all day. Unclench your fingers.' Holmes glanced down in surprise. He seemed to have forgotten about his broken wrist.

'Even Watson has concluded the truth,' said he. 'What is your agenda in choosing these compromised men?'

'No agenda,' said Andrew.

'What are you two atoning for?' I asked.

Holmes looked at me in surprise. 'A good question, Watson.' He pinned the brothers with a glare. 'Answer him.'

James flushed deep red, and Andrew began a careful examination of a small gold ring on his fourth finger.

'We have an older brother,' he sighed. 'He was set to inherit the title and the estate. But he was a serious man, unpleasant actually, with rather odd religious leanings. A fanatic of sorts. So, one day we hired some friends of ours who are actors. We staged a . . . a . . . thing.' Here Andrew tried not to laugh but a giggle came from his brother. He continued, 'We convinced our brother he was having a vision. As a result, he joined a monastery, renounced all possessions, and is a monk to this day.'

Holmes and I stared at the brothers in amazement. Holmes suddenly laughed.

Andrew shrugged. 'A happy monk, from all reports.'

'He was not a very nice man,' said James.

'So, you see,' said Andrew, 'not exactly a terrible crime. And we have put our fortune to good use.'

'Parties and balls?' I remarked.

'Yes, pleasure,' said Andrew. 'But we have also provided public parks in fourteen cities, with more in the planning stages. And three libraries.'

'All right, enough,' said Holmes. 'Are you finished, Doctor? Those wires . . .'

'I have immobilized the fingers so that you do not move the carpals. This is for forty-eight hours only. After that, the wires will come off and you will begin rehabilitating the fingers with prescribed movements which I shall teach Dr Watson to perform. It is an unusual course of treatment but is your best chance for a full recovery. I realize you will not stop working, so these are here for protection. Do you understand?'

'Ah!' I exclaimed. 'At least I do, Doctor.' It was a clever solution.'

'I give you a short time only, Mr Holmes. After that, you

must follow my instructions, or lose your music forever. Do you understand?'

Holmes stared at him doubtfully.

'You know the legend of Cinderella? Your carriage turns into a pumpkin in forty-eight hours. That is all the magic I can provide.'

I wondered if Holmes knew this fairy tale. Apparently so, because he nodded. 'Understood. Thank you. But I doubt that I can clear this case in just two days.'

As Dr Meredith began packing his medical kit, Holmes asked me to retrieve my notebook and take notes, as we would learn more from the Goodwins. But before the doctor could leave, a small commotion ensued at the front door, followed by the patter of feet up our stairs.

Heffie O'Malley burst into the room, Mrs Hudson on her heels.

Heffie was scrubbed clean and glowing and was wearing a nicely tailored schoolgirl uniform, her wild red hair escaping from a plait into a diaphanous cloud around her face. Her cheeks were flushed, and her eyes shone with excitement.

'Mr 'olmes!' shouted the girl.

'I am sorry, gentlemen,' said Mrs Hudson. 'I could not stop her.'

'Mr 'olmes, that job you sent me on. That was a right horror, but I fixed it. I fixed it good!'

Heffie paused and took in the five of us in the room, Holmes on the sofa with his bandaged arm, the terribly polished Goodwins in their costly attire, and Dr Meredith and his extensive supplies.

'Wot the bloody 'ell is going on 'ere?' she wondered. 'And 'ave you got any food?'

James Goodwin was on his feet, transfixed by the girl and offering his chair. He smoothed his patent leather hair self-consciously. 'Mademoiselle! Please be seated! You are flushed. May I find some tea for you? Biscuits? A brandy?'

Heffie eyed him from head to toe, and then laughed. 'I only drinks champagne afore six. Oh, sit down, you silly git.'

CHAPTER 19

Pack of Foxes

en minutes later, our sitting-room had been cleared of all guests. I opened the window, as the scent of James Goodwin's cologne was giving Holmes a headache. But the snow outside had turned into sleet and it chilled the room in an instant. I closed the window.

Heffie was eager to tell her story. Holmes, his face white and drawn from his ordeal, lay back on the sofa, nevertheless listening with intense interest. Here is what she related.

Shortly after Holmes had deposited Heffie the previous night at Lady Eleanor's school, she was offered a bath and issued with a nightgown, slippers, shoes and the school uniform which she now wore. She was introduced to Judith, with whom she was temporarily to share a room.

This arrangement did not suit the senior girl at all. Judith, in fact, was quite the double-edged sword, according to

Heffie – radiating intelligence, propriety and charm when the headmistress was near, but revealing quite a different personality the moment Heffie was alone with her.

It transpired that Judith was a gifted fabricator, and Heffie quickly ascertained that the girl had in play several businesses on the side, not the least of which was operating as a kind of brothel queen, brokering the services of some of the more attractive senior girls to eager workman at a nearby packing factory. For this, Judith used several rooms in a boarding house which sat between the school and this factory.

Heffie was no mean hand at chicanery herself and signed on immediately as a member of Judith's gang. Judith had apparently managed to hide these activities from the headmistress, although Heffie had not had the time to discover all. She did learn, however, that one of the male teachers who visited the school twice weekly as a music instructor had begun to suspect something.

Judith told Heffie that she had planned to ruin this teacher, whom she was poised to name as the culprit. She would claim, in a day or so, that he attacked her in a fury when she refused his marriage proposal, but that she had been afraid to point the finger. It was a brilliant plan, delayed by Heffie's arrival on the scene.

I was astonished that the girl had discovered this much in a mere twenty-four hours, but Holmes was not.

'Excellent work, Heffie,' said he. 'I presume you told no one, as we agreed?' He shifted uncomfortably on the sofa.

'I tol' no one,' she said, 'like you said. Nobody would

believe me if I done so anyways, 'cuz everybody over there thinks Judith walks on water. Even poor Lady Eleanor is bamboozled. They all are. But I saw what's what, an' there you are.'

'Remarkable!' I said.

'Could I have a sandwich? An' a whisky, please?' asked Heffie. I called down to Mrs Hudson for some food and tea. Heffie waited for me to sit down again, then continued. 'That Judith, she's a smart one, and mean, as well. I could handle her meself, but the girl has friends there, a gang, like; and, girls, you see, we can be dangerous in a group. It's kind of like a pack o' foxes. We 'ave sharp teeth.'

Holmes nodded. 'You do. Excellent work,' said he with a smile.

'Foxes don't run in packs,' I said. 'They hunt alone.' Holmes frowned at me.

'Well, it's up to you, Mr 'olmes. I done my bit.'

'Indeed, you have, Heffie, and it was a wise move to leave. What is the name of the teacher whom Judith was set to ruin?'

'Jerome O'Keefe,' said she. 'But she won't have any luck there. I scared 'im off.'

'How did you do that?'

'Tole 'im that 'e was right about the brothel, but that the whole school was in on it and 'e'd best look elsewhere for work, or they'd ruin 'im.'

'Did he believe you?' asked Holmes.

'Seemed to. Wise man.'

'Did you have time to discover if any of the other teachers

were involved?' Holmes absentmindedly was rubbing the upper arm above his splint. I could see he was in pain.

'No. But I run out o' time. My guess is none of 'em. Like I said, Judith's a smart one.'

'Poor Lady Eleanor,' I remarked. 'I doubt she has any idea of this.'

Holmes sighed. 'Our work is done. We will have to let the lady know. That will come as a blow. But better that she learn what Judith has been up to and remove the worm from the apple. I hope the school is salvageable.'

'Wot's "salverjibble" mean?' asked Heffie.

'Saved. The question remains whether the rest of the school is still working as designed? Can something good be restored?' said Holmes.

'Oh, seems so, Mr 'olmes. I think it was only Judith and a few of 'er close friends. Four at most. I'd say the rest o' the girls are straight out aimin' to go into service. Poor fools.'

'Not something you'd consider?' I said.

She looked at me as though I'd proposed she sprout wings and fly. She turned back to Holmes. 'Anything else I can do for you, Mr 'olmes? You look to be laid up for a bit. You need a hand, do you?' She paused, with a mischievous grin. 'That's a joke. Hand. Heh heh.'

Holmes did not respond. I looked over and his eyes were closed. Had the pain and all the morphine managed to finally knock him out?

Heffie looked embarrassed. 'Sorry. You ain't tippy-top right now, is you?'

Holmes did not answer the question. He opened his eyes halfway. 'Heffie . . . I have more work for you. In the meantime, let me pay you for the Judith case. Watson, there is money in my desk drawer.'

'You are planning to report this to the police, I presume,' I said, unlocking the desk after retrieving the key from his watch chain.

'Not while Billings is in charge. Have you had a look at the manifesto that he is distributing among the force?'

He indicated 'Might Is Right' on a side table.

'That thing you lifted from Officer Fleming? Now when could I have done that?' I remarked with more irritation than I meant.

Heffie yawned. I turned my attention to paying her, and Mrs Hudson arrived with sandwiches and tea. It was dark outside by now. It transpired that the school had taken Heffie's clothes and burned them, so that all she had was the schoolgirl clothing which she was wearing.

'I can't go back 'ome in this kit,' she remarked, mouth full of ham sandwich. Once again, Holmes invited her to stay downstairs with Mrs Hudson. Exhausted from having been up all through the night on her Judith case, the girl retired early, but not before a parting shot: 'You were so worried I didn't stitch 'im up right, Doc. Look at 'im now. You ought take better care of that man! 'E's a sorry sight, 'e is!'

The room was suddenly very quiet. I turned to Holmes. His eyes were closed, and he was breathing heavily. Heffie was of course right: he did not look well at all. I removed a blanket from his bedroom and covered him with it. He did not stir.

I contemplated bringing bedding from my room upstairs and remaining here in the sitting-room to keep an eye on him. I glanced at the pamphlet on the table, but I was too tired to read. As I considered my next move, the silence was rent by the splintering crash of glass breaking as a brick smashed through one of the front windows looking down onto Baker Street.

'What!' cried Holmes, instantly awake. He and I leapt to our feet, he tangling in the blanket and nearly tumbling, me reaching into my pocket for my revolver without even a split second of thought. But my gun was upstairs, still in my valise.

We both stared down at the object. It was rectangular in shape, with newspaper wrapped around it. Holmes approached it and gingerly poked at it with one slippered foot.

'Careful!' I cried. 'Might it be a bomb?' The anarchists leapt into my mind.

'It's a brick,' said Holmes. 'You can see here, this corner, sticking out.'

'Thank God,' said I.

The curtains flapped and a blast of cold air rushed in from the broken window.

'Quick, Watson, look down in the street. Careful!' Partly concealed by the curtain, I peered out. The street was empty. I turned and Holmes had picked up the brick with his good hand and was holding it near a table lamp. He looked shaky.

'Give me that and sit down,' I said, and taking it from

him I unwrapped the paper which had been tied with brown string. It was a carefully folded page from the newspaper, and inside was a note on plain white paper.

The note said, simply, '*Devil!*'

'The newspaper, Watson. That is the real message, I wager.'

Remarkably, the newspaper was not wet, only slightly damp. Given the sleet, this missive must have been carried here under a wrap. The newspaper clipping was from *The Times*, a mere four hours ago.

As I unfolded it, a large illustration was revealed. It was taken from the photograph of Holmes earlier this morning on our doorstep, accompanied by the enormous black dog looking fearsome. The artist had added fangs. I held it up and Holmes regarded it impassively. He collapsed back down on the sofa, closing his eyes.

'Zanders again. Read it to me, if you please, Watson.'

'The caption reads "*The Devil of Baker Street with his hound of hell, on the prowl again!*" Oh,' I said, 'I guess he has dropped the Faust reference.'

'"Hound of hell" is much better. Read on, please.'

'"Sherlock Holmes, whom the police are calling a plague upon the department, leaves his home at 221B Baker Street" – my God, Holmes, they've given out your address! – "with a new partner in crime, a dog so vicious that it is rumoured to be the Black Dog of legend, the Hound of Hell. All of London is advised to keep clear until the police can ascertain the movements of this avowed 'champion of justice', whom they say has moved to the dark side."'

I shook my head and regarded my friend, who now lay still, ghostly pale, eyes at half mast, taking this in. In his current state, he looked far from dangerous. But it was never a good idea to underestimate Sherlock Holmes.

Mrs Hudson and Billy burst into the room, and the landlady cried out in dismay at the broken glass, the flapping curtains and the icy rain splashing in on the rug and furniture.

'Billy, there are loose boards in the basement. Bring them up, and a hammer and nails,' said Holmes. 'You and Watson can keep the rain out, at least.'

'Right away, sir,' said the page, and ran off.

'Oh, Mr Holmes,' wailed Mrs Hudson, crossing the room and examining the broken glass. Holmes arose with difficulty, crossed to her and put his good arm around her shoulders.

'There, there, Mrs Hudson,' said he in an uncharacteristically tender moment. 'It's just a broken window, after all. Some young hooligans, no doubt. We'll patch it up tonight and have the glazier out in the morning.' She choked back a sob.

'Where is Heffie?' he wondered suddenly.

Billy came back in with a piece of wood to cover the window. 'She took off, Mr Holmes. Soon's she heard the noise. Ran off down the street after 'em, she did.'

Holmes seemed less surprised at this than I was. Neither was he worried. He nodded to me, indicating Mrs Hudson, and sank back down on the settee. I dutifully escorted the lady back to her ground floor flat, hoping my comforting words would put her at her ease. I offered her a sedative, which she declined, accepting a tea and brandy instead and insisting I partake with her.

I was eager to get back to Holmes but lingered a moment longer in her bright yellow kitchen, which struck me in that moment as a haven of domestic sanity after a day of madness. A bouquet of cheap daisies brightened one corner, and near the oven, a rack of freshly baked scones for the morning steamed the chill air above them. I smiled. Our landlady was forever trying to entice Holmes to eat.

Mrs Hudson warmed her hands on her teacup and looked up at me with tear-stained eyes. 'Thank goodness you are here, Doctor. It is not the same without you.'

'Have there been other threats?'

'No. But he does not do well alone—' Mrs Hudson studied my face, 'although he may have convinced you otherwise. I realize you are married, Doctor, but perhaps if you could just look in, you know . . . a bit more often?'

I nodded. I would. And I would not leave him in this state.

CHAPTER 20

Might Makes Right

 had pitched camp in one of the larger chairs in the sitting-room in order to stay close to Holmes. As soon as the window was patched, he had closed his eyes and could not be roused, whereas I was awakened several times during the night to thunder, and the lashing of rain and sleet against the windows and the board we had placed over the broken pane. A draught crept in around this makeshift repair and at one point I added a second blanket to Holmes, returning to my uncomfortable chair.

It was close to nine in the morning when I was awakened from the depths of a dreamless slumber by Mrs Hudson. It seemed to me that I had slept only an hour, so completely exhausted was I from the day before. Our landlady shook me gently. 'Doctor! Doctor Watson!'

I started, struggling to remember where I was, and why

I was in a chair and not a bed. All the events of the last two days came back in a rush. It felt like a month had been packed into forty-eight hours with Holmes.

I looked over at the sofa. He was gone! I heard voices coming from his room, and a moment later an elf-like, dapper fellow with blond curls, whom I recognized as our barber, John Wheeler, emerged. His shop, a block south on Baker Street, was our favourite and I had continued to patronize it even after my move.

Wheeler left Holmes's room with a small satchel and a damp white towel. He saluted me as he passed through the sitting-room on his way out. 'Doctor, good morning! Ah, you could use a trim. Come and see me!'

I rubbed my stiff neck, all in a fog, as I attempted to make sense of the barber's presence in Holmes's bedroom. Mrs Hudson thrust a cup of coffee into my hands. 'Drink, Doctor.' She nodded in the direction of his room. 'He's eager to see you.'

I stumbled to my feet, then was obliged to move aside as two workmen carrying a pane of glass the size of our broken window entered in a wave of plaster dust and wiry, East End energy. How had I slept through this continuing parade? What a contrast to my quiet home in Paddington!

I escaped by carrying my coffee into Holmes's room. He was reclined on the bed in a clean shirt and waistcoat. His dressing gown was thrown over all, and his splinted wrist rested on a pillow. I noted that he was freshly shaved, with hair combed, which explained John Wheeler's visit. Of course! Holmes had always been somewhat catlike in his attention to grooming, and I knew well from my wartime shoulder injury that a one-armed shave was a questionable proposition at best.

My friend was blessed with a remarkable resilience, and he looked as sleek and rested as if nothing untoward had happened to him in months – if you did not notice the bandaged hand, of course. Lestrade's files were spread on his lap.

'Ah, Watson, you slug-a-bed! You are awake at last!'

He set down a file, snatched my coffee cup with his one good hand before I could object, and drank it down.

'Not awake yet,' I remarked testily, rubbing sleep from my eyes. He set my now empty cup among three empty ones on his bedside table. 'You, however, should be resting.' I said.

I ducked back into the sitting-room. 'Is there any more coffee, Mrs Hudson?'

'But I just gave – oh, I see. Yes, I'll be back with another pot, Doctor.' Thank goodness for Mrs Hudson, who knew our patterns only too well. I picked up the '*Might Makes Right*' pamphlet and returned to Holmes.

'Where is Heffie?' I wondered.

'On another errand,' said he. 'I asked her to find out a bit more about Judith's side business. Oh, and Watson – she followed the brick throwers last night.'

'That was dangerous. We should not have allowed it.'

'Ha! Try to control the wind. Heffie knows to keep herself safe. In any case, it was a group of society women who were gossiping among themselves about ridding the city of people in league with the Devil. And about their card game the next day.'

'Ladies? They were out at night, alone? Let me take a look at that wrist.'

'Yes, Watson, you *are* behind the times! Women are not all retiring violets. *Ouch!* What are you doing?'

'Checking that the circulation in your fingers is adequate. Can you feel this?'

'Yes, obviously, Watson.'

'Good. Well, I am relieved she did not run into terrorists. Just readers of Gabriel Zanders, no doubt!'

'It will not be terrorists who take down civilization, Watson. It will be a gullible public – average, normal people, manipulated by misinformation and driven by fear.'

'That is a cheery thought,' I said. 'I had a look at this pamphlet. Its author, Ragnar Redbeard, whoever he is, would be more than happy to take down civilization. He thinks tyranny is justified. Redbeard! Sounds like a pirate!'

'It is a pseudonym. Social Darwinism, is what this is called, Watson. Survival of the fittest as applied to the social order. The weak should be destroyed. That includes the poor, the ill, the unlucky – that is, of course, most of the population, if not all of us, if considered over time.'

'But . . . Darwin? I thought you believed in evolution, Holmes, as a scientific thinker.'

'A scientist doesn't *believe in* theories, Watson. One examines them for inconsistencies with evidence, then adopts them as a working premise until a more accurate one appears. Evolution as a theory maps to the facts far better than any other. And so I embrace it.'

'The scientific method. Of course. But what is *Social Darwinism?*'

'Something entirely different, Watson. Survival of the fittest, for them, is justification for rampant bullying. There have always been autocrats, dictators, and despots. They believe they deserve whatever they can take from others. The weak do not deserve to live.'

'Listen to this,' I said, reading from the pamphlet: '"If a man smite you on one cheek, smash him down; smite him hip and thigh, for self-preservation is the highest law. Give blow for blow, scorn for scorn, doom for doom, with compound interest liberally added thereunto. Eye for eye, tooth for tooth, aye four-fold, a hundred-fold." Why, this is life in a wolf-pack!'

'And hardly logical, when you consider it fully. I am sure there are Social Darwinists who wear spectacles.'

I laughed.

'I jest, but it is troubling, Watson. There is a rising wave of this thinking in our country. Mycroft brought it to my attention. Billings is just one example, as is the unknown person who stands behind him. If this philosophy were to take hold among the police, it would be exceedingly dangerous.'

'I cannot imagine there are so many sadists in the population,' I remarked.

'Sadism is not a requirement. Lack of empathy and a desire for power is all. And above all, fear. Just run-of-the-mill human weaknesses, in an unfortunate, but all too common combination.'

'I don't see how fear connects.'

'To a person who feels threatened, the illusion of immense personal power has great appeal. When fear is coupled with jealousy and helplessness, as it often is, the foundation is laid.'

'One must feel quite downtrodden, then. But who is so hopeless?'

'Watson, help me on with my clothing as we talk, would you please? We must get underway. There is much to do on our case today. Find me a frock coat, please.'

I went to his armoire and looked for his usual city attire.

'For us, Social Darwinism is despicable, ridiculous. But Watson, you must remember that we are men of privilege, with the benefit of a good education and the ability to earn our keep in comfortable circumstances and relative safety.'

'Except that you risk your life daily,' said I. 'There are any number of criminals in London and elsewhere who would gladly see you dead.' I espied several black frock coats and selected one.

'That is not the point.'

'And I risked my life at war, Holmes.'

'I do not forget this. But we both do this by choice, Watson, and arguably for a higher purpose. Consider the extreme poor in London. Many are sleeping on the streets, many are weak and unprepared, unable to defend themselves or their possessions, or those they love. Imagine yourself in such circumstance.'

'Here, try this one.' I held up one of his frock coats.

'Imagine that you and Mary were crowded into meagre public lodgings, or even on the street, with leering and violent men and women surrounding you, jealous over any happiness or possessions you display. Angry over anything you have that they do not. You are perhaps injured or weakened from starvation or illness. The few possessions you manage to obtain are stolen from you regularly.'

I shuddered. This described thousands in London, including the poor wretches I'd seen yesterday. 'But even so, Holmes, I would still not wish to beat others into submission. Only to find a way to earn my keep and remove my wife and myself to more protected ground.'

'Would you not feel fear?'

'Yes, of course. But still I would never—'

'Yes, but that is *you*, Watson. You are made of solid stuff, my friend, and discount your own valour. The lesser man might justifiably feel a combination of fear, despair and resentment. Ah, this cursed wrist!'

The brace would not fit inside the narrow sleeve. I would need to find another coat. I helped disentangle him from this one.

'Hatred could build in him to where a philosophy such as this seems reasonable,' Holmes continued. 'Where civilization fails, this "might makes right" mentality prevails.'

I returned to the armoire. 'Holmes, we here in England are civilized people!'

'Watson, my good fellow, civilization is a thin veneer. Thinner than one would like. The British are no more immune than anyone. Surely you witnessed barbarism during your army days? I mean, outside any official battle.'

I paused. I had indeed witnessed cruelty, callous behaviour in the face of a wounded enemy, looting, and worse. Many things which I would consider shameful.

'I see that you have. And from officers? English "gentlemen", correct?'

'Some,' I conceded. 'But these were moments of extreme duress.' I rifled through his armoire. All the black frock coats seemed to be identical. Did none of them have more generous sleeves?

'But you took no such advantage of your wounded enemies. No stealing from dead comrades,' said Holmes.

'Good God, no!'

'Of course, you did not. But you saw it. And more of it that you would admit.'

'But this Redbeard suggests more than taking advantage of the weak! If I were to follow his ideas, I should beat a man to a pulp for buying the last good lamb chop at the butcher's before me!'

'Never mind, Watson, we must focus on our case. I have been reading the police files.' He picked them up and thrust them at me, one after another. 'A Devil Tarot card was found in Anson's deathbed. But no Tarot card in the reports from Benjamin. And none here, for Clammory.'

I waved them away. 'I shall read those later. Let us find you a coat.' I took two more out and held them up. 'These all look the same.'

'None at Danforth's murder,' Holmes continued, his eyes

burning with excitement. 'Then the one we discovered at Enrietti's. Yet . . . I sense this killer would like to be found.'

'Well, that Lucifer letter to the Goodwins seems to confirm your theory.'

'Ah, thank you, Mrs Hudson.' Our landlady had appeared, as if by magic, handing me another cup of coffee. She placed a second cup for Holmes next to his bed, eyed the frock coats, encircled his bandaged wrist with a gentle hand, and immediately intuited the problem. She took the two coats I held and hung them back up.

'The letter adds weight but is not confirmatory, Watson. Another coat, hurry.'

'Let me finish my coffee, Holmes. About that letter, is it not odd that the Goodwins waited and only presented it to you now? They seem suspect to me. Could it be that they themselves have written the letter?'

'I do not think so, Watson. It is more likely that they will be targets, and soon.' He looked at our landlady, now standing behind me. 'Oh no, Mrs Hudson, just no!'

She was holding up a tweedy sack coat she had plucked from the armoire. It was looser in cut, but typically country wear. Mrs. Hudson shrugged, laid it on the end of the bed, and left us.

'Not that coat, never in the city!' He turned back to me. 'I digress. The Goodwins are unusual, to be sure. First, the Lucifer handwriting is like neither of theirs. Nor is the language. Neither observation is conclusive but consider this: the Goodwin brothers live privileged lives, enjoying both the ripe fruits of high society and also the deep satisfaction of influence in Parliament. And they are philanthropists of the first order. They are handsome, popular men about town, and— I said no!'

I held up his tweedy sack coat. 'Holmes, this the only coat you have that will fit over that wrist! Put it on.'

With a glare, he complied. 'I have not entirely dismissed the Goodwins. But as I was saying, they enjoy great personal freedom and a sybaritic existence. This does not fit the picture.'

We had moved from Holmes's bedroom into the cluttered sitting-room where Holmes began searching for something. 'My gloves. Black, fingerless. Help me find them, please. The killer, I believe, is a frustrated, angry and vengeful person, and even more to the point, highly organized. Possibly with a need for order. That was true of both alphabet murderers I mentioned earlier.'

I smiled as we rooted through the considerable clutter with which Holmes surrounded himself.

'The Goodwins' house is perfectly neat,' I offered.

'They have servants!' said Holmes in irritation. 'And entertain frequently. Of course it is!'

'What about Titus Billings?' I asked. 'Is it possible he is responsible for this crime wave?'

Holmes had located his fingerless black knitted gloves and was now pulling them on.

He sighed. 'Unclear. He is no mastermind. The nature of these murders – and the surrounding tragedies – shows elaborate planning and delicate execution. Does that seem like Billings to you?'

'No,' I admitted. 'Here, let me help.' I put on the right-hand glove for him.

'Titus Billings is after something else. His *raison d'être* is power. Absolute personal power. So no, Watson, I think it is more likely that Billings and our case are simply parallel developments. But Billings is a liability, to be sure. His need for dominance has set him against this investigation, a position he will never relinquish voluntarily. I underestimated this investment when I confronted him at Scotland Yard.'

'It would seem so, Holmes.'

'Yes, and I have paid for it.' He looked down at his gloved hands. The injury was now largely concealed. 'But why has Mycroft not delivered news on who supports Billings? I sent word to him last night enquiring as to his progress.'

'I might have something for you there,' said I. 'When I was at the Goodwins', I overheard Billings trying to intimidate them by implying a connection to someone highly placed. A cousin, I believe, to the Queen.'

'What? Why did you not mention this?'

'I could not catch the name, it was whispered, deferentially—'

'Well, what good is that, Watson, without the name? The Queen has many cousins.'

'Andrew Goodwin replied that the man was their cousin as well! That stopped Billings in his tracks.'

'Interesting. I wonder who it is. Watson, bring me my "G" file. Let me see what I have on the Goodwins. Meanwhile, look them up in *Debrett's*.'

In a moment, he was poring over one of his indexed notebooks in which he kept track of people of interest while I paged through *Debrett's*. Our searches both revealed that the Goodwins were, in fact, related somewhat circuitously to the Royal Family. Second cousins to a foreign, highly placed Royal, who shall remain unnamed in this narrative.

'Well, this adds to their allure, surely?' I remarked, embarrassed at my own desire to be invited to a party on Grosvenor Square.

'It may also make them even more envied. They could very well be the "G" on the killers's list of targets, although I do not think envy is sufficient motive for this string of murders. No, there is something deeply personal at the root of these killings. If all the victims had harmed others, we must find out who and how. Something in these facts will relate to our killer. We do not yet know what Danforth the elder had lurking in his past.'

'But Danforth was killed by his oldest son, Charles. Charles is in gaol. He could not have killed Enrietti.'

'He is not the man we seek. That is an unfinished avenue of this investigation. Our master villain set off Charles Danforth in some way. In fact, a visit to him in gaol is on my list for today. Come, our coats, Watson! We must be off.'

'We are not taking a single step in the direction of Scotland Yard, Holmes!'

'Your concern is admirable but irrelevant. Danforth has been removed to Pentonville where he awaits trial. It should not be a problem to slip in. I am friendly with someone there.'

'I don't like it, Holmes.'

'Nevertheless, we must go.'

We stood in the hallway donning our ulsters, hats and scarves. As he struggled with his ulster, Holmes gave a quick glance of disapproval in the mirror at his country attire. I found it amusing that one who cared so little for public opinion nevertheless took such pains with his clothing.

He called for Billy, who appeared instantly.

'Billy, hail us a cab, then take this note to my friend Mr Clifford Smith-Naimark at *The Times*' archives. Tell him it is urgent and collect what he has for you by four p.m. today. And deliver these two other notes as well. Wait for a response.'

Billy nodded and dashed off.

Mrs Hudson approached with our umbrellas and two pocket lanterns. 'You'll be wanting these, gentlemen. It's a pea-souper this morning. And wetter than a duck in a downpour.' She gently patted Holmes's injured arm. 'You take care, Mr Holmes.' He smiled at her, then turned and took my arm with his good one.

'Come, Watson! Let us be off! The game awaits!'

PART FIVE

BACKWATER

'There is some soul of goodness in things evil,
Would men observingly distil it out.'
—William Shakespeare, *Henry V*

CHAPTER 21

Cat and Mouse

rs Hudson had not exaggerated. An unseasonably dense, greenish-yellow fog had followed last night's storm, converting an ice-frosted London into an opaque mystery. No four-wheeler was available, so we bundled into a hansom, its lack of enclosed cabin making for a very chilly ride through the murk. To my surprise, Holmes directed the driver first to an address in Kensington.

'Watson we shall detour from this case briefly to inform Lady Eleanor Gainsborough of the facts surrounding her prize pupil. I cannot imagine it will please her, but I feel I at least owe her the report. And then . . . onto our main task!'

We were forced to inch along as the driver could see no more than a few yards before him. Holmes was taut with impatience, drumming the fingers of his right hand on his knee.

'I am surprised you took on Lady Eleanor, Holmes, given how busy you are just now.'

'Perhaps a mistake, Watson. But I have committed and must follow through.'

'I wonder why did she not call the police about the attack on the girl?' I said.

'Perhaps in some way she suspected a ruse and did not wish to risk scandal.' He paused, and smiled at me. 'Or perhaps she has heard of Titus Billings and thought better of it.'

'Odious man! But I sense she has a particular admiration for you, Holmes.'

He shrugged. 'The public response to me has been polarized of late, Watson.'

'Hers was particularly ardent,' I persisted.

He waved the thought away. Our cab continued at a snail's pace. Few were on the road, as driving about in this deep fog was dangerous. The gaslights along the streets remained lit even in daylight, pale orbs glowing in the fog like out-of-focus moons, helping us keep to our route.

I put this minor peril out of my mind and turned my attention to the case, which seemed as impenetrable as the mist through which we were travelling.

'Holmes,' I ventured, 'I still cannot understand why the murderer would send such a letter to the Goodwins.'

'There is something of the showman in our killer, Watson. He is proud of his work and wants attention, admiration. People who kill in series like this usually accelerate their game, shortening the time between murders, making each more gruesome, or in other ways creating a growing sense of horror. For them, it is a kind of theatre. They have been known to send notes to the police.'

'Like the Ripper!' I exclaimed. 'Then why not this time?'

'Perhaps he has. Perhaps Titus Billings has ignored it and will not say. Or it could be that this highly intelligent killer believes an idiot is currently in charge of the police force. Billings has, after all, appeared to fumble this investigation. Perhaps the killer miscalculated by sending his letter to the Goodwins, who did not announce it to the press, but rather kept the threats private.'

'I see,' I said.

'Our killer has an agenda and is playing a long game. I have theories. But what worries me, Watson, is that the killer may attract a macabre following. When murderers receive a lot of press attention, imitators may get ideas. All the more reason to close this case quickly.'

Soon we arrived at an elegant home at Courtfield Gardens. It was a graceful four-storey building in the middle of the block, with columns on the front portico, impressive but not ostentatious. A Gothic style church across the street barely visible through the mist impressed me as a sinister apparition from a dark fairy tale. I shook my head at the fanciful thought. I had not had enough sleep.

We were admitted by a maid and left to wait in an enormous first floor reception-room, which, unlike the building's exterior was nothing short of astonishing. It was like standing inside a life-sized 'cabinet of curiosities', so popular in years gone past. The walls were papered in a riot of greens and hung with paintings of wild animals and the stuffed heads of an actual lion, ibex, black jaguar, and one beast I couldn't identify – perhaps an anteater.

A marble fireplace was flanked by two tall ivory tusks, intricately carved with animals spiralling up the long shapes. Aside each were tall glass cases in which were housed dozens of delicate hand-blown glass orchids, each with a beautifully handwritten label. On tables under the animal heads was a magnificent collection of shells – twisting, delicate, iridescent – and by the window, a gilt-edged set of large, illustrated books, one open to a painting of an orchid.

There were no chairs, only a large flat item that looked like a mattress, surrounded on three sides by carved wooden-backed bolsters upholstered in a silk paisley of bright reds and pinks, shot through with golden threads.

I recognized it as a *majlis*, a type of Eastern divan on which one lounged rather than sat. What Englishman would fling himself down on such a thing in company with those he had just met? It might be better suited to the lounge of a Turkish bath, not a sitting-room in Kensington.

We stood awkwardly until a tall butler with a faint blond moustache and an expression of practised neutrality entered, directing a footman to take our things. Then suddenly into this remarkable room swept the lady we had met yesterday, wearing an embroidered kaftan of green, her beautiful dark hair tumbling down her back in the manner of a Pre-Raphaelite princess. Even at her age, she was a stunning creature. She quickly wiped away a tear.

'Oh, Mr Holmes! Thank you for coming! And you as well, Dr, er – I am surprised you have arrived so quickly!' She rushed to Holmes and embraced him. He stiffened in alarm and, I assume, pain.

'Oh, I am sorry!' said she, patting the splinted arm. 'Your arm! A cast?'

'It is just a temporary measure. A touch of arthritis, madam,' said Holmes. 'What did you mean, "arrived quickly"? I came to bring news of Judith's attack. I received no summons.'

'Your girl! She ran away. And my Judith . . . but we are at cross purposes. We shall have tea in the solarium, and clear up this mystery.'

We dutifully followed the lady to her solarium, an enormous and whimsical space constructed in the atrium of the grand house. A steamy heat inside this room allowed for an array of tropical plants and even trees to flourish in abundance. I heard the sound of birds and looked up to see five bright parrots perched in limbs at least twenty feet above our heads. The oppressive fog, visible through an intricate glass and ironwork roof, provided an eerie canopy of opaque greenish grey light, giving the effect of being inside an aquarium.

And, indeed, one whole side of this atrium contained an actual aquarium, fanciful in design, with filigreed decoration echoing the patterns in the roof. Weedy green fronds waved amongst fluorescent corals and brightly coloured fish. This was clearly the home of a formidable collector, and one with an artistic sensibility.

In the centre of the room was a grouping of gigantic, carved teak armchairs, to which Lady Eleanor guided us and bade us to be seated.

'This room and the one you were in display just part of my late husband's vast collection,' said Lady Eleanor. 'Lord Gainsborough was an amateur naturalist and used his fortune to help collect and document various rare species. He travelled world wide and donated more than a thousand specimens of flora and fauna to the British Museum.'

'I noticed the labels on the cases there, and in here as well, inscribed in a lovely hand,' I said. I felt like a small child perched on my oversized chair, and although he said nothing, I sensed Holmes was growing impatient.

'Yes, that is my doing,' said the lady. 'I helped my husband catalogue his collection, as well as his donations. I began as his secretary, you see. It was a natural fit. I am known for my handwriting.'

Holmes managed a polite smile. 'But to the point, madam, and before I tell you our news – why have you summoned us here?'

'Judith has run away. Your girl has as well. I think there may be a connection and I am terribly worried.'

Holmes and I looked at each other.

'Madam, perhaps Judith's leaving the school is for the best,' said Holmes. 'I have difficult news for you but shall not insult you by delaying further. Heffie left your school to report to me. I am afraid she discovered that Judith, your prize pupil, is a duplicitous young lady. She is running a brothel business from inside the school. It involves four other girls, servicing local workers and using rooms in an adjacent business.'

At these words, the lady turned white. A storm of emotions flickered across her beautiful face in rapid succession – surprise, pain, outrage, anger. It was clear that she had not known.

Holmes continued. 'Apparently she has managed to hide this from everyone else at the school. Heffie gained Judith's confidence and learned that the story of the attack was untrue—'

The lady gasped. Holmes pressed on.

'She told Heffie that she had falsified the attack in order to trap the school's visiting music teacher. He had discovered Judith's activities and threatened to reveal her when his own advances were rebuffed.'

The lady's eyes glistened with tears. She seemed to grab onto this fact like a drowning man reaches for a lifeline. 'The music teacher? Mr Pembroke? Oh! We . . . we *must* find Judith,' said she.

I reached out to take her hand, but she withdrew it, turning instead to Holmes and taking up his good hand in her own. He stiffened.

'Please, Mr Holmes,' she said. 'Judith probably ran away once she knew that Heffie had discovered her. Or that awful man – that teacher! Whatever Judith has done, there is something good inside the girl. Redemption is always possible! I know it. Please, will you help me find her?'

I became aware of a slight meaty odour in the room which floated through the dense smell of orchids.

Holmes frowned slightly and freed his hand. 'Madam, I am on a very pressing case at the moment. There is a vicious murderer at large, and—'

Suddenly, a loud sound – which to my ears evoked the giant drawbridge of a castle suddenly being let down, although I had never heard such a thing – came from somewhere in our immediate vicinity. Perhaps right behind me. I leapt up and turned, as did Holmes, looking in the same direction. There was nothing there.

'Sit down, gentlemen. It is just Belle.'

What on earth? We both sat. I felt a little sheepish.

'I suppose the disappearance of one unfortunate young woman cannot possibly compete with a case of murder,' said Lady Eleanor. 'Or murders. Nevertheless, I must beg you, Mr Holmes. Please.'

I felt a strange pressure on my ankle followed by a sharp pinprick, and looked down to see that the enormous, spotted paw of some giant animal had reached out from under the large teak chair on which I was sitting and wrapped itself around my foot, its claws pricking the inside of my ankle.

With an involuntary yell, I shot to my feet.

Holmes was standing, too, staring aghast at the giant fur appendage curled around my ankle. Something was under my chair. Something feline. Something like—

'Belle!' cried the lady. 'Let him go. Down, Belle. Belle, no.'

The paw slowly uncurled from around my ankle and retreated beneath the chair. The sound of an idling motor engine rumbled from down there.

'It is just my cat, Belle. She is harmless, unless you attack me. She is very protective.' Lady Eleanor smiled wanly. 'It is a comfort, since my husband died such a horrible death.'

'Cat?' I edged away from my chair.

But there was nothing quite like a 'horrible death' to rivet my friend's attention. 'Your husband, Lady Eleanor?' asked Holmes, fixing on the alternate fact. 'I read that Lord Gainsborough had a heart attack his sleep.'

Horrible, perhaps to the widow. But what kinder way to go, really?

But before she could answer, my chair itself suddenly moved, and out from under it oozed a spotted animal – one who had compressed herself into such a small space that Holmes and I were further astonished at her actual bulk as she unfurled herself.

Belle was a leopard. A fully-grown leopard wearing a jewelled collar She sat down a few feet away, curling her tail around her legs, and regarded me with flat, yellow eyes. Even seated, her head was three feet off the ground.

No one moved.

Belle yawned, showing four-inch fangs, then turned to lick herself energetically on one shoulder. Holmes and I, frozen in position, looked at each other.

'Belle is quite tame,' said Lady Eleanor. 'My husband brought two leopards from South America to the London Zoo four years ago. One was pregnant but died shortly after giving birth to Belle, whom I then raised by hand. She is a sweet girl unless, well, as I said . . .'

I shuddered. I did not even like house cats, for their sudden pouncing. This was in another league entirely.

Holmes coughed. 'I am allergic to cats,' said he. 'Perhaps we could return to the parlour.'

The lady smiled at us in understanding. A moment later, the cat having been banished to her 'room', Lady Eleanor and I sat rather uncomfortably near the floor on the Arabic *majlis*. It was awkward in the extreme. I kept glancing at the hall which led to the solarium.

Holmes declined to join us in repose on the *majlis*. Instead, he roamed the room in his nervous manner, stopping here and there to glance at the unusual collection of objects as he proceeded to ask our distraught hostess a series of questions. I struggled to retain my dignity on the awkward seating.

'You referred to a horrible death, Lady Eleanor. Did the papers get it wrong?' asked Holmes.

'Yes. It was terrible. I—I— Oh, I can't. It just . . . I just . . .' She covered her eyes and turned from us. 'The papers said one thing, but the truth is another. You see . . . He was in the bath when he died. We had just had the house electrified.'

I anticipated what followed.

'Do sit with us, Mr Holmes.'

'No, thank you.'

'My husband put a lamp into the bathroom. I told him not to. But—'

'It fell into his bath and he was electrocuted?' finished Holmes.

'Yes.'

'Were you in the house at the time?'

'No, I was out.'

'The servants?'

'All three were at market. We had been planning a party.'

'Did the police consider foul play?' Holmes paused, a large piece of something like lava or coral in his hand. He set it down.

'They concluded there was no foul play. They did ask me to prove I was elsewhere, and I did. I was with a lady friend and we were—' Her voice broke. 'We were shopping for gloves on Oxford Street. I bought some pale blue ones . . . with a little rose . . . Oh, if only I had been here!'

'You could not have foreseen this, Lady Eleanor,' I said.

'Was it ruled an accident, then?' continued Holmes.

'Yes. My husband was a difficult man. But the thought of him being murdered . . .' She fought back tears. 'The lamp just fell in, apparently. It must have been terrible for him. Our solicitor got the story changed for the papers. Out of consideration for me.'

Holmes was silent for a moment. He glanced at me. Then, 'Madam, I must ask you a few questions about your husband. I do not wish to be indelicate, but I would like to set my mind at ease about something.'

'Ask whatever you like.'

Holmes paused, standing before the front window. The fog behind him was now brighter, almost an absinthe green.

'Precisely how did he amass his great fortune?' he asked.

She swallowed, then answered readily enough. 'My husband was what you call a business speculator. He bought and sold other businesses. He had an uncanny knack for knowing when a business was in trouble, and for – I don't know – transferring funds from one bank to another. At least, I think so. I was not privy to the details. As a woman, you know . . .'

'And how was he regarded by colleagues in his field?'

'He had few colleagues of his stature, Mr Holmes. He kept his dealings quite private. Even from me.'

'Was he well regarded? Liked, perhaps?' asked Holmes. 'Many friends?'

She hesitated. 'Admired, yes, very much so. Liked? That is a question I cannot answer. He was rather like you, Mr Holmes, in that he did not bother much about public opinion. And he socialized rarely. Collecting was his passion.'

Holmes turned to a table standing in front of the window. 'Ah, I see you have Sanders' *Reichenbachia*!' said he, pausing at four gilded volumes displayed there.

'What is that?' I asked, not following his rapid digression. I thought the Reichenbach was a waterfall somewhere.

'Four volumes on orchids, lavishly illustrated. Sanders' take on leading orchidologist Heinrich Reichenbach's work,' said Holmes, once again displaying the arcane nooks and crannies of what he called the 'little empty attic' of his brain. This diversion struck me as odd. But Holmes rarely did anything without purpose.

'Orchids have a sinister history, do they not Lady Eleanor?' he asked. 'Orchid hunters have been known to die or disappear out in the field.'

'I don't know, Mr Holmes. I think of them simply as

beautiful flowers. As you can see, they were only one of my husband's passions.' She gestured vaguely to the room.

'Very lovely labels,' I said, nodding towards the glass cases. Her icy glance told me how lame was my repeated gambit.

Holmes continued. 'Were there any businesses which – or, rather, *people who* – resented your husband's transactions? Anyone harmed, left destitute? Anyone with their dreams dashed or their family fortunes sold on the block?'

'My goodness, I would hope not! None that I know.'

'Was Lord Gainsborough a Luminarian?'

'That word is familiar. What is it?'

'An honorary society. You have heard of it, then?'

'Yes, I have heard the word,' she said.

'Was it through your husband you heard the word?'

'I am not sure. I may have read of it in the papers.'

'It is a secret society. They are not in the papers,' said Holmes.

'Well, then, I suppose I heard the word from Peter.'

Holmes moved to a side table. 'Did your husband fraternize with the Goodwin brothers?'

'Mr Holmes, I do not understand what you are getting at. Peter's – my husband's death is still a fresh wound. And now this news of my dear Judith—'

'My apologies, Lady Eleanor, but I must insist. I have good reason. The Goodwins?'

'Goodwins? Why, yes, he knew them. He mentioned them once or twice. I have, of course, read of their famous parties.' She attempted a smile.

'Did you ever attend one of their parties?' I interjected. 'I have heard such wonderful things.'

'No,' she replied, coldly. Holmes glanced at me in annoyance. I shrugged.

She rose to her knees, to escape from the *majlis*, and presumably from me.

Holmes extended his good hand and drew Lady Eleanor to her feet. As I struggled to my own feet after her, he continued the barrage of his questions.

'What about after your husband's death, Lady Eleanor? Did you yourself suffer any accidents, receive any threats? Any sense of personal danger to yourself? A loose carpet on the stair? A near miss of some sort? Anything whatsoever threatening?'

My friend, in his eagerness, had become something of a human Gatling gun.

'You frighten me, sir.' She moved away from Holmes and now took up his former place, silhouetted by the front window. Her slender figure was erect, and I imagined her expression resolute. Despite her fears, this was a lady who would not be crushed by ill fortune.

'Let me think,' she said. 'Why, yes! Now that you mention it, I suppose there was something. I put it down to carelessness. Not long ago I was nearly run over in the street. I was distraught, grieving. I looked up just in time.'

'Run over? By what?' Holmes asked eagerly.

'A four-wheeler. Driving far too fast.'

'Where? When?'

'In front of the house, here. Last week.'

'Did you see the driver? Did it seem intentional?'

'I did not see the driver, no. Intentional? It had not occurred to me, but I suppose it is possible. I did get a glimpse of the man inside the carriage.'

'Can you describe him?'

We were both facing the lady, our backs to the door leading from the hall. I suddenly caught that scent again. I turned around. Belle sat in the doorway, staring at us. Perhaps she had escaped her 'room'.

'Do you mind? The cat,' I said.

'Leopard. Oh, Belle, shoo,' said Lady Eleanor. 'She won't hurt you.'

The cat slunk away.

Holmes and I took up other positions, so that we could keep an eye on the doorway. He turned back to the lady. She might have been smiling, but backlit as she was against the window I could not quite see. I supposed every visitor reacted in this way to Belle.

'Madam,' said Holmes, 'the man in the carriage?'

'I caught only a glimpse. A large man. Tall, very heavy.'

'Tall?'

'His face was high up in the window.'

'Moustache? Beard?'

'Clean shaven,' she said. 'Though I could not swear to that.'

'Hair colour?'

'I . . . I don't know. He was wearing a top hat. That is all. It was so fast.'

'How do you know he was heavy?' persisted Holmes.

'I . . . well . . .' She put her hands up to her lower cheeks. 'Heavy here,' she said. 'Jowls.'

Holmes shot me a meaningful glance. I understood that he now feared Gainsborough might well have been a victim of the Alphabet Killer. And that the lady herself could be in danger.

'Excuse me, Lady Eleanor, I noticed a telephone in your hallway. May I use it, please?' Holmes asked. She nodded, and he left the room briefly.

She looked after him, distraught. We lingered in uncomfortable silence until Holmes returned from the telephone.

'Madam, I am afraid I am on a very pressing case at the moment. I have called Inspector Gregory Lestrade of Scotland Yard, a fine man with whom I have worked many times. He and his men will be here shortly. If my theory is correct, I fear you may be in danger. Someone will stay with you until I can close this case.'

'Me? Why? Why would I be in danger?'

'It is complicated. Please believe me and accept this protection. I must be off now. If you would kindly ring for our coats?'

'Mr Holmes, please! I want no police in this house!' exclaimed the lady. 'Imagine, with Belle? And – well, who knows if they are honourable men? Sensible men? Sir, can you not send someone in your place – perhaps this Mr Wilson here—' she waved dismissively at me – 'to investigate and stay with me yourself?'

She placed a delicate hand on his good arm and took hold, her face turned up to his, pleading.

Despite my irritation, I had a sudden flash of my wife Mary, vulnerable and taking comfort from me when she was a client of ours on a dangerous case, and before we fell in love.

'Mr Holmes, my husband left me well looked after,' pleaded the lady. 'I can pay anything you wish. Please!'

Holmes gently untangled himself from her. 'I am sorry, Lady Eleanor, I cannot stay,' he said. 'Good day.'

Stumbling through the dense fog, it then took us fifteen minutes to flag down a hansom on nearby Gloucester Road. Few were hiring the two-seaters in this weather, and few were on the road. As we departed Kensington, I mused on what felt like an escape.

Lady Eleanor was not the first woman to desire close personal attention from the great detective, nor would she be the last. Whether for them it was a kind of hero worship, the allure of fame, or the challenge of attracting a man who seemed immune to their charms, I could never tell. But none could sway Sherlock Holmes when pursuing his case or his quarry in his own way.

Holmes directed the driver to Pentonville Prison, where he intended to question Charles Danforth. We rode for a few minutes in silence, inching through the treacherous brume, our ulsters soon dripping with moisture.

I held up a hand before my face. Even at arm's length I could see tendrils of fog in the way. 'My God, this weather!' I exclaimed. It was extreme, even for London.

'Orchids,' said Holmes.

'What about them?'

'Consider this, Watson. Six years ago, a tragic series of deaths occurred in the Amazon. It was an orchid-collecting expedition in which eight men went in and only one came out alive. It was a dangerous area, but so many disappeared and never a trace was found. Murder was suspected, but if I recall correctly the case was never closed. If Lord Gainsborough had a hand in this—'

'Oh, I remember reading about that. But it was some time ago.'

'Watson, please recall that we are considering each victim as having a past evil deed to their credit. If this orchid disaster was his doing . . . well, you see my point. And, of course, there is his known philanthropy later. This fits squarely into the victim profile. Lord Gainsborough, it would seem, could very well be our "G".'

'But the date of his death . . . would he not have been the first? And then out of order, alphabetically?' I asked. 'It happened roughly when the Anson killing did, correct?'

'Yes. But, except for this, Gainsborough hits all the marks.'

'And the peripheral deaths? Could they all be by the same hand?'

'Some, perhaps. Not directly, but possibly inspired by or in some way caused. It would be too coincidental if they were not, Watson.'

'Then you fear for Lady Eleanor's safety, Holmes? Even all this time after Lord Gainsborough's death?'

'Who knows? But Watson, I will not make the same

mistake as with Mrs Danforth. I warrant that suicide is not in this lady's future, she seems made of stronger stuff. However, if her husband's death is connected, and if she is targeted by this ongoing killer and his plans, at least I can rest easy knowing that she is safe.'

We continued in silence for several minutes through the increasingly opaque fog which mirrored our thinking. Or at least *my* thinking.

'Holmes,' I ventured at last, 'you are not allergic to cats, are you?'

He laughed. 'Not at all,' said he. 'Although we may have made a narrow escape from some claws, nonetheless.'

He glanced sideways at me. A smile flickered over his face and was gone.

CHAPTER 22

One Flask Closer

entonville Prison was a far cry from Kensington and a long ride in the open two-seater hansom through the freezing damp. We arrived cold as a herring on ice, and through prior arrangement were ushered into a small room where prisoners met with their solicitors or their family members, when allowed.

Charles Danforth sat in a wooden chair, wearing handcuffs and leg chains. He looked considerably less menacing than he did in Holmes's sitting-room, now slumped in striped, ill-fitting prison wear, hair awry but not yet shorn for incarceration, as his trial had not yet taken place. His pale face reflected fury mixed with despair, and bloodshot eyes glared at us from under bushy brows.

We were seated on stiff wooden chairs, facing him. It was colder in this room than outside.

'Mr Danforth,' began Holmes, 'I am here to try to

understand the circumstances which led to your actions some days ago. What was it that set you in a rage against your father?'

The man stared at us but said nothing.

'I understand you thought you had been cut from the will.'

No answer.

'Of course, your family reports that there were strained relations between the two of you, leading to the incident.'

Still nothing. The man's lips curled in a sneer.

'But something specific arrived to transform this ill will into a murderous fury.'

'Get away from me,' the prisoner said.

Holmes sighed and rubbed his injured arm absentmindedly. He glanced at me. 'Ah, it is chilly in here. Do you have your flask, Watson? I could do with a sip of brandy.'

I carried a flask of brandy with me at all times. Although it was often a joke when people said such things were 'for medicinal purposes', in my case it was the literal truth.

I removed it from my pocket, wondering if Holmes was flagging. He took a quick sip, handed it back, and turned to the prisoner. Danforth stared at my flask like a man parched, following it with his eyes as I replaced it in my pocket. Ah, of course.

Holmes continued, 'Tell me about your father.'

Danforth was silent again.

'Something must have set you off. Surely your solicitor tried to find some mitigating circumstance that could affect your sentencing?'

'Give me a drink,' said Danforth.

Holmes consulted his pocket watch. 'I would like to offer you something in exchange for your detailed and candid information. I believe I have something that you would appreciate.'

'A drink.'

'No.'

'A curse on you!' The prisoner spat. We both pulled back. The noxious spittle missed us both, thankfully.

'You realize, of course, Mr Danforth, that you will very likely hang, or if not, then suffer a long sentence of hard labour?'

Danforth did not reply.

'Hard labour, you may not be aware, is often the tread-mill, as it is here at Pentonville, on which many men founder and die. Elsewhere, it might be crushing stones into gravel with a hammer, which breaks strong men's backs. Or you might find yourself turning a crank to a quota, all alone in your cell, until you collapse. Or perhaps picking oakum until your hands are turned into raw, bleeding meat. Day in and day out, until you are dead.'

Danforth gaped at us in horror.

'That is right. Most people are unaware of the details of a hard labour sentence,' said Holmes casually.

I was not unaware and I shuddered at the reminder of this sad reality. I recalled a year ago when Holmes himself was threatened with such a sentence. Sadly, given time at hard labour, it was the strongest and most resilient men who would last the longest, and therefore suffer the most.

'I would choose hanging,' murmured the prisoner, his eyes glassy.

'As would I,' said Holmes. 'Hard labour is often a slow death sentence. But you may not be given the choice.'

He paused, allowing the words to sink in. 'Mr Danforth, it is possible I could help you to receive a sentence of time without hard labour . . . at one of the less draconian institutions.'

I wondered if Holmes really had the power to do that.

'I am listening.'

'I ask you again. Tell me about your father. The relationship was strained before the murder. Why?'

'My father was despicable.'

'I understand Sebastian Danforth was a highly respected MP, made his fortune in paper, was an amateur poet, and was being considered for Queen's honours for his donations to – what was it? – literacy programmes for the poor. Everyone should learn to read, wasn't that it?'

'He was vermin.'

'That is a harsh judgement. Why?'

'Blackmail. He dealt in letters. Letters of all kinds. He enjoyed ruining people. A sadist, actually. He was still at it when he died.'

A violent murderer who tortured his wife was now denouncing his father as a sadist. What ghastly goings on took place behind society doors.

'Interesting. Letters. So you killed him with a letter opener. *Piquant*,' said Holmes. He withdrew his cigarette case and offered it to me. I declined, then realized he needed me to

228

light one for him. I took a cigarette, did so, and handed it to him. He took a long draw on it. Danforth watched him hungrily.

'He concealed his true nature well,' said the prisoner.

'So many criminals do. Is that why you killed him? You must have known about his blackmailing for a long time. What set you off on that particular night? Did he threaten someone you cared for?'

'No.'

'Certainly not your wife.'

'No. What do you mean by that?'

Holmes shrugged. 'Nothing. Why did you think your father had cut you from the will?'

'He did not, as it turns out,' said Danforth, bitterly.

'Yes, but why did you think he had?'

'Give me a drink and I will tell you.'

'Tell me first.'

'And a cigarette.'

'Yes, to both. But talk first,' said Holmes.

'Telegram.'

'You received a telegram. Now we are getting somewhere. What did it say?'

'It said "Your father sees you. David will inherit all now."' And also—'

'*Sees* you?'

The man looked down.

'You took that to mean that he somehow saw, or at least knew of, some criminal behaviour of yours? Burning your wife Constance with cigarettes, perhaps?' asked Holmes.

Danforth started, his chin trembled. A tear escaped his eye and rolled down his cheek. He yanked at his hands, cuffed to the chair, but could do nothing to stop it. 'Do not speak her name!' he roared, turning wild eyes in Holmes's direction. 'I will kill you.'

Holmes sighed.

'In any case, you believed your father had changed his will. How might the telegram sender have learned of your misdeeds?'

The prisoner yanked his hands in a paroxysm of anger.

'Again, Mr Danforth, who do you think could have informed him of this? Might your wife Constance have done so? Or is that what you believed at the time?'

'No! Constance would never tell.'

'Why not?'

'The shame.' He grimaced at the memory, and a look of hatred contorted his features. 'She deserved it. She knew it.'

I felt a wave of revulsion. Fiends like this often convinced themselves they were 'made' to do things by others.

'I see,' said Holmes. 'Women can be infuriating. Unfaithful. Treacherous.'

Of course he could not mean that.

'Oh, she was, she was!'

'Perhaps it *was* she, in fact, who told your father?'

'Never, I say. She would never.'

'Hmm. What else did the telegram say?'

'Said my father got a letter. But my father then denied it.'

Holmes stiffened. 'I see. This telegram – anonymous, I presume?'

Danforth shrugged.

'Did you not try to trace it?'

'No.'

'You just believed it and acted,' marvelled Holmes. The guard had stepped away. Holmes leaned in to me. 'Watson, how full is that flask?' he whispered.

'Completely full, minus your small sip.' I took it out and held it in such a way that it could not be seen by the guard, who had been posted just outside the door, and who regarded us periodically through a large window.

At the sight of it, Danforth's eyes gleamed. Yes, alcohol surely had this man in its grasp.

'We shall give you all the brandy in this flask if you recount *verbatim* the telegram you received,' said Holmes.

I shook the flask. The liquid sloshed. Danforth licked his lips.

'Word for word,' said Holmes.

Danforth closed his eyes. 'It said, "Your father sees. Constance ruins all. You are burned. David now inherits everything."'

'That is all? Nothing else?'

'No. Give me—'

'At the time, who did you think sent you this telegram?'

'Perhaps some snitch in my father's solicitor's office. Someone who knew of the revised will.'

'Which was non-existent.'

'How was I to know that! You asked me what I thought. Now give me the drink!'

Holmes held up a gloved hand. 'No indication of the sender? Not an initial? Nothing?'

'Yes. Yes. An initial. No name. Give me—!'

I waved the flask at him but held it back.

'What initial?' insisted Holmes.

'It was . . . it was . . . "L"!'

'Ah!' cried Holmes, triumphant. 'So *devilishly* clever.' He nodded to me. *Lucifer.* 'Time to go, Watson!'

In a moment, Danforth was gulping down the brandy. I stood to block the guard's view of this forbidden interchange as I poured it down his throat. One part of me despised the man, but at the same time I pitied him.

As we departed Pentonville, Holmes directed me to flag down a four-wheeler. We were lucky to get one. It was now two in the afternoon and I hoped he would direct the cab driver to Marylebone and home. To my disappointment, he gave the man an address in Notting Hill, the home of Theodore Clammory, the third – or possibly fourth – victim of the Alphabet Killer.

As our carriage moved off, I asked Holmes if indeed he had the power to get Danforth imprisoned elsewhere.

'It is a moot point, Watson. The man will surely hang.'

CHAPTER 23

Zebras

ur next stop was Notting Hill. Mr Theodore Clammory had suffered a typically violent death at the hand of our quarry. He had begun a chain of barber shops, made a fortune, and then donated half his income to provide services to veterans of the Boer War, of which he was one. He had been found in one of his barber shops with his throat slit by a straight razor, next to his chief barber and business partner, similarly dispatched.

We headed south-west on Marylebone Road, in the direction of his home.

'Watson, we progress. I begin to form a picture of our killer, and absolutely to confirm my theory. Danforth was compelled by that mysterious telegram from 'L' to kill his father, and the elder Danforth's history as a secret blackmailer fits the pattern perfectly. Philanthropists with dark pasts. We have only to confirm that Anson, Benjamin and Clammory similarly comply to the model.'

'And then what, Holmes?'

'And then . . . we shall hope that the evidence somehow reveals something telling about the killer.'

We at last arrived at a beautiful new terraced home. Not so long ago, Notting Hill was known for its pig farms, but over recent years it had grown rapidly from a rural to an expensive neighbourhood filled with parks and green spaces, and newer, elegant homes. As graceful and as these new four-storey buildings were, however, the dense fog which continued to cling to the streets gave even this area a feeling of foreboding.

We rang. The door was answered by an elderly woman of indeterminate age, pale, wizened, and garbed in a nun's habit, complete with wimple. Her face resembled those of the dried apple dolls I had once seen in an exhibit of folk crafts that Mary had insisted on visiting.

We introduced ourselves, and Holmes explained that he was investigating a series of murders which now appeared linked, 'Including that of the late Mr Clammory. Are you a relative, madam?'

'Sister,' said the woman, 'Sister Bernadette.' Behind her, the house was dark and curiously empty. Nothing, not an umbrella stand, nor a table, nor a mirror was visible from the door.

'I see. And are you related to the deceased?' prompted Holmes, gently.

'Yes. Are you deaf? My name is *Sister* Bernadette, and

Theodore Clammory was my brother.' Her voice was like rustling dried leaves. "I suppose I will have to invite you in. But be quick, I am very busy.'

Minutes later, we sat with her in a once grand but now entirely inhospitable room. It had beautiful walls decorated in the French style with elaborate boiserie panels and glittering brass lights with crystals, none of which were lit. The intricate wooden floor was chipped and bare, and the few pieces of furniture huddled near the window were old and cheap, as if rescued from some seedy hotel. The fireplace was dark and there were no other lights. Several candles sat unlit, with only a dim glow barely penetrating from the front window. The afternoon had grown dimmer, the dense fog now the colour of mould.

It was as if this nun was serving penance.

We sat, growing increasingly cold, while she succinctly and with even less charm than the furnishings, answered Holmes's questions. Sister Bernadette was the only relative of the successful Theodore Clammory. She had temporarily left her nunnery, St Cecilia's in the Loire Valley in France, to return to London to dispose of his estate, the proceeds of which she, as sole beneficiary, was in the process of donating to her order.

When Holmes asked her why she did not simply hire the family solicitor to take care of these duties, she replied, 'There is no one connected with my brother whom I trust.'

The room was icy. I wrapped my scarf higher around my neck, worried that Holmes, so lean and with his recent injury, would be suffering more than I in the cold. But he seemed impervious, and simply pressed forward with his questions. In due course, he found precisely what he needed.

'If you don't mind my indelicacy, Sister, I must ask you some personal questions.'

'And I may answer them. Or not.' I detected a flicker of a smile from the pinched face. I noticed that her eyes were a startling blue, and I wondered what she had once looked like before becoming Sister Bernadette.

Holmes smiled back, but his posture revealed, at least to me, a touch of impatience.

'How did your brother make his fortune, precisely? It takes a lot of money to open a series of establishments all through London, and even, I am told, in Birmingham and Manchester. I presume that you were not raised in wealth?'

'Why? Because I took my vows?' The nun stared at Holmes with eyes narrowed, challenging him.

'All right, let me begin with another, more general question. Can you please relate to me your brother's history? What made him go into the business of opening a series of barber shops?'

The nun snorted. 'Well, Theodore had to do something after his disastrous time in the army. And he fell in with a despicable character.'

'What disaster befell him in the army?'

'The Boer War?' I asked. 'I am a military man myself.'

'Both my brothers – Thaddeus was there, too – were at Majuba Hill,' said Sister Bernadette. 'Now, that was a disaster.'

It was indeed. In February of 1881, in a notoriously ill-prepared move, the British lost more than 200 men to fewer than ten enemy casualties.

'Some say both of them behaved dishonourably in the field. Tried to turn tail and flee, it was said, though they were hardly the only ones. Apparently an orderly tried to stop them and they nearly decapitated him in response. A witness saw it all, but he was discredited and later died, knifed in an alley in Bordeaux while on leave.'

'Knifed by whom?' asked Holmes.

The nun shrugged, but her expression indicated she had her theories.

'I see,' said Holmes. 'Do you think this rumour is true, about your brothers' attempted desertion?'

'My brothers were without morals. I pray for their souls daily.'

'Do you recall the name of the man knifed in the alley?'

'No. I turn my eyes to God.'

'Yes, of course,' said Holmes. 'What happened to your brothers after this?'

'Ultimately, both received their due,' said Sister Bernadette, a small bitter smile contorting only the lower half of her face. 'Thaddeus died while abroad, not long after, of dysentery. And you know what happened to Theodore.'

We did. His throat was cut from ear to ear. I somehow intuited that this did not displease his sister. Whatever beneficence she might have harboured may have been beaten out of her by later life events. I wished to give the woman the benefit of the doubt.

'How then, did your brother arrive at his successful business?' asked Holmes.

'He and I inherited our parents' estate. I gave all my share to my Order. With his, Theodore bought this house and began his business with that horrible Ignatius Johnson. My brother's lifestyle rivalled that of royalty, he was so self-indulgent!'

'In what way?'

'This house. His appetite. He ballooned into a caricature of himself; indeed, he was once portrayed in *Punch*!' said the nun, the thought as distasteful as though he had run naked through the pigsties that used to fill this once muddy and disreputable area.

'And can you tell me more about his partner in life and death, Mr Johnson?' asked Holmes.

The lady recoiled in disapproval. 'That was his chief barber, and my brother had an unhealthy relationship with him. Theodore financed a series of shops specializing in all sorts of self-indulgent grooming for a certain kind of man.'

Holmes and I looked at each other, puzzled.

'A dandy?' I asked.

Her rheumy eyes flicked over to me, then up and down, taking in my clothing, shoes, hair, everything. Apparently, I met with her approval and she answered, 'Yes, those kind.'

Holmes hid the raised eyebrow he flashed to me. This woman! I held back a laugh.

'They were successful?' asked Holmes.

'Who was successful?' snapped the nun.

'The shops. They did well?'

'Wildly,' said she. She flicked her tongue as if to discharge a bitter taste. 'His fortune grew. I suggested to him that he indulge himself a little less – Theodore loved his parties and his feasts – and instead donate to a worthy cause.'

'You were here often, then, in London?' asked Holmes.

'I visited once in a while.'

'Of course, you were hoping he would donate to the Sisters of St Cecilia?' said Holmes sympathetically.

'I was, but it was not to be. He set up a fund for the relatives of those who died in the Battle of Majuba Hill. It quite polished his reputation. But I knew the underbelly. Oh, I knew.'

'Theodore was motivated by guilt, then?' I suggested.

Her eyes flicked once more to me. 'My brother did not suffer from anything like guilt. Obligation, perhaps. He had been pressured by others.'

'I see,' said Holmes. 'Let us turn to his recent murder. Were you present at the investigation?'

There was the sudden, eerie sound of flapping nearby, from the hall just outside the room. It was disturbing. The light from the window had dimmed further and the room was now shrouded in darkness.

'Yes. I was staying with my brother at the time,' said the woman. 'I do not think the police expended much effort.'

'Why is that?'

'Well, Ignatius Johnson was clearly the culprit.'

This puzzled Holmes. 'Why do you say this? He was found dead next to your brother.'

She shrugged and chuckled, a particularly mirthless

huffing sound that reminded me of a cat choking on a piece of meat. 'Just my theory. Although it would have been difficult for him to confess. After killing my brother, he slit his own throat.'

The flapping sounded again.

'What is that sound?' I asked. 'Are there pigeons, Sister?'

'Yes. There is a flaw in the ceiling upstairs. They keep coming in.'

I cleared my throat and pulled out my watch. 'Holmes, I think we should best—'

But he was not to be deterred. 'Ignatius Johnson left no note?'

The nun shook her head.

'About Johnson, have you any detail on his wound?' asked he. I thought this unlikely, but my friend's instincts were correct.

Her eyes glistened. Not only did she have detail, but she relished it, clearly. 'From ear to ear,' she said, licking her lips. 'Sliced. Deep. Almost to the bone.'

'Slit his own throat from ear to ear, to the bone?' said Holmes in disbelief. 'Why, I would imagine that is rather hard to do. One might, er, fatigue halfway through.' He pantomimed doing that with his good hand.

Sister Bernadette smiled and made the same gesture but finishing the swoop triumphantly.

'Impossible, I would say', said I. 'Speaking as a doctor. Are you sure it was quite literally ear to ear, or perhaps just a general description of the wound?'

'Oh, yes,' said the nun. 'I saw it. It was ear to ear.' She

pulled back her wimple and indicated a point just at the base of each tiny, hairy ear. 'Here . . . all the way to here.' She replaced her wimple, eyes gleaming, rather gleeful about the whole thing.

'Thank you very much, Sister!' said Holmes abruptly rising. 'Watson, shall we be off? We have additional stops. We can see ourselves out.'

We stood up to go, but Holmes turned again.

'Oh! I am sorry, but I have one more question, Sister. Was a Tarot card left at the site of these deaths, by any chance, or did you see one in the house?'

'Tarot card!' she said with disgust. 'No! Those are the works of the Devil!'

'Indeed. Good day, Sister,' said Holmes and we walked to the door of the room. I peered down the darkened hallway and, some twenty yards away, to the front door, lit from above by a clerestory.

I glanced up. Nothing flying was visible, but that was not to say they weren't there. The notion of bats crossed my mind. Holmes must have had the same thought. We exchanged a look and made a dash for it.

Once again in a cab, this time a hansom again, we had no opportunity to get warm after that chilly visit. It was not the mere cold, either. There was something decidedly unhealthy in that house. My heart sank when Holmes gave the cabbie an address in Bermondsey. It would be a freezing trip across the river.

'Holmes, do you think that Sister Bernadette may be

involved some way in her brother's death? Might she have killed him?'

'No. She was left-handed – did you notice how she demonstrated cutting one's own throat? The police report stated the cuts were by a right-handed killer. Lestrade, who has taken lessons, managed to get at least this noted.' Holmes flashed a smile. 'I looked at the photographs from the Clammory carnage. Clammory and Johnson were both in barber chairs, draped as though for a shave, both with necks slashed ear to ear, as described by that gentle nun.'

'Ha!'

'But Johnson also had a wound in the stomach, and much less blood from the neck wound,' Holmes pointed out.

Our hansom made good time through elegant Knightsbridge, our driver aiming for Westminster Bridge for our crossing to the South Bank and on to Bermondsey. I was so exhausted, hungry and chilled at this point, I kept an eager eye out for a hot chocolate or a coffee stand. They were everywhere except when you needed one. The fog had thinned just enough for me to spot one at last, and I insisted, against Holmes's objections, on buying us both a steaming hot drink. We were soon rattling through the dense mist again.

'So he was stabbed, then dragged into the chair and the job was finished, do you think?' I said.

'Yes. Perhaps he walked in on the scene, struggled with the killer and was stabbed. Or, if he was close to Clammory, perhaps he was an intended victim. Remember that this killer wants someone close the victim to die as well. I suspect two killers in this instance, or one very strong one to drag the barber after stabbing him.'

'But you knew all this going in. We have learned nothing of use here from the Sister!'

'Not true, Watson. We have made progress! We know of a previous transgression on the part of the victim, a cowardly if not downright evil deed during the Boer War, for which Theodore Clammory's philanthropy seems to have been an attempt to make amends. That is the pattern exactly. And we confirmed the second death was someone the victim cared about.'

We rode for a few minutes in silence. I thought of the terrible tragedies that seemed to follow, one upon the other.

'The pattern, yes.' He sighed. 'Although no card. No Devil.'

'Are you sure, Holmes?'

'Lestrade was on this one. He was thorough. No card.'

We looked at each other.

'Bats, though,' I said.

'Pigeons,' said Holmes. 'Never start your theory with a zebra when a horse explains it all.'

'Except when on a case with Sherlock Holmes.'

He nodded.

'Bats,' I said.

We tried not to laugh.

CHAPTER 24

Fabric of Doubt

e entered the smoky, industrial Bermondsey area and immediately the acrid smell of leather tanning mixed with the burnt sugar odour of the Peak Freane biscuit bakery wove pungently through the fog to make our nostrils sting. Our next stop was the Benjamin Fabrics warehouse. There, James Benjamin and his wife Bertha had been found hanged, side by side, apparent suicides. Benjamin had been a leader in his industry, with almost a monopoly on a certain coveted type of chintz fabric. I had a vague image of ribbons and flowers, perhaps mentioned by my wife.

'Watson, this morning in the police files I read an interesting fact about Benjamin Fabrics,' said Holmes as our four-wheeler rattled through London. 'Some years ago, James Benjamin bought out two of his competitors, combining three companies into one larger one. A newspaper called this "gaining a stranglehold" on the production and distribution of this particular fabric.'

'Stranglehold? Well, that is certainly telling!'

'But there is more. One of the businesses he absorbed was that of his own brother, who subsequently hanged himself. Benjamin, a bachelor, then married his own brother's wife, whom he apparently coveted from the first. His business subsequently soared, though had a dip recently.'

'Well, there is the dark deed you seek, Holmes. For what type of philanthropy was this man known?' I wondered.

'His was not precisely a philanthropy, but he did set up a generous pension for his employees. This was lauded in the papers as a model business practice, which more companies should adopt.'

'A man of mixed, er, accomplishments.'

'As we seem to discover, Watson, each Luminarian's past transgression seems to connect rather poignantly to the method of their dispatch.'

'Here is a question, though, Holmes. If the Goodwins selected their honourees on the basis of dark secrets in their past, how did they, and then how did the perpetrator of these crimes, have this information?'

'An excellent question. Consider this. Those who are being recruited are invited to the parties. A large quantity of alcohol, *ganja* and perhaps other intoxicants are provided. From this, one can infer that indiscreet confidences might have been shared. The Goodwins are far more nuanced than they appear. Dark secrets may have been carefully elicited by them – remember that my brother has pointed

out their sophistication in politics. Assuming the killer starts with the Luminarian list, he then seeks out these buried stories of evil-doing.'

'Unless the killer is one of the Goodwins. I presume that is why you don't ask them?'

'For the moment, yes, Watson. But let me ask you something. Do you suspect them?'

'I would find it hard to believe.'

Holmes smiled but said nothing.

We arrived at our destination in Bermondsey. An enormous yellow-brick building loomed up out of the fog with the sign *Benjamin Fabrics* over the door. However, not only was it closed for business, but the doors were locked with chains and several padlocks, and the ground floor windows were boarded up.

We traversed the circumference of the building with no luck. At last, Holmes found in an adjacent close a side door that was neither boarded nor chained. He tried the handle, then sighed. 'Ah, Watson, we face defeat. I cannot pick a lock, hampered as I am.' He rattled the door impatiently with his good hand. 'I don't suppose you could . . . oh, of course not! You haven't a criminal bone in your body.'

'If you mean lock-picking, Holmes, you are correct, I could no sooner do that than rob a bank. However, step aside.'

Holmes looked at me quizzically. He moved aside and I gave the door a mighty kick. There was the sound of splintering wood and it gave way. But before we could enter, a tall, muscular man in filthy corduroy with hair like greasy straw rounded a corner at the end of the close and ran towards us.

'Wot you be wantin' here?' he shouted. As he reached us I noticed he was brandishing a cosh, with a look of menace on his pockmarked face.

I stepped in front of Holmes, raising my stick in a defensive pose. 'Stand down, man,' I said. 'We mean no harm.'

He shrugged, and after a moment sizing us up he lowered the cosh, staring at the broken door which now hung from its hinges. 'Cor, look what you done!' He looked down the close towards the main street, cupped a hand to his mouth and shouted, 'Police! Police!'

'There, there, good fellow! We are not thieves. I have urgent business here,' said Holmes. 'I have come to see about some fabrics.'

'So you kick down the door? Ain't you figured it out? We're closed.'

'But I have an appointment. Is there an office nearby?'

'The whole business is shut down. Nobody wants to buy nothing from a house of death. There ain't no appointments.'

'How would you know?'

'I'm the watchman. 'Til the family can sell this place,' the man said. He glanced down at the damage. 'You'll pay for that bloody door.'

'Give him cash, Watson,' Holmes said to me, then turned to the man. 'While my friend finds some change, do tell me, is the fabric still inside?'

'It is.'

'*Everything* is still inside?'

'I just told you, yes. The Benjamins killed theirselves in there. No one has set foot in since. And no one is going to.'

Next to me, I could feel Holmes tense in anticipation.

'Sir, my name is Mr Brahms. I am a fabric buyer. I don't care one whit about any "house of death". That is so much superstitious nonsense to my mind. I wager the new owners of this place would be furious if you turned away someone who could bail them out of the financial trough they now find themselves in.'

'I can't let no one in.'

'It can do no harm. Mendelssohn here and I know there are some chintz designs based on Chinoiserie that would suit our buyers down to the ground. Don't we, Felix?'

Felix Mendelssohn? I nodded, holding back a smile.

The man hesitated. 'You might be thieves.'

Holmes sighed. 'I say, sir! Do you really think that Mr Mendelssohn and I could hide huge bolts of fabric in our ulsters here and steal away with a fortune hidden on our persons? No! We shall simply look over the stock in order to make an offer to your employer. We may very well be interested in a large purchase, a very large purchase indeed, if the price is right.' Holmes pretended to rub his hands together in excitement as if thrilled at the thought of acquiring a quantity of fabric at an excellent price. It was a reasonable simulation, given that his left hand was immobile.

'Wot about this door, then?'

Holmes smiled at me, and I felt in my pocket for change. Finding some, I withdrew it and began to count it.

'Have you the keys?' asked Holmes of the man.

'Yes, but I ain't goin' in there.' He kept his eyes on the money.

'You do not need to. Felix, pay for the repair.'

I handed the man some coins. His face lit up and he pocketed them with pleasure. His tune changed instantly.

'There ain't no lights in there. They electrified, but the electricity is turned off.'

'No matter. We have our pocket lanterns with us. You have yours, Felix?'

I nodded. 'That I do.' I could not for the life of me remember Brahms's Christian name.

After a charitable donation of several more coins, the fellow volunteered to be our lookout. In a moment, we found ourselves alone in a vast, deserted warehouse. As predicted, there were no lights inside, and given the late hour and dense fog, the few windows in the building afforded little illumination. It was nearly pitch black.

'Brahms and Mendelssohn, Holmes?' I whispered as I fumbled in my ulster for my pocket lantern. Reaching for his own, Holmes chuckled, and I marvelled at his stamina and humour in the situation.

I lit our pocket lanterns. Mrs Hudson had been wise to remind us. Every sensible Londoner carried them on such treacherously foggy days. They had, on more than one occasion prevented our being run over by a carriage, and in one instance allowed us to find each other when we were separated in a terrifying chase through Regent's Park in complete obscurity.

'Hold them both, would you, Watson?' said Holmes, handing his to me.

'I shall go ahead of you, then. What are we looking for?'

'Stairs. The police report says the bodies were found up on the second floor. I am hoping everything has been left undisturbed.' We spent some minutes peering around the ground floor, through large storage and packing-rooms, and a warren of offices and hallways, lit only by our dim little devices which I held in front of me. But at last we found the stairs, ascended to the second floor and arrived in a long hallway.

'Now where, Holmes?' I paused, with both lanterns aloft.

'Hurry, Watson, before that fellow outside changes his mind. We are looking for the owner's office, and a small showroom just off it. Turn left, here. I have the photographs of the crime scene with me and a vivid image of the police report stored right here.' He tapped his forehead.

We made our way carefully, eventually finding the darkened office and a door leading to the showroom. The moment we entered, and before our pocket lanterns could reveal anything, the pale reek of death hit my nostrils. It was faint. The couple had died here nearly a month ago, and yet the unmistakable odour was there.

I held up the lanterns up, casting a dim light on the entire room.

'Ha!' cried Holmes, grabbing one of the lanterns from my hand.

My breath caught. There were two nooses, bizarrely fashioned from strips of bright floral chintz, hanging in the centre of the room. Each had been slashed, presumably to free the bodies, but remained grotesquely in place. I lowered the lanterns slightly, and there, beneath the nooses were two wooden chairs, lying on their sides. The Benjamins had hanged to death here, side by side.

'We are in luck! The scene is intact, or nearly so. I shall be able to determine if this was suicide or murder!' Holmes was beside himself with delight, shining his lantern around the room.

My own reaction was revulsion. The incongruous cheer of the loops of fabric hung from the ceiling, their pattern of bright pink and red roses, with blue ribbons dancing across a white background, made the improvised nooses all the more sinister. In the dim lights of our lamps, these strange instruments of death gave a macabre and horrifying aspect, as though a child's party had been transmuted into a dire tragedy.

'All right, Watson,' said Holmes cheerfully. 'The police concluded suicide, or at least did so officially. Apparently despondent over declining profits and pushed to the brink by a deal gone wrong, this couple supposedly did away with themselves after a client cancelled a large order.'

'Something does not feel right about this,' I said.

Holmes laughed. 'Ha, Watson! You are a master of understatement. Death by chintz! No, of course it does not feel right. We are remarkably fortunate that little has been touched. Superstition has for once worked in our favour.' Holmes's enthusiasm could occasionally feel quite out of place.

'Here, take my lantern again and follow me with both our lights, Watson. This injury is inconvenient.'

'Of course, Holmes.' I took his lantern and held both near him.

He looked about him in the gloom. 'Now, let us see if we can reconstruct what happened here.'

He approached the two nooses and examined them. 'Hold the lights closer, please.'

I hesitated.

'What are you standing there for, Watson? You have been at a murder scene before. You look transfixed.'

'Sorry, Holmes. It is just . . . this fabric. Our new kitchen curtains are exactly—'

'Put your mind on the problem, Watson! Hold the light here.'

I did so and he carefully looked over each noose in detail. It was now after four in the afternoon, and we had been going since early this morning with nothing more than coffee and a hot chocolate. His stamina was legendary, especially when on the trail, but as I have mentioned elsewhere, I had not the professional enthusiasm he had, and I had grown hungry and tired.

But not so Holmes. Energized, he proceeded to examine the room in great detail. I followed him with the lanterns, in and around bolts of fabric, thumbing through sample books, peering closely along the window ledges, down on the floor to peer at the floorboards, even into the cracks between the floorboards.

He next inspected the upended chairs – and two comfortable upholstered chairs sitting on an expensive-looking small rug, evidently where clients were seated and shown samples of the costly wares.

Between these two chairs was a small table on which rested two empty coffee cups and a pewter plate of biscuits. I held one of the lanterns close to the plate.

'Interesting! Every biscuit is broken,' said Holmes.

Holmes continued his examination. I followed him around the room a second time, as he moved in fits and starts, examining and re-examining walls, pattern books, an ashtray, the rug – wordlessly, but with the small murmurs and exclamations which so often accompanied the process.

Holmes returned to the small table twice. Finally, he stood still in the centre of the room, below the nooses, thinking. I waited patiently. At last, he spoke.

'Well, it is clearly as I expected, Watson. Murder. All the signs are here. Two people committed the murder – one very large, the other possibly smaller, but I am not certain of that. The footprints are scarce, the carpet is barren, and the police have trampled through here with their usual lack of discretion.

'However, I have a fairly clear picture of what transpired. The nooses were fashioned from an available bolt of fabric, in no hurry, and they were cut to size and the remnant of the bolt stashed behind these others here. If Mr Benjamin had created the nooses, why would he hide the original bolt of fabric like this? No, it was done in secret, and then the nooses themselves were hidden in a handier spot over here – see the scrap of selvedge lying here, and the corresponding missing bit on this noose? – and then the nooses were brought out. I am thinking they may have been presented, presumably for dramatic effect.'

'Dramatic effect?'

'Yes. Whoever is committing these Alphabet Killings has made certain the victims suffer. Imagine watching these nooses go up, knowing your fate was sealed.'

'Cruel, then.'

'Our perpetrator is fuelled by rage yet behaves in a very calculated manner. Next, two chairs were placed under the nooses. Mr Benjamin was ordered up onto the chair and went willingly, and there the noose was placed around his neck. There was no sign of a struggle in or around his chair.'

'Why on earth, Holmes? Why would he not struggle?'

'There are three possibilities, Watson. One, he did not believe the perpetrators would go through with the act. This is possible but unlikely. Two, they could have held a gun to him, and he feared death by gunshot over hanging.'

'Hmm. That would not have been my choice,' I remarked, even remembering the gunshot wounds I received in my army days. Hanging, I understood, was exceedingly painful.

'May you never have to make such a choice. The third possibility, and perhaps the most likely, is that he was told his wife would be spared if he cooperated. He was sadly wrong.'

Holmes moved to stand by the upended chair on the right. I shifted the lights to remain near him.

'Mrs Benjamin was second to die. She entered the room with a tray of refreshments. Upon entering, she saw her husband, either standing on the chair or, more likely by then, dangling dead from the noose.'

'Why more likely?'

'Because there was no sign of a struggle on the chair which held Mr Benjamin. If he had watched what happened next, that would not have been the case.'

Holmes walked to the door and I followed.

'She then dropped her tray of refreshments here by the door, and was seized, dragged into position, and forcibly put into place, while kicking. There are marks here, by the door, and—' he dashed back to the chair – 'over here, on her chair. A handkerchief was inserted as a gag in her mouth. You can see, it is clearly on the floor near her body in the photograph provided by Lestrade. Her chair was then knocked away, and she was hanged to death next to her husband.'

I took the lights and moved to the desk, where I glanced down at the police photographs, which Holmes had laid there. 'Yes, I see.'

'The murderers retrieved the refreshment tray and put all back on it, except of course for the coffee which had spilled over there by the door. I found traces in the cracks between the floorboards, although the killers had attempted to clean it up. They placed these items on the table where they would have been put for the visitors.' He moved to the table and I joined him there.

'The fact that all of the biscuits are broken is further proof that the plate was dropped.'

'Why would they set all this up?'

'It is obvious, Watson. To make the investigators think that the visitors had come for their scheduled viewing and had departed before Benjamin and his wife supposedly committed suicide. The police report states that there was no coffee in the pot although they drew no conclusions from this. It was empty, of course, because it was spilled near the door, and the visitors – our murderers no doubt – were not interested in refreshments. They were merely interested in getting on with the business that brought them here. The biscuits are broken, too, for having fallen near the door.'

'Interesting,' I said.

'The police report also remarked that there was a large order for fabric on the desk here, with the word "cancelled" written across it.'

'It is not there now.'

'Very good, Watson. It was removed as evidence. Lestrade noted that it was written in a hand which did not match Benjamin's or his wife's, but this observation was disregarded. The leading investigator felt this proved that the last visitors had cancelled their order, and then left, thus giving the Benjamins a reason to commit suicide.'

'It was definitely murder then,' I said, in awe at my friend's remarkable abilities of observation and deduction. Although at this stage in our friendship, this really should not have surprised me at all.

'Yes. Now if only I could tie this in absolutely with our series. It is likely, it is promising . . . but it is not certain. And we must be certain, Watson.'

'What would consist of proof to you, Holmes?

He paused. He crossed to the visitors' chairs and stood by the small table.

'Proof that the Devil has come for his due?' said he, turning towards me with a smile. I followed him there with our lights.

He lifted the tray and picked up something from underneath. It was the back of a card with a blue filigreed design. He turned it over. In the feeble light of our pocket lanterns, the familiar figure on the card seemed to dance and wiggle, mocking us as we stared at it.

'This will do,' he said with a smile.

It was, of course, The Devil.

CHAPTER 25

Deep Waters

he fog had thinned at last but darkness had fallen when we left the Benjamin Factory Warehouse. Cabs were scarce in dingy Bermondsey, but I managed at last to secure us a rickety hansom, which lacked the usual blanket, and we headed for Baker Street. It was a long, icy ride north and west, and my friend retreated into a state of contemplation, his eyes closed. I shivered throughout the ride, willing our driver to find the shortest route.

We arrived soaked and freezing, and Mrs Hudson greeted us with relief at the door. 'Two notes came for you, Mr Holmes,' said she. 'The fire is lit and I've some food for you upstairs, Doctor. I'll bring up some tea. See that he eats, will you?'

But Holmes had already bounded up the stairs to our sitting-room. I thanked our landlady and followed, finding him still in his wet coat, tearing open the first note.

'From our toxicologist, Watson! Ah, yes! He reports on what he found in the ammoniaphone. Hmm . . . "A rare substance," he writes, "which I believe to be a biologically derived toxin, possibly marine, powdered . . . chemical analysis indicates an extreme vasoconstrictor . . . could easily cause instant cardiac failure." Clearly the cause of death, then. He adds that it is not unlike a Hawaiian poison of mythic legend he once encountered.' Holmes set down the note. 'Interesting. Possibly marine. The sea? A sailor? Or more likely someone with prodigious research skills.'

He closed his eyes, lost in thought. I hung up my own dripping coat and gently eased him from his. I was shaking with the cold and could not wait to get warm.

'Sit down by the fire and dry off, Holmes. Doctor's advice!' He ignored me and began to pace the room, thinking. I sat close to the hearth and leaned into the warmth, trying to rub feeling back into my numb hands.

'This poison, Holmes. The Goodwins had a collection of seafaring items in their study,' I remarked. 'Some relative of theirs. An explorer, I believe.'

'Go on.'

'That is all, really, Holmes. I know no more. They had a harpoon, a sextant. A brass diver's casque.'

'They said nothing more of the man?' asked Holmes. 'Were they close to him? What relation?'

'A distant uncle, I think. And this relative was lost some time ago.' I then espied the roast joint on the sideboard. My stomach growled. 'Oh, and James said he was more of a Jules Verne man, himself.'

'Hmm,' said Holmes. He ripped open the second note.

I applied myself to making two thick sandwiches. 'Verne is a bit fanciful for my taste.' I put one of the sandwiches on a plate and handed it to him. 'Eat something, Holmes.' He ignored me and read the second note.

'Good news! The Goodwins are en route to the South of France. I urged them to take themselves far away for a time. If they are the "G" on the list, they will be safe.'

'And if they are involved, Holmes?'

'Ah, you suspect them now, Watson? If they are involved, then the killings will stop. Now . . . let me jot some notes from the day.'

Immediately he set to writing on the blackboard in a fury, the *rat-a-tat-tat* of the chalk like an angry woodpecker. At the force of this onslaught, and without his second hand free to steady it, the blackboard began to move around the room, Holmes following it with feverish concentration.

I knew better than to laugh at this curious dance, so I got up, found the brick from the night before and positioned it like a kind of doorstop at the base of the blackboard, keeping it from escaping his aggressive ministrations.

Holmes remained facing his blackboard as I remarked, 'What of Lady Gainsborough's husband? The naturalist. The poison?'

'I have already thought of that.'

'Of course, Gainsborough was dead before Enrietti's murder.' I added, setting a sandwich on a table near him. He said nothing.

'What about—'

'Watson, I do not require help thinking!'

He continued in silence for a while.

Finally, I could not resist. 'You have sent the Goodwins away. Will they stay, do you think?' They did not seem the type to scare off easily.

'One hopes. Mycroft will have added his voice – oh, why have we not heard back from my brother?'

I shrugged and started in on my sandwich like a schoolboy who had been left at school over the Christmas holidays. Holmes left his untouched. He remained at the blackboard for some minutes, then at last collapsed into a chair opposite me. He looked dangerously fatigued.

'Holmes, there is one ray of light. There have been no bombs detonated in London today. Did you not say there had been one planned for Borough Market? You and Vidocq have managed to avert that, at least. Take heart, Holmes, you have most likely managed to save lives with that information.'

'At least we know that Vidocq followed through in informing Mycroft.' He paused. 'Therefore Mycroft is likely to be still in London.'

'You were expecting to hear from him?'

'Yes.' Holmes leaned in to the fire, finally aware that he was still cold and wet. He struggled with his jacket and I took it from him and helped him into his dressing gown.

'Is that unusual?'

He nodded, staring into the flames. Mrs Hudson entered with tea.

'Nothing else came, Mrs Hudson?' asked Holmes. 'Billy is not back?'

'No, and no. You would hear of it from me,' said she. 'Now eat and drink something. It is inconsiderate of you to make Dr Watson and me worry about you like a child who doesn't know to come in from the rain.' Holmes looked up at her in surprise. She departed with a look of remonstrance.

'I have been duly scolded,' said he with a smile.

'She has a point, Holmes. Take a care.'

Holmes considered his sandwich, thought better about it, and took a sip of tea.

'It is time I brought up my concerns about Mycroft,' I ventured.

'What concerns?'

'Well, I am not always convinced he has your best interests at heart.'

'Why should he? He has more important things on his mind, Watson.'

'You noticed that the Goodwins do not feel entirely comfortable about him,' I added.

'Nor I about them. But, Watson, my brother is not an easy man. He does not *care* if one feels comfortable around him. Do not distract me with this fuzzy thinking.'

Just then, Heffie burst into our sitting-room in a shower of wet garments and youthful enthusiasm. She was ready to report to Holmes what she had found out about Judith in following her throughout the day.

'Hungry?' I interrupted. 'Sandwich?'

'Oh yes, please!' In a moment she was eating with gusto, to Holmes's considerable annoyance. He wanted her report immediately.

She gamely complied, put down her sandwich, and began.

'I picked up 'er trail easy enough from one of 'er regular customers. I followed 'er all today, like you asked, Mr 'olmes. That fog! She easily found a new kip not too far from me. She was sometimes doing jobs for a fellow in Holborn.'

'What kind of jobs? What fellow? Man named Fardwinkle, by chance?'

'No, not him, but one like 'im. Errands. Procurement. Small change.'

'Quick work, Heffie, excellent!' said Holmes. 'But what else have you learned?'

'She's a girl 'o many ideas,' said Heffie. ''Course, you got to be, in a position like we is.'

'But she is not in your position,' said Holmes, kindly. 'Judith was being educated and groomed for service, was she not? With promise of a good posting?'

'Charity is all well an' good, Mr 'olmes, if you looks close at the person you is tryin' to 'elp. She ain't doin' nothing of the sort, not Judith. In service? She'd sooner slit yer throat. She got scams all over town. Gotta admire 'er in a certain way. She's a good l'il actress, she is.'

'Perhaps the stage would a better career path for her,' I said.

'Where is she now?' demanded Holmes.

'I dunno. She gimme the slip late today. 'Ard to do. The girl is good.' Heffie at last took another big bite of her sandwich.

'*Where* did she give you the slip?'

She held up a hand, chewing.

'Let her eat, Holmes!'

'Shmiplolia.'

'What?'

She swallowed. 'Fitzrovia.'

'Fitzrovia! Where exactly?'

'Charlotte Street.'

Where Victor Richard's shop was. At the epicentre, or so Holmes described, of the French anarchist community.

Holmes considered this. 'French,' said he.

'What about French?' I asked.

'Lady Eleanor mentioned the girl speaks French! Heffie, did anything political come up in your conversation with Judith? Bombs? Anarchists? Anything like that?'

'No,' said Heffie. 'And she don' seem the type.'

'Why?'

'She . . . she's jus' about money. Money and 'erself. Those blokes – ain't they got bigger fish to fry?'

'Yes, I would imagine her interests are entirely pragmatic. But one never knows.'

'Wot's "pragmatic"? asked Heffie.

'Practical.'

'Right. That's 'er.'

'Heffie, you have done an admirable job. Carry on, would you, please? Rest downstairs again tonight and see if you cannot pick up the trail tomorrow. And keep me informed of Judith's whereabouts and anything you can learn of her. I will find you a job with the police one day, young lady, I promise.' Holmes took a note from his desk – I did not see how much – and handed it to the girl. Her eyebrows shot up in surprise at the amount. She grinned and stuffed it down the front of her dress.

Billy appeared in the doorway, looking chagrined and unhappy. I furnished him with a sandwich and he held it in one tight fist, while reporting that after doing the errands for Holmes, he had tried to look for Mycroft Holmes, but he was neither at home, nor the Diogenes, nor Whitehall. There was no trace of him and no one knew where he was. Heffie, who had leaned up against a bookcase and took all this in, said, 'Let me look for 'im, Mr 'olmes. I might 'ave some better luck.'

'No, Heffie, please continue with Judith for now. I am not yet worried about my brother. Now, go and get some rest.'

Once both young helpers were gone, he closed the door. 'Judith!' he exclaimed. 'Working the dark side of the street, even as she studied for a place in a rich man's home. Oh, what mischief she could do there!' He shook his head ruefully. 'I am afraid that Lady Eleanor's hope for her *protégé* is ill-founded. Judith is far beyond rehabilition, I think. And well mixed up in this case.'

Just then Mrs Hudson knocked and delivered us a package.'

Mrs Hudson,' said Holmes, 'you don't mind having Miss O'Malley again tonight in your spare room? I am sorry to impose.' She nodded, and with a brusque thank-you, Holmes closed the door on her quickly.

Not to be deterred, Mrs Hudson opened it right back

up again. 'Get him to rest, Doctor,' she said, and closed the door again.

Holmes tore open the strings of the package. A thick batch of newspaper clippings, photographs, lists and maps fell out. 'Mr Clifford Smith-Naimark has delivered! Information on all the victims so far. A clue, perhaps *the* clue, could be somewhere in these papers.'

'Can it not wait 'til morning? You need to rest.'

'No, Watson, I need to be three people! There are so many threads in this case. I must make notes from what we learned today . . . and then tackle these files.'

He took the pile to a small table next to his blackboard, angled a light upon it, and began his work.

I lingered there for another half hour, drinking a small whisky to calm my nerves. Then, seeing that he was occupied in a manner I knew only too well, and which could last for hours if not the entire night, I rose to go to bed.

'Good night, Holmes. Do not strain, my friend. This case is a marathon, not a sprint.'

'Wrong metaphor, Watson. It is an ocean. And these are very deep waters. '

I did not know then how dark and deep those currents would become – and in only a few short hours.

CHAPTER 26

Into the Mud

awoke to Holmes standing over me in bed, a lamp in one hand and excitement lighting up his features. 'Hurry!' he cried, shaking me by the shoulder. 'Get dressed. Warm clothing. We must leave in five minutes!'

'What . . . what time is it?'

'Four a.m. We must make low tide.'

'Tide? Where? Holmes, I have had barely five hours of sleep!'

'The Isle of Dogs. Get up!'

Ten minutes later, we were racing east in a cab. The weather was chill and grey, but minus the killing fog of yesterday. Dressed in the warmest clothes I had with me, at Holmes's urging I had also donned an old pair of Wellington boots pulled down from the attic. My own pair had moved with me to Paddington, but Holmes had a spare pair – too big for me, but serviceable. We were going to the foreshore of the Thames, some distance away.

Along the way, Holmes explained that we would be following up on the Anson murder. Long before inexplicably seeming to have drowned in his bed, Horatio Anson had been a titan of shipbuilding during the lucrative years of the '50s and '60s, his shipyard situated on the Isle of Dogs. The next slip over from Anson Shipbuilders had belonged to a rival's company, which Anson acquired in a less than friendly move.

Our cab became ensnared behind an accident involving two omnibuses, and the alternate route chosen by our driver was blocked by construction of a new set of mansion flats. Even our London cabbie had trouble moving us towards our destination. Holmes was vibrating with impatience, checking his watch again and again. The Portland Road underground train station was visible just ahead. 'Quick, Watson, the train!' cried Holmes, and in a moment we were in the bowels of the earth, rattling east towards Wapping.

I rarely travelled underground, preferring to walk. For Holmes, it was always a cab, night or day, and cabs were a luxury to which I had quickly become accustomed during my time with him. He only used the underground rail when, like today, time was of the essence.

As we steamed forward through the tunnel, I commented that I had heard that a new electric train would be soon travelling from the City to Stockwell. It would surely be more hospitable than the sweaty, noisy carriage in which we now found ourselves. Perhaps faster. Certainly quieter.

Holmes said nothing but pulled out a map drawn in pencil and consulted it.

'What exactly leads us to this precise location today, Holmes?' I asked.

'Our letter "A" and Anson's profitable shipbuilding company. The rival he destroyed, Thomas Linville, had the adjacent river slip. If I am correct, we will learn something important today.' He took out his watch. 'If we make it in time.'

'Or do not drown,' I said, only half joking. In fact, drowning was only one danger of immersion in the Thames. The river was so polluted from sewage and industrial waste that few who fell into the stew ever again enjoyed full health, if they were not poisoned outright.

'Horatio Anson had mud in his airways when he was dried off, put into nightclothes, and placed into his bed, already dead from drowning. Fortunately, the autopsy on Anson was conducted by Chester Wilson, a rare man of real science. Wilson examined the mud samples from Anson's airways under a microscope. The particular pollution and the diatoms were consistent with the Thames.'

'How did Anson ruin his rival?' I asked.

'He didn't just ruin Thomas Linville: Anson "capsized him", said the papers. In 1864, Linville had just completed his masterwork, a magnificent, 500-ton iron steamboat, the *Queen of Egypt*. The night before her maiden voyage, a bomb detonated onboard and she sank into the Thames, taking eight souls with her. The bomber was never discovered. This effectively sank Linville's company. His shipworks were sold two months later to his neighbour and rival, Horatio Anson.'

'I see. Was Anson not a suspect at the time?'

Holmes shrugged. 'Some papers theorized that he had sunk his rival, but no charges were brought.'

From Wapping, we took a cab east. The morning sun was just coming up, forcing us to squint into the cold light. We picked our way down through grimy Limehouse and into Millwall, through dank and muddy streets, with dark cottages set among looming factories. Icy scum and mud lined the roads in heaping piles. I thanked heaven for the fickle London weather, and no dense fog today. As we neared our destination, the scent – a heavy oily mix of burning fat, chemical smoke and metallic vapours – filled our nostrils and was to make our next foray a living nightmare.

We arrived near to our destination, but then it took several minutes to find our way past a warren of warehouses, dreary industrial structures and the Ferry House Pub at last to an entry point at the end of Ferry Street. The Thames shore was not accessible everywhere, but there were alleys and a few unlocked gates that were known to sailors, dockworkers, mudlarks . . . and Sherlock Holmes.

We slipped through a narrow passage and a creaking wooden gate, taking steep stairs down to the shore itself, visible only at the lowest of tides.

The bottom half of the stairs was normally under water, and those steps were coated with slime. Even in the Wellingtons with their ridged soles, it was treacherous going.

Three steps from the shoreline, I slipped and landed heavily on the bottom step, painfully bruising my tailbone.

We found ourselves on the cluttered shore, comprising a broad strip of greyish brown sludge next to the lapping water of low tide, and above that, mounds of what were, essentially, centuries of refuse.

Holmes had a pencilled map in hand, showing the locations of Anson and Linville's shipyards. He headed off westwards, the shore curving steeply around to the right.

Already, the Thames was lapping in and out, wetting a wide expanse of the mud, rubble and boards. I had never been this close to the water before and was surprised at the sheer volume of detritus, pieces of cement, old iron rope and bolts, screws, broken bricks, shards of pottery and glass, timber and rocks. Whether one walked on the mounds of rubble or close to the water through viscous mud, either way, the footing was precarious.

We began on the ooze, our feet sinking in an inch or more, the muck gripping like a live thing. Memories of the Grimpen Mire came to my mind. Holmes glanced at me. 'Don't worry, Watson, there is no quicksand here,' said he.

As we picked our way forwards, he continued to relate the Horatio Anson saga. 'I read last night in the clippings that in the '60s this area was filled with shipbuilders, mostly gone now. Anson and a man named Thomas Linville were at the top, in heated competition. But Anson was responsible not only for "capsizing his rival". Shortly afterwards, Linville hanged himself, leaving a wife and three children destitute.'

I stumbled in the mud. 'Can we not move to drier ground, Holmes?'

'It will be harder going, but very well. Hurry, Watson.'

We moved farther from the water up onto the mounds of debris. He was right, of course. Sharp rubble, shards of glass, iron scraps and shells made for terribly uneven footing.

'What happened to the surviving Linvilles?' I asked.

'It is a sad tale. After the father, the mother committed suicide. There were two young children who were sent to London to live with two different sets of family friends. A third, a boy, was away at University, and I read that he also killed himself.'

I found it necessary to keep my eyes on my feet. Holmes's ill-fitting boots made navigating this rough terrain even more difficult.

'One tragedy after another,' I said. 'Horatio Anson's story certainly fits the Luminarian pattern of past dark deeds, then,' I said. 'If indeed he killed off his rival's business.'

The sound of children's voices floated across the river and I looked up to see, directly across from us on the opposite bank, several filthy children raking through mud and debris. An older man moved among them, his harsh voice issuing commands, though I could not make out his words. He struck one small child, who tumbled forward into the mud, then rolled free and dodged a second blow. The boy reached into his pocket and handed something to his abuser.

Mudlarks! In search of anything saleable – old coins,

bits of chainmail, intact pottery or silver, building material, even on occasion pieces of jewellery. In addition to the foul air, the shore itself stank – dank, fishy and vaguely dirty – and I imagined life spent searching here every day. The city was full of low-level scams and dark trade just beneath the surface of the bustling metropolis.

I looked up and Holmes had moved out of sight around the sharp bend of the shoreline. 'Hurry, Watson!' His voice floated back to me over the sounds of the rushing Thames, the horns of barges, metallic clanking of chains and the dull roar of nearby factories.

I stepped back onto the mud. My feet sunk up to my ankles, and the viscous stuff pulled with considerable force. There was now an inch of water covering the mud. Was the tide coming in?

I struggled after Holmes. As I rounded another bend, a new pungent and sickening smell wafted down the river. I sneezed and moved my scarf to cover my nose. 'What is that odour?' I exclaimed, as I arrived at Holmes's side, half fearful of coming upon some giant beached and rotting sea creature.

'The slaughterhouse, Watson. It is right over there.' He pointed across the river to an enormous structure slightly upwind of us. Even from here, I could hear the lowing of cattle and the occasional loud bray. I shuddered.

Feeling suddenly cold around the ankles, I looked down. The water had risen a good two inches! As it receded, something bright and golden caught my eye. I bent down to pick it up. It was a perfectly preserved ancient gold coin.

As a boy, I had been fascinated with old coins. I looked at it closely. A treasure! King Charles I, was my guess.

'Holmes,' I exclaimed. 'Look! This is over two hundred years old!'

But he was once again out of sight around the next bend.

'Watson!' His voice was high pitched, excited. I pocketed the coin and plunged forward.

Holmes was squatting down on a long, slick set of flattened boards up near the brick walls, peering at something closely with his magnifying glass. The boards slanted down to the water and once formed the slips to which the ships were moored. The wind had come up and it blew his ulster wildly around his thin, wiry body. Above him were the much worn and nearly illegible words, 'Anson Shipbuilders'. Other than large yellow brick buildings above us, once workshops and foundries, there was not much left but these few ghostly reminders of once-bustling shipyards.

Along the defunct slip were remnants of long pieces of iron rope made of threads sturdy enough to hold vessels in against the strong current, and there, under the shiny moss-covered wall, was something that had set Sherlock Holmes on fire.

'What is it, Holmes?'

'Look!'

Embedded in the long parallel slats of wood were disused iron rings and other rusted fittings. Holmes was bent over a set of these rings, examining scratches on them with a feverish excitement.

'Horatio Anson was chained alive to these rings right

here,' said Holmes. 'See how the rust is worn away. Something metal abraded the surface. Handcuffs, I'll warrant!'

I moved closer to see. Next to these iron rings were shallower scratches on the wood. They were light in colour, contrasting to the worn timbers into which they had been scored. Holmes pointed to these. 'His left hand, look! Scratches on the wood as he struggled.'

He rose and moved excitedly several feet towards the water. 'And down here, his feet were fastened! This piece of rope is not old at all. New, in fact. And see these dents where his feet beat against the boards as he thrashed about.'

The horror of this death struck me. Imagine being chained down to the ruins of your once thriving business, the exact location where you had destroyed your rival. Helpless, pinioned, as the filthy tide came in. My God, the sheer terror.

I glanced across the river. The mudlarks and their keeper, who had been there moments ago, had vanished. The mud flat where they had been standing was now a shining pool of water.

Water sloshed around my feet, then receded. We were up against a twenty-foot high brick wall. I looked up and noticed the waterline in the bricks – at least ten feet above our heads! It was a sheer seawall, and we had nothing to climb out with, nothing to grab onto.

The water washed in again. Was it higher?

'Holmes . . .' I said. Could he have got the time wrong?

But he was oblivious, bending over a piece of wood embedded in concrete.

'Look here!' He pointed to an adjacent board. There, in very rough scratches, were the letters, "L–I–N–I".'

Another, stronger wave washed in, definitely up to my ankles now, covering the letters.

'Blast!' said he, standing up. '"L–I–N–I" – I think he did not have time to write the V. Anson must have been trying to write "Linville". This is it, Watson, this is what we needed!'

'Holmes! The tide!'

He looked up, distracted. 'So soon?' He wiped his hand on his coat and pulled out his watch. He looked straight at me.

'My watch has stopped. What time do you have, Watson?'

'I left my watch at Baker Street!' I had not wanted to lose two on this case.

He stared at me for a moment, then back at the way we had come.

I heard the sound of horns coming from the river. The water was now washing up to our ankles and lower calves, then not fully receding, leaving us sloshing through a couple inches of water.

We looked at each other again.

'Run!' Holmes shouted, and took off back the way we came.

The curve of the shoreline being so extreme, we could not see ahead of us to our entry point but had to merely plunge forward. I had the impression we had come rather a long way. Holmes, with his long legs and boots that fit, easily outpaced me, and I started to fall behind. Then my foot caught under a board, one of the slips. A wave rushed in with such force that it nearly knocked me down, twisting my leg and causing my ankle to jam under the board, catching there and holding me fast. The wave receded, but I could not pull my foot free.

Holmes was ahead of me by a good twenty yards. 'I see the stairs!' he shouted.

I pulled sharply again, to no effect. Shifting position on the slippery mud, I struggled, but my foot was firmly stuck. The next wave came in and knocked me to my knees, wetting my clothing up to the thighs. I tried in vain to free my foot. Another wave and I could go under!

Holmes saw me now.

I just glimpsed him racing towards me when the next wave hit. I was knocked over but managed to keep my head above water. This time, the water did not recede. It was now about two feet deep.

The smell was horrific. Raw sewage. Dead fish. Oil. Industrial waste. If my head went under, all would be lost. The cold was numbing. The thought of drowning amongst this rubbish in the filth of the Thames filled me with terror. I looked out across the river. A wall of water. Rising.

One strong hand was suddenly under my arm. The tide ebbed, just for a moment, and Holmes knelt down. His good hand gripped my trapped ankle hard, and he twisted and yanked. I cried out, and the boot slipped off my foot. I was freed, but one foot was bare.

The next wave came in, this one stronger. We clung together, feet spread wide for balance, and still it nearly knocked us down.

We would clearly never make it back to our entry point. And now I had only one boot. Cutting my feet on the iron filings and sharp stones could prove fatal. Holmes squatted down. 'Climb onto my back!' he cried.

I was shorter than my friend, but not small, and my compact physique was solid. I was unsure if he could carry me.

'No, run! Save yourself, Holmes!' I cried.

'I'm not leaving you here.' He hunched down, his back to me. 'Get on. Now. Or we both die!'

There was no time to debate. I climbed up onto his back. He staggered upright and moved towards the wall nearest to us.

Another wave came in and rocked him. It was up to his upper thighs now, and mine as well. It was all he could manage not to be swept out with it.

The steps were in sight but a good thirty yards away. The water already covered the bottom two. We would never make it.

The next swell knocked us against the wall. Here, at least, was a series of iron rings. Holmes grasped the nearest with his good hand. I reached out and grabbed one as well. It was just in time, for the force of the next swell would have knocked us both off our feet.

I slipped off his back and clung to the ring. Above were several more.

'Climb, Watson, and get help,' he cried, unable to do so himself with only one functional hand. I clambered up the rings towards the embankment, then looked up. Two weather-beaten faces peered down at us.

'Landlubber,' said one, in disgust. A looped rope dropped down within reach.

We were saved.

Some fifteen minutes later, we sat near the fire of the Ferry House Pub, facing an old sailor named Nash, a near-toothless character with mahogany-coloured skin, tiny bloodshot blue eyes, and a lopsided grin. 'I seen you two go down,' said he, 'and I kept track of the time. When you didn't return fifteen minutes ago, I figured you for a couple of fools. But you ain't mudlarks, you're dressed too nice for that.'

Holmes and I exchanged a look. We were a bit dandified for mudlarks.

'Ever' so often, me and Jamie see some go down – kids for fun, boys showin' off for a young lady. They don't all come back. Keeps me haunted, an' I vowed to keep watch for fools like you. Though Jamie don't agree. He says it's "natural selection", like Darwin. "Stupid deserves to drown," sez 'e. I don't think that way.'

'Ever see anyone come out carrying a body?' asked Holmes. 'In the night, probably?'

The old sailor shook his head. 'I stops lookin' come nightfall. People down there after dark are generally up to no good. They can fend for themselves.'

Holmes said nothing but before we left, he took down the man's name and address. 'Expect a thank-you from me,' he said to Nash.

As we exited the Ferry House, me limping with a single

boot, it started to pour. At this point, anything to rinse us off was a blessing. It took us thirty minutes to find a cab dirty enough to allow two Thames-soaked, reeking travellers to climb aboard. Even then, the cabbie made us sit on a blanket that looked like it had been trailing through the streets for weeks.

Upon our return to 221B, I was never so happy for a hot bath in all my life. Holmes went first, at my insistence, but at last I lay comfortably soaking in the warm water of Holmes's newly installed bathtub off the main hall. My peace was broken by a sudden exclamation from Holmes in the next room. 'Idiot!'

Before I could guess at this, he burst into the bathroom in his dressing gown, face flushed. He was holding a letter from Oliver Flynn.

'Holmes!' I protested. 'Hand me a towel!'

He did so, and I flung it over myself in a vain attempt at dignity. It sank into the water, laying over me like a napkin that has fallen in the soup. But I was not ready to exit my bath. Not after our recent escapade.

'Listen to this,' he roared. 'This fool! Oliver Flynn writes back to me. In person, he knows me as a French artist named Pierre Vernet.'

'What?'

'Later. But I wrote to the esteemed Mr Flynn *as myself* – Sherlock Holmes – warning him of danger and suggesting he decamp to Paris until the Luminarian case is resolved. This is his reply!'

'Go on,' I said.

'"My dear Mr Holmes – While I've heard of you, of course, and your brother has similarly warned me of impending danger, I'm afraid my theatrical commitments, not to mention my theatrical life, make a sudden trip to Paris out of the question. If I reacted to all the dangerous 'lists' I am on, I would be forever 'on the lam', as the Americans say. Now, what fun is that? Please come to my party this evening as my guest."'

'Well, a word to the wise does not pertain,' I said. 'Will you go?'

'Sherlock Holmes will not go. But Pierre Vernet, who has been before, will.'

At my puzzled look, he explained. 'Pierre Vernet is one of my disguises – a French artist with anarchist leanings. I will go tonight as Vernet. Will you join me, Watson?'

'Of course, Holmes. If I can only finish my bath. And perhaps get a little rest?'

Holmes looked up, having forgotten entirely that he had barged in on my bath.

'Oh, I am terribly sorry. Yes, a rest. We will discuss this more later.' He got up and started out of the room.

I began to move my towel, but replaced it again when he popped back in.

'Watson, we are stretched very thin on this case! I have sent Heffie off to track down my brother.'

'Good. Now give me a fresh towel and get out of here!' I said.

PART SIX

OUT OF THE FRYING PAN

'There are few things wholly evil, or wholly good.
Almost everything, especially of governmental policy,
is an inseparable compound of the two; so that our
best judgement of the preponderance between them
is continually demanded.'

—Abraham Lincoln

CHAPTER 27

Aesthetes and Anarchists

he London weather was as fickle as any young person only half in love, for it was now a clear night, icy, with stars twinkling in an inky sky. As our carriage rattled towards Chelsea and the Embankment home of Oliver Flynn, I girded myself for the unknown. Next to me in the carriage was a man I hardly recognized.

Holmes was attired in a costume I had never seen. With considerable help from me, he had donned an evening coat of black velvet, an alarming red brocade waistcoat with sparkling jet buttons, a cravat of blood red silk, and a red rose in his buttonhole. He managed to slip black kid gloves over his wired fingers, and added a perfect moustache courtesy of his theatrical kit. It looked as real as my own, though smaller and in the French style. Even his hair was somehow different, now loose and curling forward onto his forehead. Gold spectacles completed the transformation. Had I not assisted him in the preparation, I would never have taken 'Pierre Vernet, French artist' for Sherlock Holmes. Fortunately, he looked nothing like his other invention, 'Stephen Hollister'.

As Vernet's English doctor and friend, 'Hamish MacAllister', I was attending this party in more or less my own persona. As I am no actor, this was the best we could do. Holmes had suggested some small changes in my own appearance, in case Richard or either of his two men were there, although he thought they would probably not notice. I had combed my hair back and also wore some tinted theatre glasses which Holmes had on hand, and he darkened my eyebrows and hair with some of his theatre paints. A quick glance in the mirror and I did not even recognize myself! I felt silly, as though I was going to a fancy dress ball in the midst of a murder investigation. Which, in a sense, I was.

As our cab drove southward through the city, I brought up once again the subject of Holmes's elder brother. At this point, Holmes was more annoyed than worried at Mycroft's failure to communicate and at Billy's failure to turn up any trace of him.

'Sometimes, Holmes, I get the feeling that your brother is not playing fair with you. With *us*,' I said. 'Maybe, in some way, this is all a game to him.'

'Mycroft does not play games.'

'Have you considered the heavyset man in the carriage that nearly ran down Lady Eleanor after her husband's death? You can't tell me that Mycroft did not pass through your mind when she described him. Even the jowls!'

'Jowls? Don't be foolish. That describes half the men in England over forty! Sorry, Watson, I make light of your concern. Despite our differences, and despite whatever Machiavellian machinations my brother may engineer in service of the Empire, Mycroft is ultimately a man of integrity.'

I said nothing. Holmes glanced at me. 'Still not convinced, Watson? If Mycroft were behind this diabolical set of murders, he would be the last person anyone would suspect. The fact that you have thought of it is almost proof that he is not.'

A person can be blind where family is involved, I thought, but kept it to myself. And while there was clearly something dark between the brothers, Mycroft was family – Holmes's only family, as far as I knew.

Holmes was staring at me. He often seemed to read my mind.

'Family loyalty can be misplaced, Watson. We do not, after all, choose our family.'

'But we do choose our friends,' I said.

'We do, indeed. In my case, in the singular. I shall never believe ill of you, Watson.'

'Nor I, you.'

Holmes smiled. But there was a touch of sadness I could not interpret.

We pulled up to an elegant four-storey house on Flood Street near the river, overlooking the historic Apothecaries

Physic Garden, where medicinal plants had been grown for over two hundred years. While in medical school, I had once attended a rather drunken party there after midnight, with samplings better left undescribed. I had not thought of it since, and it now seemed a lifetime ago.

In short order, I was standing in exotic foreign territory, a place I never expected to be in all my life. The interior of the house was bright and artistic, an unusual mix of the conventional – ferns and overstuffed furniture – and the bohemian, with outré sculptures, a hookah, and Morris-style wallpaper in blues, greens and reds. Everywhere were colourful Impressionist paintings, theatre posters, and photographs of famous stage stars.

I never expected to find myself in the home of Oliver Flynn. The man had a remarkable reputation – one quarter literary genius, one quarter hedonist, one quarter Socialist, and one quarter family man, with a wife and two children. There had been scandalous rumours about his alternate romantic life, but those did not concern me. I was eager just to see this fascinating man in the flesh.

Our mission here was to convince Flynn to leave town with his family before suffering the fate of the Luminarians ahead of him on the list. And Holmes also hoped to uncover the dark secret that placed Flynn on the list.

We were welcomed and offered a choice of champagne or absinthe. Holmes was almost instantly enfolded into a knot of men that surrounded our host Oliver Flynn at one end of the room next to the fireplace. Left on my own, I more fully took in my fellow guests.

Around me were foreign creatures of all types and ages, and styles. The women, who mixed casually and individually with the men, were attired in what Holmes had explained to me en route was 'rational dress'. Espoused by the female artists, writers and progressives of the day, the style omitted corsetry, that bane of my generation's existence (and even worn by some men – though never me – for its 'character building properties'). Instead, the ladies glided from room to room in loose gowns of flowing linen, chiffon and silk, fresh flowers in their hair and encircling their wrists. Boldly savouring their champagne, they smoked cigarettes in ivory holders.

Some of their gowns had low *décolleté*, many were embroidered in exquisite handwork, and all were surprisingly flattering. It seemed that a bevy of Shakespeare's faerie queens had descended from their nightly escapades and had alighted at this gathering – faeries with strong political opinions. I found them exhilarating.

Despite the late hour, many young children, seemingly unattended, scurried throughout the party, snatching cakes from trays and playing hide-and-go-seek in and around the furniture. Their peals of laughter interrupted serious conversation, and one little girl returned again and again to a piano, banging on it until gently removed by a beautiful Titania – only to repeat the action a few minutes later.

The men were a curiously mixed lot, young and old – dandies, theatrical types, rough-hewn workers, intellectuals, and a few conservative professionals. I stood alone at a table of refreshments where I had a better view of our host. Oliver Flynn did not disappoint. Tall, with long, flowing, almost Shakespearean locks, he was attired in a gaudy purple velvet suit, with a red cravat, loosely tied and fixed with a large amethyst halfway down his chest. His shirt was unbuttoned, showing a rather improper amount of flesh. While theatrical, the ensemble was also strangely flattering. His enormous liquid brown eyes, almost like a sad spaniel's, swept back and forth over his rapt audience, willing their attention. I could picture him atop a craggy mount, reciting fiery poetry in the moonlight. All he required was a jewelled sword and a kilt flapping in the wind.

The man was charismatic, there was no doubt. An adoring group of twelve – all men, including Holmes as Pierre Vernet – were hanging on his every word. I edged closer to catch what he was saying.

'The form of government best suited to the artist is no government at all. It is said that the highest achievement to which man can aspire – the freedom to create art – is only available to a few. But that will change in the coming age of machines.'

Machines? I was under the impression that artists of his ilk abhorred most machinery and thought the Industrial Revolution had been a terrible threat to craftsmanship. I edged closer.

'Mankind is enslaved to business. To manufacturing,' Flynn said, his voice a melodious blend of Irish lilt and Oxford education. 'They are harnessed, yoked to the inter-ests of others. Even machines designed to remove menial work end up enslaving the hapless worker. But machines must not rule us, they are meant to be our slaves!'

'Hear, hear!' exclaimed several young men.

All right, I thought, that was understandable. Holmes's escapade in the Lancashire silk mills two years ago came to mind, where child workers darted dangerously between bits of machinery to keep the mechanical looms humming. What a contrast they were with the playful children at this party.

Flynn continued. 'Then each man . . . and each woman . . . will be free to create art, make beauty, and appreciate life as it should be lived. For what higher calling is there than art and beauty?' The small group around Flynn burst into applause. I had seen enough.

I looked around for something to eat and found a tray of cheese biscuits.

A high-pitched male voice called out. 'Hamish! Hamish, darling, come!'

Darling?

I looked up to see it was Holmes who called me, now surrounded by a group of five young men. They looked to be of university age and crowded in close to Holmes in the manner of gentlemen theatregoers surrounding an adored actress. I caught a flash of lace, a manicured hand, a man taking snuff, another patting Holmes's arm. Holmes snatched one man's lace handkerchief mischievously. He blotted his brow as if it were a sunny day in the garden and he had grown too warm. The handkerchief was snatched from his hand and waved in the air with a comment I could not hear and then a gale of laughter.

I must have been staring for Holmes caught my eye, beckoning me with a crooked finger and a wink. Reluctantly, I made my way over to him.

'This handsome fellow is my friend and colleague, and . . . also my doctor . . . Dr Hamish MacAllister,' Holmes said to the group as I arrived. They turned and surrounded me in an instant, hemming me in. Holmes saluted me with a touch to his forehead and vanished. His mocking smile infuriated me. Oh, we would have words later!

The group pressed in close. 'Oh, Doctor, Doctor!' said a man in a lavender evening coat and matching cravat. 'What kind of a doctor *are* you?'

'An army surgeon,' said I in my gruffest voice.

This, strangely, caused a ripple of laughter.

'A medical doctor, then!' said another 'Because . . .'

'Let me guess. You have a toe . . .' I said.

A beat as they took this in, followed by a roar of laughter. Why? I wondered.

'Oh, I have a toe!' said one.

'Me, too,' cried another.

I looked around for Holmes. He was nowhere to be seen. I endeavoured to disengage but was cornered.

'Pierre said you were a writer.'

'Are you a poet?'

'Poet?' I laughed. 'Not me!'

I shall admit here that I have privately dabbled in verse and was a secret admirer of Sir Walter Scott's heroic poems. But even Holmes did not know that. Although who was I fooling? Holmes seemed to know everything about me.

'Doctor, you need a flower!' said a short young man with a Scottish accent. He grabbed me by the arm, pulling me away from the group.

It was a relief to be out of that knot of men, and yet this was another mocking stranger under the wrong impression, or so I thought.

'I do not need a flower,' I said, irritated.

But he had already plucked an orange rose from a bouquet on a side table and proceeded to snap off most of the stem. He leaned in to insert the bloom into my buttonhole.

'Do not mind them,' he said, *sotto voce*. 'They so rarely get to tease. This flower is not a label, it is a reminder.'

'Of what?'

'Of man's highest aspirations. You see, nature cannot be bested. No painting, no poem, no sculpture, no symphony – no work of man is more beautiful than this simple creation. Though we may aspire.' He smiled. 'Charles Rennie Mackintosh taught me that.'

At my puzzlement, he added, 'He and his wife, both great artists, are my friends. I am Dr James Duncan from Glasgow. Yes, a medical doctor, like you. Do not judge us, Dr MacAllister.'

'I . . . yes . . . I mean, no . . .'

He smiled and vanished into the crowd. I was chagrined at my reaction a moment earlier. I could certainly manage a little teasing without losing my temper.

I was then distracted as a squealing group of entirely naked children ran through the party. When I looked up from them,

I found myself staring into the eyes of a roughly clad French workman with two days growth of beard, small steel glasses and greasy, messed hair. The man leaned in, took me by the arm, and propelled me away from Oliver Flynn and his group. 'Come with me!' he whispered in a French accent.

'Let go of my—' I started, but then realized who it was! 'Vidocq! What are you doing here?'

'Shh!'

He did not let go of my arm until we were outside on a balcony overlooking the Apothecary Garden. Beyond that, the Thames glittered in the moonlight. The river was lovelier when it was not about to engulf one, I thought.

Behind us, through two doors, and in two salons, the party bubbled along.

'Watson,' he growled. 'Do not say my name. Here I am Jean DeGuiche.'

'And I am Hamish MacAllister. You were warned to leave town.'

'Eh?' He shrugged in that Gallic manner. 'I have the, how you say, *unfinished business.*'

'What?'

'A young *anarchiste*, name of Vadim, he arrive from Paris yesterday. He is very, how you say, *enthusiaste*, but also a bit stupid. He makes the bombs. I am tip off, and follow him here to intercede.'

'Intercept, you mean?'

'He have a bomb with him tonight.'

'Here, at the party? Why? Oliver Flynn is on their side, is he not?'

'In theory. Monsieur Flynn work with Louise Michel, some of the *anarchistes*, to help the poor. Build schools. Orphanages. But he does not realize where some of this money actually goes.'

With a nod, he indicated the second salon opening onto this balcony. There Oliver Flynn now held sway with a different group: serious men and women of the ardent intellectual type. There were one or two workmen who looked like they had come to the party directly from their jobs in construction, others of a more scholarly bent, sporting dark clothes, faces that never saw daylight, and serious frowns. Pamphlets, marches and unison chants came to mind.

'See the man in the yellow shirt?' He nodded towards Flynn's coterie. 'Vadim. Look what he carries.'

At the far side of this group stood a handsome fellow of perhaps nineteen or twenty, wearing a bright yellow shirt. A canvas bag with something heavy inside hung from his shoulder. Mycroft's warning at the Diogenes floated back to haunt me – 'inexperienced young men . . . one will blow himself up accidentally'.

'Does he plan to detonate this bomb here, at this party?'

'I do not think so.'

Clinging to Vadim's arm was the only woman in the group. She was blocked from my view, but I caught a glimpse of long, dark hair.

'Why bring a bomb here?' I asked.

Vidocq continued. 'He do this to show off to friends. And to impress some girl he meet only yesterday,' he sighed. 'It is always the girls.'

Ah, these Frenchmen. Thank goodness such immaturity was behind me. The group shifted and I had a clear view of the girl. She turned to beam at Vadim, confident, teasing. My, she was a beauty!

Upon second glance, there was something familiar about her. It was then I noticed the dark mole on her cheek. *It was the young woman from Hyde Park! The one who had handed me the Tarot card.*

'It's her!' I cried. 'She's . . . she is working with . . . she's going to set off the bomb! Tonight! Here!'

Whoever this girl was, whatever her connection, I knew only that she must be working with the person carrying out the Alphabet Killings. She would kill Oliver Flynn, next on the list, and any number of his friends and family. I had to find Holmes. I looked wildly about for him.

He was nowhere in sight. I turned back to Vidocq, but he had left me and was elbowing his way through the crowd towards Vadim and the others. *Where was Holmes?*

There was no time to lose. I followed Vidocq but became entangled in the crowd. As I pushed through, I found him exchanging harsh words in French, one hand gripping the startled young man in the yellow shirt.

I saw at once that Vadim's lovely female companion was missing. And so was his canvas bag. The bomb!

I caught a flash of dark hair as the girl made her escape through a far door in this second salon. I tried to follow, but again was hampered by the crowd.

I emerged in a long hallway, doors all along it. Coming

towards me were two drunken partygoers, an artistic dandy arm-in-arm with a serious female anarchist. They stopped to steal a kiss which lurched into a passionate embrace as they completely blocked the narrow hallway. 'Excuse me!' I shouted, pushing them aside.

'Barbarian!' cried the woman.

I checked one door after another. Nothing. Then I spotted the canvas bag discarded on the floor at the end of the hall. It was flattened. Empty!

I opened the door nearest to it and dashed in, stumbling over a stack of books placed in my path. I recovered, only to find a dagger pressed to my chest, just under the breastbone. A quick upward thrust and it would be over. I did not move.

The beautiful young woman from Hyde Park glared up at me, the dagger held firmly in her right hand, a crude bomb with a timer in her left. She smiled. 'Hello, Dr Watson,' she said, savouring the moment. 'That disguise is no disguise at all.'

'You are here to kill Oliver Flynn!' I said. 'The "F" on the list!'

She looked surprised, then laughed.

'But why kill all these other innocents?'

'Why not?' said the girl. 'The bomb goes here, or the bomb goes there. A lot of people either way. A party or a market place. This will receive more attention.'

'And is it attention that you want?'

'Not me,' she said. 'My employer. And now – goodbye.'

'Goodbye . . . *Judith?*'

She paused, raising an eyebrow and smiled at me. I looked past her and gasped in relief.

'Holmes!' I cried.

My ruse worked. She turned to look, and I grabbed her knife hand and twisted it. The knife nicked me but tumbled to the ground. She screamed and kicked me, hard, and we both dived for the weapon. She flung the bomb away and I followed it with my eyes, fearing that we and the entire house would go up then and there. She got to the knife first and slashed at me, cutting the back of my hand badly. I cried out but managed to grab and twist her wrist. She dropped the knife. As I lunged for it, she seized the bomb, kicked me hard in the ribs, and escaped through the window.

I righted myself and grasped my bleeding hand. But before I could pursue her, Holmes and Vidocq burst into the room.

'The bomb?' Holmes cried.

'She has it!' I nodded at the window and Vidocq took off after the girl.

'Your hand!' said Holmes. The cut had nicked the dorsal vein and it was bleeding profusely. I ripped off my tie and Holmes bent down to help me. With one hand apiece, we managed to bind the wound.

'We must get everyone out of the house,' he said. 'Vidocq told me you recognized the girl from the park. She's here to kill Flynn.'

Holmes managed at last to convince Oliver Flynn of the danger, and in a few tense minutes, with the help of the persuasive Dr Duncan, we had the entire party – guests, children, servants, everyone – moved across the street to the Apothecary Gardens. The police had been summoned and a bomb specialist was en route. Several of the woman, led by the kindly and beautiful Mrs Oliver Flynn, were in the process of putting the children to bed in a neighbour's house down the street.

As we stood regarding Flynn's house, Holmes said, 'I should have followed up more aggressively on the girl after you got that card, Watson. I dismissed her as a hired messenger and focused elsewhere.'

'Holmes, you are only one person. There have been so many paths in this case. And you have been blocked from getting much police help.'

'For what little use that has been recently,' he said bitterly.

We heard a shout from the roof. There stood Vidocq, waving at us. 'She is gone. The bomb is here!' he called down to us, pointing to a place behind him on the roof.

'Save yourself, Vidocq! The house is emptied!' shouted Holmes.

'I am dismantle!' returned the Frenchman. He gave us a jaunty salute and disappeared from view.

Not five seconds later, the bomb detonated with a roar and the roof of Oliver Flynn's house caved in. I stared at it in shock.

'Vidocq,' I whispered. 'My God! He had no time to escape!' Holmes stared at the smoking ruin. He shook his head sadly. 'It does not appear so.'

I watched smoke and a few flickers of flame arise from

the ruined top floor of the house. I had never liked the man. But I would never wish him such an end.

'He died a hero,' I said. 'But what about Flynn and his guests?'

I needn't have worried. 'The Langham! The party moves to the Langham.' Oliver Flynn's voice carried over the noise of the crowd. 'How can I thank you, Mr Holmes?' he called out to us as he approached..

I looked at Holmes in puzzlement. 'Not *Pierre Vernet?*'

Holmes shrugged. 'I had to reveal myself, Watson. He would not heed the warning from Pierre Vernet.' He turned to Flynn as the flamboyant Irishman arrived to face us. 'You are not going to the Langham, are you? As I told you, the murderer will soon learn he has not succeeded in killing you and your family.'

'I have sent my man to Victoria. He is securing tickets for us to go to Paris on the dawn train. We shall hide with a friend until that time, and in Paris you may contact me at *Le Meurice*. I do not want to run like this, but I am listening, Mr Holmes. We will be safe until you or your brother send word.'

CHAPTER 28

Conflagration

ur carriage rattled north to Baker Street through the empty streets. A deep exhaustion and sadness settled over me. Holmes, however, was still at work.

'We are barely keeping apace, Watson. This Alphabet Killer is now in a hurry, but the "F" is safe for the moment.' He removed his moustache and glasses, and the rose from his jacket. He took out a comb and returned his hair to its normal style. I removed the rose from my own lapel and he handed me his. I stared for a moment at the two flowers, then looked at him.

'Holmes. You . . . ?'

'No.' A moment. 'Surely you know me by now, Watson.'

I smiled. No, I would never know him completely. It felt wasteful to toss the flowers out the window. I laid them on the seat for the next passengers to find.

'Are you sure Flynn was the "F"?' I wondered.

'Yes.'

'What, then, was his secret crime? I asked.

'What does it matter?'

'You have wanted to confirm each of the others!'

'Flynn has funded several anarchist groups, one of which is responsible for fourteen deaths in a bombing in Dublin.'

'Funded? But did he know how the money would be used? That is not so direct, is it Holmes? Not like the others.'

'I do not know. In any case, we are on to "G" now.'

'But if G is Gainsborough, then that one is already dead.' I said. 'But if the G is Goodwin—?'

'They are in Nice. They were less inclined than dear Mr Flynn to ignore my suggestion to take temporary refuge.'

'Then you have eliminated them as suspects?'

'Not entirely, Watson. But they are at least safe if they are *on* the list. And if they are involved, they are disconnected from events here. Either way, it serves my investigation. I am rather surprised they complied. It suggests their innocence, in fact.'

'But does not confirm it?'

'No. Which brings us to the girl tonight. She was introduced at the party as Judith.'

'I was right, then! As I confronted her, Holmes, I had a sudden intuition. I called her Judith!'

'And?'

'She . . . she seemed amused.'

Holmes shook his head. 'I thought the Hyde Park girl

was merely a messenger, but she appears to be a principal in this case. Her connection to Lady Gainsborough bears re-examination. We know from Heffie that Judith is duplicitous, entrepreneurial and intelligent. But there must be someone behind her, Watson, there must! To what degree has this young woman been involved, and at whose behest?'

'Lady Gainsborough?'

'Or the late Lord Gainsborough. Or another?'

'And her motive?'

Holmes shrugged. 'Depends on her history – love, money, revenge? Money, most likely. Consider this. The writer of the Lucifer letter was a literate person. It took at least two people to manage these killings – and to drag Anson to the shore and bind him there, to force Mrs Benjamin to join her hanging husband, to drag Clammory's partner, wounded, up onto the barber's chair. A highly intelligent, articulate, and very strong individual is involved. There is not a single killer but two or more – a group. We are close, Watson, so very close!'

The carriage rattled on and we passed Hyde Park. Speakers' Corner at this hour was deserted except a for a lone woman, standing on a box, exhorting in the darkness to no one. A brisk wind had come up. The nearby trees were now fluttering wildly and her skirts blew around her.

'I must look into Fardwinkle when I can. Although the style, the flavour, the nuance . . . Fardwinkle feels wrong. I shall set Heffie on Judith's trail tonight.'

'Holmes,' I said. You say the killer has sped up his agenda. If your theory that A and G were Anson and

Gainsborough . . . G is already done and that brings us now to the letter H. Might that be "Holmes"? Your brother is on the list.'

'Mycroft can look after himself,' said Holmes.

He waved off the thought. Our carriage pulled up at 221B. Billy, who had been awaiting us outside in the cold, ran up to us.

'Sir! Sir!' he cried. 'Heffie!'

'What about her?' asked Holmes.

'A note from her,' Billy said, handing a slip of paper up through the window.

He read it and blanched. 'When did this come?'

'Just now, sir!'

Holmes turned to me, his face white. 'My brother's house is on fire!'

There was no traffic at that hour and our cab thundered south towards St James and Holmes's brother's flat. As we rounded the corner, we became aware of a great fire burning just down the street on the ground floor of a stately residential building opposite the Diogenes.

Holmes gasped. 'Mycroft!'

We pulled up between several police and fire vehicles. The firemen were wrestling with a large hose and, through the large front windows, I could see bright orange flames flickering behind heavy drapery. Even as I watched, one of the drapes caught fire.

We dismounted the vehicle and saw a young fireman seated on the kerb, his face blackened. He was being tended to by another for a burnt arm.

'Anyone in there?' cried Holmes.

The wounded fireman, partially in shock, looked up at Holmes and nodded. 'A man's body. The girl. I couldn't . . .'

I turned to Holmes, but he was gone. To my horror, I spotted his thin frame, black coat flapping behind him, racing towards the burning building. He paused on the landing in front of the door.

'Holmes, no!' As I leapt up to follow, two burly policemen tackled me and brought me to the ground. I lunged up and onto my knees, but they held me back. Between their struggling forms, I saw my friend plunge through the doorway and into the inferno.

'Dear God, Holmes!'

'Stop him!' someone cried.

'Nobody can go in there now,' said the policeman to me.

'But that's my friend!'

'Say goodbye. You're not going in there.'

It took three of them to hold me back. Both curtains were now burnt, and we had a clear view of the conflagration that was once Mycroft Holmes's sitting-room.

I saw Holmes's tall figure moving through the flames. He bent as if to inspect something on the floor.

'Holmes!' I shouted.

He stood again and moved uncertainly away from the window. It was hard to see. He appeared to bend down again. Or did he fall?

I was shouting uncontrollably. A fourth policeman joined us, but they could barely contain me. As I tried to break free from them, a miraculous vision presented itself.

On the landing just in front of the door appeared the tall, angular figure of Sherlock Holmes, silhouetted against the flames, carrying in his arms the limp figure of Heffie O'Malley. Behind him roared orange flames. In front of him the inky night suddenly lit up with a blue flash. A photographer!

Holmes took a step forward and paused. I noticed flames licking the cuffs of his trousers. They were on fire! Sparks rose from the material, and he stumbled.

In an instant, three firemen converged on Holmes. One scooped Heffie from his arms and two others caught him and conveyed him from the landing to the front walkway, laying him on the pavement. A man flung a thick, wet blanket over his legs as another threw one over the still form of Heffie. Their clothing sizzled and steamed.

The policemen holding me released their grip and I ran towards my friend, but a fireman blocked me.

'I'm a doctor,' I shouted. 'A doctor!' They let me pass.

Holmes lay still on the pavement, eyes closed, his clothing scorched and smoking. Unconscious? I took up his good hand and felt for the pulse. He was alive! In that moment, that was all that mattered. I stared down at his soot-blackened face.

Holmes opened his eyes. 'Watson,' he said. 'Heffie?'

I turned to see the girl sitting up, wrapped in wet blankets. She was conscious and being given water to drink. She coughed and looked over at us.

'She is safe,' I nodded. His eyes closed. Two men approached with a stretcher and I stepped back to let them through.

CHAPTER 29

Embers

he next morning, Holmes was stretched out on the divan of our sitting-room, his lower legs carefully bandaged by me, with help from another doctor on the scene. I had once again given him morphine and was keeping a careful eye on his respiration. The morning papers were spread before me on the dining table. Front page centre was a large, dramatic illustration of Holmes, standing tall in the doorway of Mycroft's home, fire raging behind him, the flames lapping the lower part of his trouser legs, sparks everywhere as he carried the unconscious Heffie in his arms. The illustrator had enjoyed a certain liberty: Holmes looked demonic.

The headline read, 'Inhuman Detective Braves Hell to Save Girl'. Below that, in smaller letters, 'But leaves brother to die in St James inferno'.

The byline, of course, was Gabriel Zanders. In it, he described Holmes as having superhuman powers to have been able to walk through flames. 'Only a creature from heaven or hell could withstand the violent conflagration through which he ventured to save a dying girl.' I shook my head in disgust. Below this was more sobering news. 'The body of Mycroft Holmes, the detective's older brother, was found burned nearly beyond recognition in his own sitting-room. The cause of the blaze was not confirmed, but believed to be a kind of incendiary device. The explosive attack was attributed to anarchists.' I felt ill.

Further down on the page the article offered theories why Sherlock Holmes 'rescued a street orphan but failed to save his own brother'. I sighed in frustration. Even in the face of heroism, Zanders persisted in pursuing his agenda of making Holmes seem both inhuman and errant.

A groan interrupted my reading. Holmes was surfacing into consciousness and I was instantly by his side. His eyes opened halfway, then closed as he was hit by a wall of pain. In my own life, of the many injuries I suffered through my army career including gunshot wounds, broken bones and pleurisy, I recall burns as perhaps the most painful of all.

Holmes groaned again. 'Morphine . . . ?' he mumbled.

'I have it right here,' I said, readying a hypodermic.

'No. No more!' He held up his good hand. 'How much have you . . . ?'

'Quite a bit, Holmes. Do not concern yourself with that.'

'How long have I been out?'

'Six hours. You were very lucky. Your clothing was on fire. Mostly first-degree burns below the knee. Some may blister. We will have to keep an eye—'

'What of Heffie!' His voice was cutting, his eyes opened wide.

'She is upstairs, sleeping. She suffered smoke inhalation but will be fine. You were just in time. Though, my God, Holmes, that was a foolhardy move.'

'I sent the girl into peril. I could never forgive—' He began to cough. 'Give me today's newspapers,' he ordered, struggling to sit up. I hesitated, then helped prop him up with pillows and handed him the papers. He fumbled, one-handed, with the large pages. 'Damn this hand!'

'Dr Meredith rewired your fingers last night. He was not happy with you.'

Holmes stared at the front page which I had laid out on his lap. He exhaled sharply in disgust. 'Zander! He cannot leave this Devil thing alone.' He scanned the article, then closed his eyes and sank back into the cushions. 'Read me the agony columns.'

'Holmes, perhaps you missed . . . It says they found your brother's body—'

'I read it. And yes, I saw the body. Please, Watson, the agony columns. Do as I ask.'

The combination of shock, pain and the drugs had addled his brain. He had come upon his brother's body, half destroyed in the fire. Why would he wish to read gossip and personal notices right now? In the early days of his practice, before Holmes had made a name for himself, before clients of all ages and means flocked to his door, he had sometimes found new cases in the agony columns. He had continued to read them for amusement, and to keep up with the rhythm of the city. But right now? Shock, perhaps. His brother was dead. I could barely fathom it myself.

Just then, Heffie appeared at the door, pale but alert and moving normally. She cast a worried look at Holmes, approached and sat near him on a chair. She reached out to touch him, but I shook my head and she pulled back her hand. 'Thanks, Mr 'olmes. I understand you carried me out o' there last night.'

'He needs rest,' said I.

'Foolish of you to go in there, Heffie,' Holmes murmured.

'Your brother, sir. 'Alf burnt up when I got there.'

'I saw the remains,' said he. 'There was not much left when I arrived. What did you notice?'

Heffie hesitated, looking to me for reassurance. I nodded. He had better hear what she had to say, the sooner the better.

'Did you see who it was?' asked Holmes.

'I don't know your brother,' said she. 'It was a big 'eavy man in a nice suit.'

'Hair. Did you see his hair?' Holmes was trying to sit up.

'Top of 'im was gone. Some kind o' explosion, I reckon. Body was more burnt than anything nearby. No face left. No 'ead, really.'

'An explosive, followed by some kind of incendiary

device. My brother normally would not miss something so obvious.' He waved the finger of his right hand in the air dismissively.

'Holmes!' Even knowing him as I did, his dissociation shocked me.

'Shoes. What kind of shoes?' he persisted.

'Cheap boots. Scuffed,' said the girl.

'Ha!'

'How could you notice that, Heffie?' I wondered.

'That is why we employ her, Watson. Good, Heffie. It was not Mycroft, then.'

'Then who was it?' I exclaimed. 'And why would—?'

'My brother wants the world to think he's dead.'

'Because he is H, next on the list after G?' I said.

'It is likely. As you said, H was next. And Lady Eleanor Gainsborough, if she is on the list, is protected by Lestrade and his men. The Goodwins, if they heeded my warning, are also out of reach. The killer grows impatient. Part of my plan.'

'Holmes, are you certain the body was not Mycroft's? It could be him in someone else's, er . . . shoes? How can you know?'

'Because of this.' He pointed to something on the page spread upon his lap.

I took it up and read, from the agonies:

'"Achy. The palace wood, the bizarre on your road, the sun at highest, entreat, request, desire. Filially, fly aloft."'

I flung the thing down. 'This is nonsense!'

'No.'

'What on earth does it mean, then?'

'It is a message from my brother,' said Holmes. '"Filially, fly aloft." Brother Mycroft. It is our code.'

'But what of the rest?'

'Shakespeare, *Midsummer Night's Dream*. "And I am to entreat you, request you, and desire you to con them by tomorrow night and meet me in the palace wood . . ." You see, I am to meet him. Secretly!'

'Well, it is not very secret if you are telling me. But when and where?'

'"The sun at highest" – he means noon. What time is it now?' He sat up, looking about him in a panic. The clock near the door had stopped at three. 'Three?' he shouted. 'Dear God, how long have I been out? I must run!'

'Calm yourself. The clock stopped.' I consulted my watch. 'It is only eleven-thirty. But where, Holmes? You are manic. You may still be in shock.'

'Bring me my boots! Heffie! Where are they? What time is it?' He continued to shout.

'Not a good idea, Holmes. Sit back down. I just told you it is half-past eleven.'

'Good. Still time! My boots!'

'Holmes, there was a dead body in Mycroft's flat. Who killed that person? And if it was not Mycroft, who was it?'

Heffie brought Holmes his boots and set them down before him. He sat down and picked one up with his good hand.

'That is of little importance, Watson.'

'Well, I am glad *you* think so. The police, however—'

'Wheat from chaff, Watson, wheat from chaff!' he shouted. 'Discerning the relevant details from the irrelevant!' He leaned down and was struggling with his one hand and bandaged lower limbs to put on the first of his boots. He was truly manic. Holmes had idiosyncratic reactions to drugs, that I knew.

'What is relevant is for you to rest!' I insisted.

''Ere, I'll 'elp you,' said Heffie, leaning down to do so. I shook my head at her, but she ignored me.

'Tie these,' Holmes ordered. Then, to me, suddenly reasonable: 'My brother must have found a corpse with similar proportions in a morgue, Watson. Remember, Mycroft has the government and all of its personnel at his beck and call.'

I was shouting into the wind with Holmes. They continued to struggle with his boots. I gently edged Heffie aside and began to help, purposely slowing the process.

'Holmes, you are not in your right mind,' I said. He picked up the paper and stared once more at the agony notice he claimed was from Mycroft.

He paused, then gasped and jumped to his feet. 'Achy! Of course! Mycroft figured it out.' He looked about him in a panic. 'A key. *A is key!* Let me see the Anson files, Watson.'

'Yes, only sit back down to read them.'

He did so, and I brought him the thick police file from the table. He thumbed through the pages in a rush. He was shaking with something – excitement, shock, madness, perhaps. This whole thing was lunacy. I wondered if this published newspaper 'message' was misinterpreted by a brain twisted by too much pain and too many drugs. I was also worried that he could die from the exertion. In the manner of a family member who accompanies a chronic drunk to a pub, was I assisting in my friend's self-destruction?

Holmes was not so far disturbed that he failed to notice my concern. 'Stop worrying, Doctor. There will be time for that later.' He continued to read, his eyes gleaming with excitement. Five minutes passed. He flung the file to the floor. 'Yes, Anson!' he shouted, 'Of course!'

He sprang to his feet, upending newspapers and files and sending them flying. He moaned in pain and staggered, and Heffie scrambled after him, ducking under his good arm to hold him up. His head swivelled back and forth. 'What time is it now?' he shouted. 'The clock has stopped.'

I was convinced he had lost all reason. We had just discussed the time. 'It is ten to twelve.' I turned my back on Holmes and reached into my doctor's bag.

'Get me my coat! I am to meet Mycroft in ten minutes!'

I glanced back to see Heffie take his greatcoat from its hook near the door and hold it up to him. He struggled into it. Could he be running into some kind of a trap? And in this desperate state? I waivered, then made a decision. My back still to Holmes, I loaded up a hypodermic and primed it.

I crossed to him, took one coat sleeve and yanked it

down. Without hesitation, I plunged a needle straight through his shirt and into his arm, injecting a strong dose of morphine, rather faster than was recommended. 'You are going nowhere in this state, Holmes,' I said.

'No!' he cried, and recoiled, pulling his arm away so quickly that the hypodermic remained embedded. He looked down at it in horror, yanked it from his arm, and flung it across the room, where the glass splintered into pieces.

'Idiot! Get Lestrade. He is with Lady Eleanor. I . . . I . . . I . . . Oh, damn you . . .' And he collapsed from the drug like a marionette with cut strings.

Heffie and I caught him and laid him back down on the sofa. We then gently removed the coat, which had only been halfway on. I checked his eyes, his pulse, his breathing. Had I done the right thing? I was not sure. I have never, perhaps, doubted my medical choices so severely. I looked at his pale face, covered in sweat. Holmes surely had not been in his right mind and was manic beyond a doubt. Was there really a coded message from his brother or was the whole thing the ravings of a man in shock?

I pulled his sleeve back to make sure the needle had not broken off in his arm. It had not. But I would do as he asked and contact Lestrade. Together, perhaps the inspector and I could figure out what would be best for my fallen friend.

I picked up the shattered hypodermic from where Holmes had flung it, determined that it was useless, and threw it into the receptacle under his desk. I locked my doctor's case. 'Watch him,' I urged Heffie, and after one more glance at Holmes I ran downstairs to send Billy for Lestrade, whom I presumed was still at Lady Eleanor's house. 'Hurry!' I urged him.

I could not leave the patient for long. I ran back upstairs, expecting to find Holmes as I had left him. Inconceivably, he was awake and standing, face alight with a feverish concentration, breathing heavily. As I entered, he finished injecting something into his arm and yanked out the needle, panting heavily.

My doctor's bag lay open. Heffie stood next to it, a piece of wire in her hand which she had no doubt used to open the lock. In her other hand was an empty medicine bottle. Traitorous girl! Her terrified eyes bored into my own, begging forgiveness. In two steps, I bounded over to her, snatching up the bottle.

Cocaine.

'Foolish girl! How much did you give him?' I found I was shouting.

'I didn't give 'im,' she said. ''E took.'

'How much?'

'All of it,' she said in a tiny voice.

I turned. Holmes stood in the centre of the room, his face a ghostly white. Sweat dripped from his forehead. His jaw was slack as he breathed in deep, rasping breaths.

'Dear God! You will kill yourself! Morphine and cocaine together can stun the heart, Holmes!'

Heffie backed away, terrified for the first time.

'I am fine!' shouted Holmes. 'Pain is *gone!*' He flexed his good arm, rolled his head alarmingly on his neck. He appeared inhuman. Uncanny. It was like Frankenstein's Monster awakening in a new, unknown body.

'Holmes! You are as far from fine as I've ever seen you! You could die from this!'

He stared at me, not hearing. Then he closed his eyes and shuddered.

A commotion from below was followed by feet pounding up the stairs. It was Lestrade. He must have been en route when we sent for him. But why? In any case, I was relieved to see help arrive.

'My God, I saw the papers. Mr Holmes, what a time!' cried the inspector. 'But more bad news, gentlemen. Oliver Flynn has disappeared. Murdered, we think. An explosion at his house last night. He escaped, but then there were bloodstains on the— er, Mr Holmes, are you all right?'

Holmes was weaving about the room like a drunkard, looking for something. He looked up. 'Oliver Flynn is safe in France!' he shouted. 'The blood is fake! I organized his disappearance. It is a ruse. He and his family are hiding until—'

'Sit down, Holmes!' I entreated. 'Help me with him, Lestrade!'

The inspector made a move toward Holmes as I closed in on my friend.

'Stay away!' Holmes roared. We both froze.

'Is it true, then, about Oliver Flynn?' asked the inspector. I nodded. He looked relieved.

'Who is with Lady Eleanor?' Holmes demanded.

'Perkins and Mead. Two of my best.' Lestrade turned to me. 'Dr Watson, he looks unwell.'

'She may not be safe,' slurred Holmes. 'Help me on with this coat.'

Lestrade looked at me and I shook my head no.

'Mr Holmes, listen to the doctor,' said the inspector. 'I am so terribly sorry about your brother, sir. The fire—'

'No! He did not die!' cried Holmes. 'Just someone in his clothes!'

'Are you sure about your brother, sir? What is the matter with you? Dr Watson, what *is the matter with him*?'

'Where is Lady Eleanor now?' screamed Holmes in a voice I hardly recognized, as he lurched towards the umbrella stand.

'At her home. I just told you!' said Lestrade, deeply alarmed at what appeared to be a mental breakdown.

'Mycroft is not dead,' said Holmes with certainty.

I was growing less certain by the minute.

Lestrade looked at me, his concern palpable. 'Doctor, is he . . . coherent? The body is clearly Mycroft. I suppose an autopsy may furnish more—'

Holmes swayed, and Heffie and I moved closer to him. I touched his arm. 'No!' shouted Holmes and he broke free from the two of us, rushing to the landing just outside the sitting-room door. He grabbed his coat that we had replaced on the rack and began struggling with it. I moved closer to him.

'At least tell me where you are going, Holmes,' I said softly, fully intending to follow him.

'The Baker Street Bazaar,' he said. 'The message from Mycroft. "The bizarre on your road. The sun at its highest," it said. *The Baker Street Bazaar at noon.* Do you see? He will be waiting for me.'

His eyes registered something behind me at the same time I heard a noise on the stairs. I turned. There was Lady Eleanor, just below us.

'Lady Eleanor,' murmured Holmes, weakly.

'Oh, Mr Holmes, thank God you are here!' She rushed up the stairs and flung herself into his arms. He embraced her awkwardly, with only one arm working.

If I had not steadied him and then gently untangled her, I am certain he would have capsized. I took her in hand firmly and held her at arms' length. She seemed near hysteria.

'There, there, Lady Eleanor,' I said. 'You are terribly upset! What brings you here?'

Holmes backed away, confused, wobbling. I hated for anyone to see him in this state, and stepped between them to block her view. 'Lady Eleanor, surely you have read of last night's horrific events? Mr Holmes is exhausted—'

'I read that Mycroft Holmes is dead. Mr Holmes's brother!'

'He is not dead, Lady Eleanor,' Holmes said.

She staggered back in surprise. 'Mycroft Holmes is *not* dead?'

I felt a movement and turned to see Holmes staring at Lady Eleanor. Through the fog of exhaustion and trauma, his eyes were pinned on her.

'The two men the police left to protect me are dead,' she said. 'They . . . I . . .'

Lestrade burst onto the landing. 'Perkins and Mead? Dead! What happened?'

'They were . . . shot, Mr Lestrade, in front of my eyes!' said the lady. She seemed partially in shock herself.

'When? By whom?' rasped Holmes.

'A stranger. A big man. Well dressed!'

'*When?*'

'Just twenty minutes ago. Oh . . .' She swooned. I caught her, and Lestrade and I helped her into the sitting-room. I sat her down on the sofa. I glanced back at Holmes, who stood motionless on the landing with a strange expression I could not translate. I gestured for Heffie to look after him. She went to him and took his arm.

'What did this man who shot them look like?' I said gently to Lady Eleanor. Behind her, Holmes and Heffie lingered on the landing.

'A terrible man. Large, very heavy, well-dressed. Oxbridge voice. I did not know him.'

My insides turned to ice. What if I had been right about Mycroft Holmes? What if Sherlock Holmes was blind to his own brother's murderous nature? If I was right . . .

I glanced at the landing. Holmes seemed to confer with Heffie. I thought of something.

'Was he wearing shiny shoes?' I asked. 'Did he have a double watch chain?'

'Yes! Yes!' the lady said.

'Mycroft Holmes!' I said.

'Perkins. Mead. My two best men,' moaned Lestrade. 'Could it be that *Mycroft Holmes* killed them?'

'Lady Eleanor, did he say anything? Anything to give you a reason why he was attacking you?' I implored.

'Yes, he did. Something about "G". Oh . . . I feel faint.'

In an instant, I poured her a brandy and kneeled before her. Lestrade stood ready to help.

'He said . . . he said . . .' She closed her eyes. 'He said that he was clearing the way to a brighter future. Eliminating the rubbish that had washed up on our shores. He said my school was a false front for criminal activity, and that I must have known. And I would pay for it now.'

'My God!' Was it possible . . . Lady Eleanor was the "G" on the list? And Mycroft was the Alphabet Killer!

'I begged him to understand that I knew nothing. I had only recently become aware that my prize student, Judith—' Lady Eleanor continued, then burst into tears. 'That . . . that awful young girl! She fooled us all!'

'Not me,' said Heffie who had entered silently and now stood across the room with her arms folded. She watched the scene with a kind of strange detachment. Of course, how could a girl like that understand the complexity of this case?

Where was Holmes? I glanced at the landing but he was gone!

'Holmes?' I called out. I ran to the landing but I was calling to the wind. I rushed back in.

'The man took out a gun. He was about to shoot me!' exclaimed Lady Eleanor.

'Excuse me, Dr Watson?' Heffie said. 'I got to tell you—'

'Not now, Heffie.' I turned back to Lady Eleanor. 'How did you escape?'

'He told me to step away from the front window. So that no one would see. As I did so, Belle ran into the room and attacked the man. He . . . he fell, and the gun discharged. I ran from the room and came straight here. He may very well be dead on the floor of my sitting-room. But I do not think so.'

'Dr Watson? Mr 'olmes, 'e wanted—' Heffie started again.

'Heffie, not now!' I turned back to the lady. 'Why do you think he is not dead?' I asked.

'Because I heard a second gunshot on the way out and a scream from dear Belle. I think it likely that my dear cat is dead and . . . I don't know . . . that Mycroft Holmes must still be alive.'

'Then Holmes is in danger,' I cried. 'Lestrade!'

'Stop!' shouted Heffie. 'Will you, for the love of Pete, *listen*? Mr Holmes just now asked me to tell you this, Dr Watson.'

'What, Heffie? *What?*'

'He told me to tell you he is heading down to the Baker Street Bazaar. His brother is there and sent him a secret message to meet him there at noon. He wants you to join him.'

'I know all that!' *Holmes knew that I knew.* My worries about his mental state doubled. It seemed certain that he was walking into a trap. But I had no time to ponder it, for at that instant there was a thundering knock at the door downstairs, then a pause . . . then a sharp crack as it was kicked off its hinges, followed by pounding footsteps up the stairs and Mrs Hudson's cries of outrage.

Titus Billings burst into the room with two deputies. Mrs Hudson was on his heels, aghast, furious.

'Sir!' she cried. 'Dr Watson, he just—'

Billings looked around as though he had walked in on the wrong play. 'Where is Sherlock Holmes?' he thundered.

'He's gone!' cried Lady Eleanor. 'Have you come to arrest him?'

'I – yes! I have come to arrest Sherlock Holmes for the murder of his brother!'

'Impossible, Billings!' I exclaimed. 'Mycroft Holmes is alive!'

Lady Eleanor turned to him. 'Are you Mr Titus Billings? The new head of police? Oh, thank heavens! Help me, please! This man is right. Mycroft Holmes is alive. He just tried to kill me!'

Billings turned to the lady in astonishment. 'Madam?'

'I am Lady Eleanor Gainsborough,' said the lady, gathering her wits about her faster than anyone in the room. 'I am in fear for my life. Please, sir, I beg you. Is there anywhere safe you can take me? Do not leave me with some random constables, as this man did.' She gestured dismissively at Lestrade. 'Mycroft Holmes is on the loose!'

'Why would Mycroft Holmes wish to kill you?' asked Lestrade. There was no time to explain to him.

'I am on some kind of list!' she cried. 'I do not understand it. Some kind of list, along with my husband and other people. The Alphabet something . . .'

Billings turned to stare at the lady. 'Holmes was blathering about that in my office. So, that fool detective, along with his brother, was behind the entire thing!' He laughed. 'Oh, the hubris! Obviously, he underestimated Titus Billings.'

'Help me, sir. Take me away. This man—' she gestured to Lestrade – 'Mr Holmes asked him to protect me, but he left two policemen, and both are dead—'

'Perkins and Mead,' said Lestrade at Billings's sharp look.

'You do not take orders from Sherlock Holmes, Lestrade. You are responsible for the deaths of those two men. You are relieved of duty as of now – permanently.'

Billings turned to Lady Eleanor. 'Madam, consider yourself under my personal protection. I shall look after you myself until Mycroft Holmes is locked up. You have my guarantee. Come, I have somewhere you will be safe.'

I put a hand up to object, but Billings shouted, 'You! I'll be dealing with you and Holmes later! Take a step closer and you'll wind up like your friend.' The nippers were already in his hand.

Heffie ran to the top of the stairs and watched them go off. I was torn. I did not trust Billings, his sadism, his need for control, his dubious actions on the case.

'Dr Watson,' said Heffie. 'Now they're gone, Mr 'olmes also asked that Mr Lestrade brings six men as fast as possible down to the Bazaar, but quiet like, no noise at all.'

Lestrade nodded. 'I'll be at the Bazaar with the men shortly.'

'But you have been relieved of duty,' I said.

'No one will have that heard yet!'

With a tinge of worry about allowing Lady Eleanor to be carried off by Titus Billings, I knew I had one priority. That was to follow my friend to the Baker Street Bazaar and his meeting with his brother, who could very well be the Alphabet Killer. I ran up to my room, gathered what I needed, and was on the street in a minute, Heffie by my side.

CHAPTER 30

The Baker Street Bazaar

he Baker Street Bazaar, a huge indoor market place, took up an entire block just a few minutes' walk from 221B. Holmes and I had once ventured there for an exhibition of Chinese porcelain, another time for a horse show, and Mary and I had attended a flower show there. It had also been the home for Madame Tussaud's eerie collection of wax figures.

Years ago, the vast main hall had been turned into an artificial ice-skating rink by means of a strange concoction of animal lard and chemicals, with painted Swiss mountains and chalets all around it. It had been a popular destination at Christmas time, safer than skating over the frozen Thames, but nevertheless took a strong stomach, for the stench was said to be fierce. This year promised a Glaciarium, a new method of creating a rink out of real ice, and the attraction was highly anticipated.

Heffie and I arrived at the main entrance on Baker Street to find it locked, and dark inside. A sign on the door proclaimed 'The return of Winter Wonderland – Holiday ice skating indoors – on REAL ICE – for the delight of old and young, boys and girls alike'. A smaller sign was added in one corner: 'Pardon us as the elves and fairies create this Wonderland for you. Closed for preparations. Will open November 30th, 1890.'

Holmes, I was certain, was already inside. And perhaps his brother as well. Mycroft's attack on Lady Eleanor made no kind of sense I could fathom, and I had to warn my friend. If my suspicions about his brother were justified, Holmes was in great danger.

How had Holmes got in? I pressed my face to the glass door, trying to see inside. In the darkness, only a small lobby area was visible. Heffie had an idea and tugged on my sleeve, motioning me to follow her into an alley behind the Bazaar. A fire escape to the first floor had been lowered to the ground, and the window above it was broken.

Eager to reach my friend, I stopped there and asked Heffie to wait in Baker Street and to warn me with a scream if anyone other than Lestrade and his men appeared. 'No, sir, I wants to 'elp Mr 'olmes,' she said, backing down only when I told her that Holmes himself had asked me to post her as a sentinel.

'If 'e said so . . . I'll do it. But—'

I showed her the revolver in my pocket. 'He is in good hands, Heffie.' I said. 'I was the best shot in my regiment. When Lestrade and his men get here, direct them our way.'

She reluctantly complied and, in a trice, I followed his path up the ladder. The window opening was too narrow for me and I had to knock out more glass to squeeze through. Mycroft certainly could not have entered this way, but Holmes had.

The jagged edges of the glass tore at my coat. The window opened into a suite of offices. Passing through them and several more doors, I found myself on a dimly lit balcony encircling the cavernous grand hall. Below me I could just make out the mechanical ice rink under construction. I had read of it, and under other circumstances would have been fascinated to see the works. Real ice, I knew, was promised, frozen by a complex system of copper piping and a cooling fluid pumped through them.

I squinted into the gloom from above, looking for Holmes or his brother but seeing no one. Dotted about the cavernous space were individual electric lights on poles, their fragile bulbs each encased in a protective cage. These threw a weak grid of light across the vast space, with darkness extending off into various corners.

From above I saw a circular wooden frame resembling a circus ring, three feet high and enclosing an area some fifty feet in diameter. Inside was a kind of shimmering black lake, dotted with pieces of floating ice. Barely visible just under the surface was a complex array of metal piping. From this construction, a large pipe emerged and disappeared into a grouping of canvas structures on wheels, like theatre flats. I could barely discern in the dimness that these were painted to resemble snowy mountains and chalets.

They had apparently decided to restore the Swiss Alps theme.

I could see neither of the Holmes brothers. Had I come in time? I strained my ears, but except for dripping water, there was no sound.

I drew my revolver and carefully descended the stairs into the grand hall, acutely aware of my visibility to anyone below. I was an easy target, but managed to reach the main floor without mishap.

I ducked behind one of the canvas flats next to a steam-driven pump. I put out a hand to steady myself. The pump was hot! Perhaps they had been testing the system, which would explain the chunks of ice. But where was Holmes?

From this vantage point, the theatrical flats created a kind of maze. Off to one side, a row of false pine trees stood in a line. Between where I stood and the rink were six lights, dimly illuminating an area about twenty feet across. An island in a sea of darkness.

'Holmes?' I whispered.

I heard the sounds of dripping water. I dearly hoped it was only water, and not blood. I was letting my imagination carry me away. I was nervous about calling out. If Mycroft were here . . .

Once again, I felt the comforting steel of the Webley in my pocket.. I knew to keep my weapons at the ready when on a case with Holmes. Perhaps even more worrying than the possibility of Mycroft's deception was the thought that Holmes, dosed as he was with morphine and cocaine, was not in his right mind. The two drugs, when used simultaneously – a combination I had witnessed only once before, during my army service – could easily prove deadly. The stimulant would prevail but place him physically in danger. The heart rhythms could be affected, and I knew well that sudden cardiac failure was a real possibility, as was a mental breakdown. And then there was his broken wrist . . .

'Watson!' The voice was low, urgent, practically in my ear. I jumped.

'Holmes!' I gasped.

'Good man. I need your help,' he whispered. 'Keep your voice quiet.'

'Yes, of course.'

'Shh! Softer yet. Stay here with me, out of the light. You have your pistol?'

'Yes.'

'Watch me closely. No matter what, do not shoot, except on my signal.'

I squinted at him. It was too dark to read his expression or condition. He sounded nearly normal.

'You are in danger,' I said. 'Lady Eleanor said Mycroft killed two of Lestrade's men.'

'Yes, I heard.'

'She only escaped because of the leopard.'

'Did Heffie tell you I was here? To meet Mycroft?'

'Yes, yes. But I already knew that, Holmes. We had just discussed it. Are you all right?'

He gave no reply. It was very cold in here. I shivered. I squinted trying to read something about his condition in the dim light.

'What is your signal, Holmes?'

There was a pause. 'The signal is "Now".'

'"Now"? Can't you think of something more distinct? "Parallelogram?". Or "fireworks"?'

'No. The word "now".' He patted my arm.

'But what if you say that word accidentally?'

Holmes murmured something I could not catch. Was he slurring?

'Holmes?'

'Watson, pay attention. Do not shoot unless I tell you to. Remember the word.'

'"Now"?'

'"Now".'

Was that a sound beyond the dripping from across the room? We waited. Nothing.

'Holmes, there is more. After you left, Titus Billings arrived to arrest you for killing your brother by setting the fire. But Lady Eleanor told him that Mycroft was still alive, and she begged him for protection. He took her off somewhere. I worried about allowing her to—'

He sighed. I felt his hand on my arm. 'But you are here now, Watson. That is all that matters. Thank you.'

'My choice was clear, Holmes. Either help her or come to you. I sincerely hope that she is in safe hands now. But Mycroft! You must face the facts, Holmes! Your brother—'

'I understand your fears, Watson.'

'But do you share them? Do you believe he has crossed the line?'

Holmes shivered. He looked unwell. 'It is so cold. We

haven't much time. My brother is hiding over there.' He pointed to a great assemblage of the theatrical flats, stacked together at the north end of the hall, visible across the darkness like a pale canvas Stonehenge. 'No matter what else happens, Watson, we will discover, here in this place, the secret of these Alphabet Killings. And something, I fear, about my brother.'

It occurred to me that even if Mycroft Holmes were not the Alphabet Killer himself, he was on the list. And if on the list, he was guilty of past harm to someone. A terrible harm. But there was no time to ponder that.

I heard the sound of crunching glass from upstairs where I had entered. Had Heffie followed, unbidden?

I looked up, but just then Mycroft Holmes stepped into the pool of feeble light from the other side. I had rarely seen him outside of the Diogenes. His corpulence usually lent his movements a ponderous quality, yet there was something strangely vital about him now – electrified, almost, with a fearsome energy. Clothed in a suit which might have cost a doctor's yearly income, and impeccably tailored and groomed, his leonine countenance projected a terrifying strength.

My eyes were drawn to his heavy jowls. Again I thought of Lady Eleanor's glimpse of the man who nearly ran her over in the street.

'Sherlock, show yourself,' said Mycroft. 'I know you are here.'

Holmes stepped into the dim pool of light to face his brother. I finally got a good look at him. He looked shaky, manic, the cocktail of drugs coursing through his system. Beads of sweat hung across his brow.

'Hello, Mycroft,' said my friend. 'You have gone to a great deal of trouble to bring me here.'

'Ah, Sherlock, I know you enjoy the dramatic. Oh, my, look at you. What have you taken?'

'Do not concern yourself.' said Holmes. 'That fire at your apartment. That was a dangerous show you put on.'

'It did not go precisely as intended. I thought you would be the first on the scene, not the girl. I nearly ran back in to save her, but thankfully you showed up to do so. A bit clumsily, I might add.'

Mycroft had observed that entire scene? He had deliberately put his brother in harm's way. I felt a surge of rage.

'She nearly died, Mycroft,' said Holmes.

'That would not have happened had you been just a little bit more ahead of the game.'

I heard a faint sound from outside. A girl's cry. Heffie! I stiffened. A sick concern washed over me. *Heffie. Standing sentinel.*

Mycroft and Holmes heard it too. Both froze in place, listening. There were footsteps, barely audible. Did they hear them, too? I raised my gun. I was to wait for his signal. But Holmes was not in his right mind. Would he even remember it? Or give it in time?

'Mycroft, you knew the transgressions of each victim, did you not?' asked Holmes, his voice shaky. 'You knew from the start these murders were more than they seemed. More than a game of of A–Z. Rather a kind of vengeance for deep wrongdoings. I would not be surprised to discover that the specific crime of each of the victims was available somewhere in your government files.'

'That is correct, dear brother. The discovery of each criminal act by the Goodwins via their alcohol and *ganja*-infused social gatherings either corroborated what I already knew or revealed additional facts about each one. As you surmised, the government does keep track of influential people and their . . . shall we say, *vulnerabilities*.'

'Which sets up an enormous question, does it not, Mycroft? Why are *you* on the Luminarian list?'

Mycroft laughed. It had a strange ring, deep and mirthless, as though Mycroft found whatever it was both laughable and pitiful. I had not heard this sound coming from the man before.

I took that moment to edge closer, crouching down behind a short piece of scenery.

'Sherlock, how is it precisely that you think the world works? In black and white?'

'In a symphony of greys, Mycroft. I am not oblivious. But there is also a world of difference between the compromises made when governing a nation and a person who venomously destroys another for personal gain. Each of these Alphabet Killings revealed a crime of that nature.'

'You are terribly naïve, Sherlock. I have always said so.'

I shifted uncomfortably from my crouched position. There was a silence. In that gap, I thought I heard a creak off to my right. Did I imagine it? Neither Holmes nor his brother appeared to hear.

I looked back at Holmes, swaying slightly from all the drugs. But he pressed on.

'The Goodwins named you for a reason, Mycroft. The transgressions of each victim I have uncovered are deeply personal. Uniformly vile. Most transpired long ago.'

Mycroft laughed again. 'Greys, you said, but still you insist on black and white? It was always thus for you, Sherlock. Your *métier* suits you well. You pursue criminals. An immediate though minor benefit to society. You kill a shark while I keep the ocean free.' He nodded at his brother.

I was now sure I had heard something. I looked around but could discern no movement outside of the light under which the Holmes brothers were standing.

'How does the death of each Luminarian serve your greater picture, Mycroft?' asked Holmes.

'You are so wrong, Sherlock. Aren't you wondering what it was that made me point you to the case, introduce the Goodwins, and insist upon your investigation? Why would I do that if I were the killer?'

'It is personal. Given that you denigrate the small crime, it is odd that you have in fact aimed your most petty offence at me.'

'Really, dear brother?' The depth of scorn Mycroft conveyed was chilling, as though years in the making. 'And what would I possibly want from you, Sherlock?'

'The satisfaction of beating me at my own game,' said Holmes. 'As you have always wanted, Mycroft.'

What happened next stunned me. Sherlock Holmes drew a pistol from his pocket and cocked it, aiming it at his brother. Holmes rarely carried a gun. I was not entirely sure how good a shot he was, especially not in his right mind.

My hand crept to my own pistol and I drew it slowly, carefully from my pocket. *Now?* Surely now. Shoot the gun from his hand. Startle him into his senses. Offer to cover Mycroft while he . . . did what?

But the word did not come. Holmes swayed. The drugs. The shock.

Now?

'But you will not do so today, Mycroft. You will come with me or die here.'

Now?

'I think not, Sherlock,' said his brother.

Mycroft Holmes could move in lightning speed when he so desired. In less than a blink, suddenly Mycroft had a gun in his hand, and for a brief terrible moment the two brothers faced each other, aiming their pistols. Before I knew it, two gunshots resounded in the empty space.

For long seconds, they stood . . . then Mycroft gasped. He clutched his chest, blood trickling between his fingers.

Holmes was upright, arm extended, his mouth open in surprise.

Mycroft sank heavily to his knees. 'Sherlock,' he said and made a gurgling noise. 'You mistake me.' He collapsed to the floor like a sack of flour and lay still.

Holmes was frozen, arm still extended. He stared at his brother, lowered his hand and looked in horror at the gun in it, as if seeing it for the first time.

I pocketed my own gun. I felt sick, unsure what to do next. Holmes looked directly at me, where I hid in the shadows. He shook his head.

'No.' He began turning in aimless circles. 'No, no . . .'

That direct look – was that an instruction? Do nothing. And yet . . .

I hesitated. His eyes glittered as he moved aimlessly. This was not the Holmes I knew. This was some other Sherlock Holmes. A man who had fallen over the edge, truly into darkness. A man who had just shot his brother in cold blood. A man with cocaine and morphine pulling the strings.

Holmes stopped circling and waved his gun in the air, as if it had somehow become attached to his hand and he did not know how to release it. He lowered his hand and stared at the weapon, transfixed.

'My God,' his voice dropped to a whisper. 'What have I done?'

Off to my left came a sudden cry of relief. Lady Eleanor appeared in the pool of light. 'Oh, Mr Holmes! I found you Thank God! . . . I am so afraid!'

I retreated further into the shadows.

'Dr Watson left me with that man, Mr Billings. But I don't trust him! Something he said. He just . . . I broke away . . . Lestrade said you were coming here . . .'

Suddenly she noticed Mycroft's body lying nearby.

'That's him! Oh, but you have killed him! Thank heavens! Mr Holmes, you killed the monster who attacked me!'

She raced to Holmes and flung herself against him, embracing him, hard. He grunted in pain. 'Thank you!' she cooed.

I watched, confused. Holmes seemed unable to understand her. He stood limply, the gun pointing down as she hugged him and then stepped back.

Her voice dropped in pitch and sounded like another woman's voice entirely. 'Thank you.' There was a metallic click as Lady Eleanor raised her arm and put her hand next to Holmes's forehead. In it was a Derringer.

'Drop your gun, Mr Holmes.'

His body stiffened. He looked up in a kind of stupor, and slowly released his weapon. It clattered to the ground.

Had she gone mad? Had he? I raised my pistol, trying to get a clear shot. *Now?* Holmes stepped to the side, glancing in my direction. I thought I detected a 'no' in his glance, but his eyes were glassy and his posture was not normal.

Lady Eleanor moved again, keeping Holmes between us. 'I know you are there, Dr Watson. Step into the light and drop your gun,' she commanded. 'Do it now or your friend dies, and I will be very disappointed. We have unfinished business.'

I stood up and stepped into the light, dropping my gun to the floor. The sound of its landing echoed through the vast hall. I was aware of the darkness surrounding us, and I sensed movement. I saw nothing, but someone *else* was there. Friend or foe, I had no idea. But I also realized that Holmes and I now faced the real Alphabet Killer, the Lucifer of the handwritten notes. The scourge of London.

'A, B, C, D, E, F . . .' said Holmes.

'And G.' Lady Eleanor smiled sweetly. 'Surprise!'

CHAPTER 31

The Bizarre

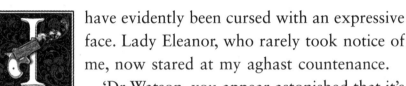have evidently been cursed with an expressive face. Lady Eleanor, who rarely took notice of me, now stared at my aghast countenance.

'Dr Watson, you appear astonished that it's a woman you have been seeking. The brains behind the murders of Luminarians. But what has been a revelation for me is how much enjoyment I got from fooling the great Sherlock Holmes.'

She turned to my friend. 'How does it feel to have taken care of the "H" for me? To have shot your brother in cold blood?' She laughed. 'A rare mistake, but one of your last. You can stop acting, Mr Holmes. Pretending to be so little affected. I suspect you may respond differently when I kill Dr Watson.'

Holmes looked up slowly, the chaos and pain of a moment ago seeming to fall from him like a cloak. He shrugged. 'It is all the same to me.'

I heard another gun being cocked, then the deep, familiar voice of Titus Billings. 'Sherlock Holmes is lying, of course. You should have witnessed the scene in my office. These two would die for each other.'

Billings stepped into the light. His left hand was held aloft, the elbow tucked into his side, as if cradling an injury. In the other hand, he brandished his cold, grey police revolver.

Titus Billings, the Law. Or a law unto himself. 'I have him now, Ellie,' he said to Lady Eleanor, training the gun on Holmes. Neither Holmes nor I dared to move, but we exchanged a quick glance. *Ellie?*

Lady Eleanor lowered her Derringer and picked up Holmes's revolver from the ground, then mine as well. The tiny woman moved from us to stand beside Titus Billings, who towered over her. What was his role?

'Keep an eye on the doctor,' she ordered. 'He's a military man.' The chain of command was unexpected: the delicate widow commanding the head of the London Police? Her voice had turned to steel, her back was straight, face rigid. This was an entirely different creature from the one we had met in Kensington. A she-devil. How had I not seen this before? And how could Holmes have missed this?

'Relax, Ellie,' said Billings. 'We only need a gun on one of them. Holmes, I think.' He smiled in our direction. A reptile. 'Have you got that, gentlemen? If either of you move I will blow chunks of that famous detective brain all over the doctor's nice white shirt.'

'Good.' Lady Eleanor glanced at Billings, then gave him

a sharp second look. 'What happened to you, little brother? Your hand?'

Titus Billings and Lady Eleanor were brother and sister!

'Ah yes, of course,' murmured Holmes. 'The ears. Siblings.'

Lady Eleanor glared at him, then turned to her brother. 'What happened?'

'Attacked by a street urchin just outside here. She got my wrist.'

'Using your own nippers by any chance?' asked Holmes, holding up his own damaged wrist. 'Effective, I will admit.'

'The little harridan,' said Billings.

'Got away, did she?' asked Holmes lightly.

There was no reply. My heart lurched. But Billings's lack of response gave me hope. He would have boasted if he had hurt Heffie.

Lady Eleanor smiled at Holmes. 'On the subject of siblings, it seems the most famous detective is now the most infamous. Mistaking your own brother for a multiple murderer!' She laughed. 'I must say, I did not quite see that coming. But Gabriel Zanders will no doubt thrill to this latest development. How does it feel to have slaughtered your own next of kin?'

Holmes said nothing. He looked ill.

'Well, before you die, are you curious about anything?' she asked, seductively. 'I would be happy to give you a little something, Mr Holmes. You have tried so hard.' She approached and caressed his face with the back of her hand. My friend managed to recoil without apparently moving a muscle.

'Still pretending that you don't find me attractive?' she said. 'Shame.'

Holmes did not respond.

'Surely you are curious about something. Something you might have missed? Something that defies logic?' She leaned in, caressing his ear.

I feared a fatal reaction from Holmes.

'I have a question!' I found myself blurting out. 'What is your reason, Lady Eleanor? Why kill all those Luminarians?'

She laughed. 'Oh, the little friend speaks. Well, Doctor, I am the rat-catcher. It is a public service, after all. Anson? Benjamin? Clammory? Danforth? Enrietti? All of them deserved to die. And believe me, I'll get Flynn soon enough. Even the great Sherlock Holmes hasn't figured out the "why" of those.'

'Of course, I have,' said Holmes.

All eyes swivelled to him.

'You were making sure the Devil got his due,' he said simply. 'Making villains pay for success stolen from others.'

'All right, Mr Holmes,' said Lady Eleanor. 'You are partly right. But only partly. Stop moving, Dr Watson! There, that's good. Remember those chunks of brains. But, Mr Holmes, you do not stand on the moral high ground. You have just killed your only family, remember?'

'I shall ever regret it, Lady Eleanor. Or perhaps I should call you simply . . . *Elaine*.'

There was dead silence. Titus Billings flushed and his expression grew belligerent. He looked from Lady Eleanor and back to Holmes.

'Yes, *Elaine* Linville,' said Holmes quietly. 'And you, Billings, are Tristan Linville, whose father Thomas Linville was ruined by Horatio Anson, a rival shipbuilder. And the rest of that sad story – and there is quite a bit of it – launched your murderous scheme.'

'Oh, you do amuse me!' said the lady, intrigued.

'It was apparent from the outset that one or more of the murders was personal to the killer. Simple revenge. But it strained credibility that they all were. My struggle was to figure which one. And what was motivating the rest.'

'More than one, Mr Holmes.'

'Yes, I understand that . . . at present.'

'You cannot know my mind, Sherlock Holmes. Nor even guess.'

'Guess, no. But I can reconstruct from the facts. Your first victim was your husband, Lord Gainsborough, when you discovered his ruthlessness in killing off rival orchid hunters. His actions reminded you of your long-time nemesis, Horatio Anson. Killing Lord Gainsborough was a well-conceived crime. But not adequately appreciated for your taste. You hid your tracks too well and found that you took little pleasure in the murder.'

'Interesting,' said the lady.

'Your husband was an evil man. But Lord Gainsborough saw the same in you and took you for an ally. The Luminarians were all compromised individuals in one way or another. When he confided this to you, he no doubt thought the two of you could take advantage in some way. You were thrilled to find that your personal nemesis,

Horatio Anson, the man whom you lived to destroy, was among the group. It was then that you hatched your idea.'

'Someone has been researching. Go on, Mr Holmes.' She smiled impassively but I could sense that Lady Eleanor was enjoying this.

'You decided to kill Anson and your husband, then you decided to hide these acts in a larger series of murders. A rather good plan.'

She preened at this appreciation of her cleverness. Multiple murderers generally want to be known, their cleverness appreciated.

'Anson, of course, deserved his fate, in your mind,' he continued. 'Not only were there three deaths in your family, but then the two youngest children were sent to live with relatives in London, never heard from again. Elaine and Tristan: Eleanor and Titus. You were given over to awful families, almost as indentured servants. Both of you clawed your way – quite admirably – out of this, you by marrying Lord Gainsborough, and you, Billings, by a slashing your way through the army ranks and aligning with royalty. Horatio Anson's murder was particularly sadistic – tying him to his own slip and letting the Thames swallow him alive.'

'You are thorough, Mr Holmes. You even went to the docks, then?'

'Elaine, this is a bad idea,' said Titus Billings.

'Shut up, Tristan,' she snapped, dropping all pretence. 'Let Mr Holmes get this wrong.'

'You arranged two deaths that were personal to you. But you had to make them seem like something else. The roster of

Luminarians was a ready-made inventory of sinners. Perhaps, as you proceeded down the list, you convinced yourself that you were actually doing the world a good turn—'

She interrupted. 'By eliminating vermin, yes, I was. You might consider me an avenging angel!'

Holmes nodded appreciatively. 'Indeed! And such brilliant work with the Danforths.'

'Wasn't that clever?' Lady Eleanor smiled. 'I had the advantage of meeting Charles Danforth and his charming, terrified wife at a garden party. I recognized the bully and his madness, and when the name came up, well, a little research . . . I have sources, too, Mr Holmes, and the Danforth will idea was hatched.'

'The suicides! And all those other deaths! Wives. Siblings. They were not all guilty people,' I said. 'Why? And how?'

'He doesn't understand, does he, Mr Holmes?' purred Lady Eleanor. 'Evil spreads, a pebble tossed into a pond of sorrows, the ripples touching all. The "how" was simple. Research. Ask Mr Holmes, he's a master at it. Research, and a small push. Like dominoes.'

'But the . . . flourishes, as one might call them,' said Holmes. 'You wanted the families to truly suffer as yours had—'

'Yes,' said Eleanor. 'Oh, yes.'

'And you wanted to be found,' stated Holmes.

'No!'

'Well, appreciated, at least. The Tarot cards. The letter. You wanted it known that these disparate deaths were by the same hand.'

'Those cards were a foolish idea,' said Billings.

Holmes looked at him sharply, then laughed. 'So you removed them from the crime scenes when you could find them! Hence, their inconsistency.'

Titus Billings's sheepish look at his sister was confirmation.

Lady Eleanor shook her head in anger. 'I told you not to, Tristan!'

She turned back to Holmes. 'Well, it is all over now. And there is one piece of the puzzle you have not been able to crack. I wager you do not know why Mycroft Holmes was on the list.'

Holmes was silent.

'He was third on my personal list, in fact. Oh, I see that surprises you. Do you know why?'

Holmes hesitated. I could see that he did not have the answer.

'I can tell you,' said a deep voice.

Everyone turned to see Mycroft Holmes rise from the dead.

There was a collective gasp from all but Holmes. Mycroft had supposedly burned to death last night, then was shot to death in front of us all just now, but he still was not dead!

'Surprise, indeed!' Mycroft waved a sticky hand in the air. 'Theatre blood. My brother Sherlock is a terrible shot. Here is the connection. Elaine and Tristan Linville's eldest brother Colin was my classmate at Oxford. We were both finalists for a scholarship, which I won. This was just around the time when the Linville family had been rendered destitute by Horatio Anson. Colin killed himself – and you, madam, blamed me.'

I looked on, scarcely believing the events unfolding before my eyes.

'Did the name of the scholarship have something to do with fire, then, Mycroft?' asked Holmes.

'Exactly . . . That scholarship was called "The Flame of Knowledge". He turned to Lady Eleanor. 'I knew you would try to kill me by fire, and I was ready. I removed all my important papers from my flat, had the entire building evacuated with full warning to take anything irreplaceable. The Greek fellow upstairs was annoyed, I am told.'

'Rather extreme, even for you, Mycroft,' said Holmes.

'It was time to redecorate, anyway.' Mycroft made a small noise that was for him, I suppose, a chuckle.

Madness.

Lady Eleanor stared from one Holmes brother to another, impressed in spite of herself. But then her gaze hardened and she raised the Derringer and pointed it at Mycroft. 'You should have stayed dead, sir. You won't escape this time. Tristan—' She turned to her brother.

'Before you do the deed, Lady Eleanor, or may I call you Elaine?' said Holmes, 'I have a question for you. We might not have found you out, had you not decided to commit these crimes alphabetically. Why did you do that?'

She laughed. 'It amused me.'

'Ah, I understand. The thrill of the high wire.'

'I enjoy a challenge. As you do, Mr Holmes. The closer to the edge . . .'

'It also appealed to her pathological need for order,' said Mycroft.

'The cataloguer. Who wanted to tidy 221B,' said Holmes with a wry smile. 'And do you intend to stop after killing my brother?'

'And you, Holmes. And Dr Watson. Do not forget my flourishes, as you call them. It had been my intention, to stop after H. But now I see myself in a different light. My primary targets are scum. It is, as you noted, a kind of service. I think I shall proceed.'

'I was right, then.'

'Yes, but you will not be here to enjoy it. Tristan, kill Mycroft Holmes. Use Sherlock Holmes's gun.'

Titus, or rather Tristan, would at last get his chance to kill. But not before rubbing it in. 'I have begun a projectile evaluation programme at the station, Holmes. Based on one of your own monographs, I believe. It will prove that your own gun killed your brother,' he bragged, 'and you will die in ignominy.'

'Well, that's progress. At least some good will come of this,' said Holmes with remarkable *sang froid*.

Lady Eleanor handed Billings Holmes's gun, then raised hers to cover us both. 'Then kill Dr Watson and Sherlock Holmes with your own gun. Self defence.'

Billings cocked Holmes's gun and took aim at Mycroft.

'Now, Titus,' said Lady Eleanor. 'Goodbye, Mycroft.'

'Now?' said Holmes.

Now!

Billings raised Holmes's gun and aimed straight at

Mycroft. The older Holmes brother stood perfectly still, expressionless, as though he knew that his nine lives had run out.

Two gunshots roared at once. Simultaneously, Holmes lunged at Lady Eleanor, pulling the Derringer from her hand.

She screamed and we all saw that Mycroft stood intact. Nothing had touched him. But Billings was on the ground, a bullet clean through the forehead.

I kept my second gun raised, transferring my aim from him to Lady Eleanor. The tiniest thread of smoke came from the barrel.

Lady Eleanor gasped and backed away. 'How . . . how . . . ?' She turned to Holmes, once again ignoring me.

'Blanks,' said Holmes. 'Mycroft's gun and mine were filled with blanks. I would have thought that obvious to you when Mycroft revealed himself still among the living.'

She looked at him, confused, then down at her brother.

Billings lay face up, sightless eyes staring into the cavernous darkness stretching above us. All three turned to face me.

'You killed my brother,' whispered the lady. With a moan, she sank to her knees beside him. I lowered my gun at last.

'What kind of crazy person would chase a murderer with a gun loaded with blanks?' I said to Holmes.

Holmes shrugged. 'One not prepared to kill.'

'And he is truly a dreadful shot,' added Mycroft. 'Sherlock, in your line of work you really must take target practice.'

'But what kind of person comes to a war zone with *two*

guns, both loaded?' asked Holmes, nodding at my second pistol.

I smiled. 'A soldier.'

He smiled back.

We heard a sharp click. Lestrade had stepped from the shadows and placed handcuffs on Lady Eleanor. She squealed in fright. 'These are just the ordinary ones, ma'am. I am not your brother.'

To my surprise, Gabriel Zanders, along with several other policemen, joined Lestrade, who directed several of his men to take Lady Eleanor away.

Next to me, I could hear Holmes breathing heavily. The drugs were wearing off, and he would soon need help. I could see the energy draining from him like melting ice. He turned to me. 'Heffie? Watson!'

I had forgotten the girl! But Holmes looked so unwell, I hesitated.

'Go and find her. I will be fine,' he said.

Two constables stepped in to assist him as I ran off. I caught a glimpse of Zanders watching the proceedings, eyes on Holmes, with an expression I might interpret as contrition.

I raced to the front of the building, now unlocked by Lestrade's men. There, across the street, I saw Heffie standing under a streetlight next to a doting young constable. They appeared to be sharing a meat pie. Spotting me, she waved.

All was well.

CHAPTER 32

221B

s a soldier, I have in the past taken pride in needing little rest, of being always 'at the ready'. In the army, the need for sleep was considered a weakness. Yet here I was, three days after the events at the Baker Street Bazaar, still taut with nerves yet utterly exhausted. I fortified myself with cup after cup of coffee, attempting to dissipate my nervous fatigue by writing up this case while it was still fresh in my mind. As Thomas Carlyle said, 'Writing is a dreadful labour, yet not so dreadful as idleness.'

A bright, cold light shone through the windows at 221B as I sat in my old chair near the fire, scribbling feverishly. It was eleven in the morning, and the door to Holmes's bedroom was closed. He had slept the better part of these ensuing days after the events at the Baker Street Bazaar, and as far as I knew was sleeping still.

Over the last three days I had attended to his burns, which now were nearly healed. Dr Meredith had visited twice about his wrist. The swelling had gone down, and Meredith gave us a refined and optimistic prognosis, along with specific finger mobilization exercises, with which I was to help Holmes regain his violin capability.

Holmes slept through all of this. I believe that his command of Morpheus was as vital to his remarkable powers as any other skills he possessed. How I envied it.

Holmes at last emerged from his bedroom as the clock chimed the half hour, still in his bedclothes and dressing gown, hair tousled, and desperate for a cigarette. Except for the brace on his wrist he looked almost exactly as he had just over a week ago when I had arrived for what I thought might be an enjoyable holiday.

'Good morning, Watson! Where are my cigarettes?' He flung himself into the chair opposite mine. I poured him a coffee.

'Eat something first,' I said.

He opened up *The Times*. 'Zanders! Well, something laudatory. Whatever on earth!' He read for a moment, then laughed. 'Now he exaggerates in the opposite direction. I am an angel of justice. A genius!' He flung the paper to the floor. 'Why can he not just tell the facts?'

'The facts do not sell papers.'

'Evidently. And how about you, Watson? Writing up the case, I see,' he said. 'How will you embroider it?

'It is a puzzler, Holmes. I have a few things I'd like to clear up with you.'

'Of course, dear fellow. Ugh, this coffee is cold.' He set it down. 'Mrs Hudson! Hot coffee, please!' he shouted.

'How did you conclude that Lady Gainsborough and Billings were siblings? Surely, just the names Elaine and Tristan alone were not enough. The two look nothing alike.'

'You did not observe, Watson? Earlobe shapes the same, first and ring finger lengths, and very faint sibilant "s"s in their voices: those were the initial clues. I already suspected, the names were mere confirmation. Eleanor and Titus: Elaine and Tristan. I regret that this last clue came rather late.' He held up a cigarette and I lit it for him.

'Mrs Hudson!' he called again.

'Patience! Did you suspect Lady Eleanor early on? When, exactly?'

'I will admit that I did not, at first. Her advances, overt flattery and neediness were calculated to blur her motives, and were well done. But gradually a concatenation of facts tipped my suspicions. First, her handwriting, and the cataloguing of her husband's collection. Both indicated a penchant for organization. You recall also that she longed to straighten up this room.'

'Many would,' I said.

'Ha!'

'And she asked you to stay alone at the school, and later her home,' I added.

'Other explanations were credible, there. But it was the discovery of the type of poison used in the ammoniaphone – something of a marine origin – that tipped the scales for me, to pun badly. After you went to bed, Watson, I looked up that Hawaiian myth to which Kepler referred. That poison was ultimately suspected to be from a particular type of coral. You recall, of course, the aquarium in the lady's home?'

'Oh, coral! Of course! How elaborate, then.'

'Everything she did was elaborate. But without a motive these were still not enough. But as I said, all was a ruse to cover up her revenge killings of Horatio Anson, her husband Lord Gainsborough and Mycroft Holmes. She threw too much decoration into the mix. Those three murders alone might have had the elegance of a Pythagorean theorem and might never have been connected. Instead, she widened the scope, propelled by hubris.'

'Hubris, indeed. Calling herself an avenging angel!'

'"Avenging" and "angel" are contradictions, are they not? I will also admit the inconsistency of the Tarot cards puzzled me for a time.'

'What has become of the Goodwins?' I wondered.

'You shall see, Watson. They and Mycroft are due here in—' He glanced at the clock. 'Ah! I must dress!'

Mycroft arrived early, informing us that he had managed to bury most of what happened in order to protect the Goodwin brothers, who may have seemed complicit when they were not. Also, it seemed that Judith, that clever young villainess who nearly got the best of me, had managed to escape to France. I registered that Holmes would not let that rest. Another trip to France was in our future.

A half hour later, all three of us sat facing the Goodwins. The two young MPs were such outsized characters that their flamboyance and youthful vigour seemed too big for this modest sitting-room. James lounged on the sofa, while Andrew paced behind him near the window, casting glances at the street below. Both wore suits of sleek, heathery cashmere and silk paisley scarves. They were like stars of the stage with their own personal costume designer.

'We owe you both apologies,' said Andrew Goodwin. 'We realize that we hampered your efforts by revealing things so . . . so incrementally.'

'You did,' said Holmes. 'Explain yourselves.'

Mycroft closed his eyes at the painful directness of this question.

'We work in government,' said James. A long pause, as though that should be sufficient.

'And?'

'It is complicated,' said Andrew.

Holmes fixed them with a stare.

'It was a mistake and we apologize,' said Andrew. 'There are a great many intersecting interests. Some of the Luminarians have . . . well, have atoned to such a degree that their contributions are such that . . .'

'Well, the security of the nation depends on . . .'

'. . . discretion, and the judicious construction of . . .'

'. . . er, of carefully orchestrated arrangements, relationships . . .'

'Stop!' said Holmes. 'You sought out compromised individuals and blackmailed them into doing favours for Her Majesty's government, while continuing the philanthropy of *your choice*. While they waited their turns to be useful, you were amusing them and stroking them socially. A kind of Robin Hood scheme, with a very elaborate carrot and stick, am I correct?'

The two brothers exchanged looks. Andrew nodded.

'These Luminarians, then, operated as high-level informants for the government?' I asked, astonished.

'That is, essentially, accurate,' said Andrew.

'But what terrible fallout from this convoluted plan! I really do not care to hear any more,' said my friend dismissively. 'It is a wonder that the government functions at all with these Machiavellian schemes in which the serpent eats its own tail.'

'Politics have never been your forté, Sherlock,' Mycroft commented.

And thank heaven for that, I thought. I, for one, found my friend's clear sense of justice – tempered by compassion – to be a beacon shining through the murk of human behaviour and morality. His results were both pragmatic and profound.

No, politics were not his forté. Nor mine, either.

I will admit in retrospect that I perhaps undervalued the Goodwins and their own brand of 'doing good'. As I reread my notes some thirty years after the actual events, I can report that the accomplishments of these two young gentlemen would outlive their legendary parties and complicated politics. Twenty-five years later, both received Victoria Crosses for bravery on the Western Front in the Great War, from which neither man returned alive. But we knew none of that at the time.

'What has become of Lady Eleanor?' I asked.

'Her trial is next week. Life imprisonment, most likely,' said Mycroft.

'And the Queen's cousin, Titus Billings's clandestine bene-factor? Has he been told of his protégé's part in these murders?' asked Holmes archly.

'Yes,' said Mycroft. 'And any further influence by this Royal person has been sharply curtailed. This case has been discussed at a level beyond him.'

'Good!' I exclaimed.

We sat silent for a moment.

'The Luminarians. Was all this your idea, Mycroft?' drawled Holmes.

His brother said nothing, which I took to be an affirmation.

'Then how did *you* get on the list?' Holmes continued.

There was an awkward pause. Mycroft was perfectly inscrutable. We turned to the Goodwins.

'Mycroft is privy to a great many secrets, as you know, Holmes,' said Andrew. 'He helped us choose some of our honourees. But then we . . . we . . .'

'We crossed the line with him when we then questioned his own, er . . .' said James.

'And you did rather threaten us, sir,' said Andrew, as if that answered the question.

'We shall simply leave it there,' said Mycroft in a tone which brooked no dispute.

How foolish, I thought, for the Goodwins to try to take on Mycroft Holmes!

Holmes laughed. 'Ah, Mycroft, how you dislike the lens

turned upon yourself. But gentlemen, a toast, at least, to the end of the Alphabet Killings!'

As if on cue, Mrs Hudson entered with a silver tray and champagne.

A few minutes later, as we sat around the fire enjoying our drinks, a philosophical question of my own bubbled to the surface and I could not help but pose it.

'Can one actually atone for a sin?' I asked. 'You gentlemen made a bargain with the Devil – or rather a bunch of devils – so do you come out on the side of the angels?'

'Does that matter?' said James Goodwin. 'It seemed a piquant thing to acknowledge the sins of our honourees while simultaneously celebrating their restitution, and then forcing them to do more good.'

'The world benefits. The net result is for the good,' said Andrew Goodwin. 'So, Dr Watson, I would say yes.'

The moral ambiguity of this case did not sit well with me. While arguably manoeuvring for ultimate good, the Goodwins nevertheless, through delay or lack of cooperation, allowed these people to be picked off. And one must also consider the peripheral deaths of people who were not involved in any way with the original crimes.

'But gentlemen,' I continued. 'Your delays, and your—'

'Dr Watson, if you please. The case is solved. Let us leave it at that,' said Mycroft Holmes. I was about to continue when I felt Holmes's light touch on my shoulder. His look suggested that this was something we might discuss further in private.

The moment passed, because precisely then, Miss Heffie

O'Malley was heard at the front door and shortly flew into the room, charged with confidence and on a mission. Her hair was tamed into a respectable chignon, and she was dressed in a conservative but flattering bright green dress, a far cry from her Spitalfields appearance.

'Why lookit all o' you!' she called out upon seeing the assemblage of serious men in the room. 'It's a regular gentlemen's club in 'ere? May a lady join in?'

Holmes had risen to his feet and welcomed her with a wave of his arm and a smile. James Goodwin, also standing, indicated a seat next to him on the settee.

'Delighted, Miss O'Malley,' said he with a broad smile. He placed a glass of champagne in her hand.

She set it on the table, and stayed standing, with a wink to Holmes. 'I've got news, she said, 'if I ain't interruptin' anything important 'ere.' We resumed our seats.

'You are not,' said Holmes. 'I think we have moved on from philosophy and into celebration.'

'Good. Then . . . there's madness over at the Yard,' said she. 'There's a kind of bonfire in the alley out back. A bunch o' pamphlets burnin'. There's men arguin' quite loud over various, and something about uniforms and 'andcuffs and proper procedure. But in all this mess, it seems I got a real job at the police station! On a regular wage, so's I can 'ave a roof and a dress and, well, Mr 'olmes, a life. I think I 'as you to thank.'

'Well, that is wonderful news, Miss O'Malley,' said Holmes, using Heffie's surname for the first time. 'You will be a valuable addition to the force.'

'Oh, please join us, Miss O'Malley,' entreated James, once again gesturing to a seat next to himself.

'Watch out for my brother, young lady,' said Andrew with a grin.

Heffie laughed. 'My eyes work fine, thank you.' She turned to face Holmes. 'Oh, but 'ere's my business! Are you free Mr 'olmes? Mr Lestrade has asked for you.'

'Now?' asked Holmes.

'Right away. Seems there's been double murder down at Borough Market. Pig seller. Trap door. Duchess. And twins.' She shrugged.

He hesitated, then flexed the fingers of his recovering hand.

'Some French detective is already down there. Says you know him,' added Heffie. 'Calls 'imself "the doc".'

'*Vidocq?*' I said incredulously. 'He is alive?'

Holmes laughed. 'Does it surprise you?'

'You comin', sir?' said Heffie.

'I am indeed,' said Holmes, springing to his feet. 'Watson?'

I was already standing. 'I am your man!'

For annotations with interesting
facts about the people, places,
and things in this novel, visit
www.macbird.com/devilsdue/notes

Acknowledgements

As always, there are many to thank.

Firstly, my husband Alan Kay, the love of my life, who bore me up during some dark times that shadowed the writing of this book.

Equally, the brilliant publisher and gentleman David Brawn, without whom there'd be no Sherlock Holmes Adventure series.

A debt of gratitude to Sherlockian friends, particularly Les Klinger, Catherine Cooke, and Leah Cummins Guinn – and also Marina Stasic, E.J. Wagner, Dan Stashower, Monica Schmidt, Glen Miranker, Andrew Gulli, Tamara Reynolds Bower, Resa Haile, Luke Benjamen Kuhns, Steve Emecz, and Julie McKuras.

Medical angels Dr Art Kowell, Dr David Reuben, Dr Jonathan Weaver, Dr Michael Broukhim, Dr Harvey Sternbach, and Dr Tony Hughes in London – for advice both fictional and real; Miranda Andrews, my hero; Christine Sofiane, Anke Lecher, and Liz Poppert who kept the transport working.

Thanks to London experts Elliott Wragg (with whom I went slip-sliding on mud at the Thames foreshore), police Historian Keith Skinner, and Isle of Dogs expert Adam Kean, all knowledgeable and generous. And especially to the deep Sherlockian and London map expert Thomas Wheeler.

Special gratitude to the literary lights Dana Isaacson, Dennis Palumbo and Lynn Hightower, who, each in their own way, make me better than I am. Also to Linda Langton and Jane Acton, who remind the person who spends days typing in her pyjamas that, yes, this is a real thing.

My Oxnardian writing buds Matt, Harley, Patty, Craig, Jamie, JB, and Bob, for sharp critiques and moral support; Ryan, Freya, Dora, and Pauline, for keeping the home fires burning; and Luke, Jaz, Kirstin, Ann C. and Ann K., Robert, Miguel, Nancy, Faye, Margo, and Lisa, for moral support and fun.

A special thank you to Carla Kaessinger Coupe and Dana Cameron for inspiring the Goodwins, and me as well.

Thank you to the gifted artist Mark Mázers who designed the beautiful drop caps, Andrew Davis for the cover, and Stuart Bache for the original design concept of the series; also to Jean Marie Kelly, Affiliate Publisher at HarperCollins US, and to Natasha Bache for her initial inspiration and her continued work on the series.

Lighting a candle for several who passed during the writing of this book, I acknowledge my mother Rosemary

MacBird, my former business partner Jim Shasky, my dear friend Paul Annett (director of the original Sherlock Holmes episodes for Granada and for whom I promised Oliver Flynn), first love Bill Kennedy, and best friend Dennis Krausnick, who gave me the honour of spending some meaningful time with him during his last weeks, talking books, poetry and Shakespeare, a world which he opened up to me twenty years ago and which directly helped me get to here.

For sustenance and inspiration, I thank my beautiful actor friends Jonathan LeBillon whose London Shakespeare readings buoyed my spirits immeasurably, Rob Arbogast, who modelled for the Holmes of this cover and inspires me, and especially Paul Denniston, who is not only my Watson but has turned himself into a genius 'grief yoga' coach and helped me with the loss of so many people I dearly loved during the writing of this book.

And finally, a special thank you to my cousin Chris Simpson, a constant inspiration, friend and helpmate, to whom this book is dedicated.

Also available

Art in the Blood

BONNIE MacBIRD

A missing child, a deadly art theft,
an unstoppable killer . . .

Sherlock Holmes is languishing and back on cocaine after a disastrous Ripper investigation. Even Dr Watson cannot rouse him, until a strangely encoded letter arrives from Paris. A beautiful French singer writes that her little boy has disappeared, and she's been attacked in the streets.

Racing between London, Paris and the wintry wilds of Lancashire, Holmes and Watson discover the case is linked to the theft of a priceless statue and deaths of several children. The pair must confront a rival detective, Holmes's interfering brother Mycroft and an untouchable suspect if they are to stop a rising tide of murders. The game is afoot!

'Dark, stylish, ingeniously plotted. Holmes and Watson live again.'

HUGH FRASER

Also available

Unquiet Spirits

BONNIE MacBIRD

An attempted murder, a haunted castle,
a terrible discovery . . .

Sherlock Holmes has found himself the target of a deadly vendetta in London, but is distracted when beautiful Scotswoman Isla MacLaren arrives at 221B with a tale of kidnapping, ghosts, and dynamite in her family's Highland estate. To Watson's surprise, however, he walks away in favour of a mission for Mycroft in the South of France.

On the Riviera, a horrific revelation draws Holmes and Watson up to the McLaren castle after all, and Holmes discovers that all three cases have blended into a single, deadly conundrum. To solve the mystery, the ultimate rational thinker must confront a ghost from his own past. But Sherlock Holmes does not believe in ghosts . . . or does he?

'*A rollicking tale worthy of Sir Arthur Conan Doyle himself.*'
HISTORICAL NOVELS SOCIETY

Holmes and Watson will return

in THE THREE LOCKS,

2020